Burning Bright

She arched against him, pushing her breasts up into his hand. Then she gave a gasp as he sank to his knees in the sand, drawing her tight into his lap. She was so slight, for all her girlish roundness, that he took her weight without even noticing it. He could feel her heart rocketing. She whimpered, her thighs splayed and quivering on his own. Lowering his lips to her hair, Veraine smiled and he let out a growling sigh.

They said nothing; they had no words in common. But he understood the language of her skin, and the little breathy gasps that escaped her parted lips. She laid her head back against his shoulder, her wide eyes staring into the forest, her pulse beating against his palm as it pressed her mound. They didn't need words. Flesh spoke to flesh in a primeval interchange that carried its own message and worked towards an inexorable conclusion.

By the same author:

Divine Torment
Cruel Enchantment

Burning Bright
Janine Ashbless

BLACK LACE

Black Lace books contain sexual fantasies.
In real life, always practise safe sex.

First published in 2007 by
Black Lace
Thames Wharf Studios
Rainville Road
London W6 9HA

Typeset by SetSystems Ltd, Saffron Walden, Essex
Printed and bound by Mackays of Chatham PLC

ISBN 978 0 352 34085 6

Contents

1 *Soul Loss*   1

2 *Stolen Treasure*   24

3 *The Rani*   42

4 *Tiger, Tiger*   66

5 *The Storytellers*   83

6 *Shinsawbu*   100

7 *The Gift of the Gods*   117

8 *Transgressions*   137

9 *Fighting Men*   162

10 *Making His Mark*   184

11 *Bring Him Back to Me*   204

12 *The Arena*   225

13 *A New Song*   266

With thanks to Karin –
www.janineashbless.com

1 **Soul Loss**

The man awoke when sunlight touched his face. He started to roll over onto his back but stiffened in pain. He tried to open his eyes. One wouldn't; the other saw only meaningless blocks of green and yellow. He groped to the back of his head where his hand encountered stickiness and swelling, and then a new agony like red lightning flashed through his skull.

Pushing himself upright he touched his eyes with trembling fingertips. Blood had run round from the back of his head and crusted in his right eye-socket, sealing it shut, but there didn't seem to be any damage there. The man coughed out a blasphemously grateful mono-syllable, then paused. He had no idea what name he'd invoked, and couldn't even remember the sound of that word. It had been uttered out of pure habit and now was gone from his mind.

This is bad, he said to himself. There was nothing in his head at that moment but confusion. No memories. No names; not one. Not even his own, he realised. He blinked his one good eye and looked down at his legs, struggling to gain focus.

What had happened?

His legs looked familiar enough: calfskin trousers laced beneath the knee, and below that bare shins, tanned and muscular and dusted with dark hair. Naked feet. He could feel the yellow sand under his heels. That was wrong – he should have had sandals on. Someone must have taken his shoes. They hadn't taken the rest of his clothes: the trousers that felt too hot in this sun, the linen tunic that might have been white once. But he had no belt, and he ought to have had some sort of weapon, surely? He looked around, trying to make sense of his surroundings. He needed to wash the dried blood from his eyes, and he needed to drink. His throat was as dry as leather.

He was, he eventually worked out, sitting in the sand of a dry streambed surrounded by dense trees. There didn't seem to be anyone else around, only the flies that were trying to land on his head. He waved them away gingerly because the pain was like a cap of molten metal sliding down his neck. The sand all around him was badly scuffed. Unless he'd been dancing back and forth across the riverbed this suggested that there had been several people here, but as to who they were he had no idea. He moved slowly around, looking for debris that might remind him, but he found only stones and driftwood – and a single pile of dung.

Horses then. But had they been travelling on horse-back, or had the thieves?

They. Why did he think he'd been travelling in company?

The man shuddered and turned away from his questions. It mattered less what had happened, he told himself, than what he was to do now. He needed water or he'd pass out again, and this time probably for good. There was no water in this river, but if he followed the course downhill it must eventually join a larger one.

Slowly he made his way downstream. For a long time there was nothing but the toil of walking and of climbing over fallen logs. It was shady under the trees once he moved away from that shallow bend, which helped. Birds croaked and squawked in the bushes, and some-times he heard what sounded like monkeys screaming.

Once he heard a deep, distant cough that made the hairs stand up on his neck, and the whole forest fell silent. He walked for over an hour, as best he could tell. He was faintly surprised at how he was able to keep going despite the pain and the thirst and the weariness. I must be a tough bastard, he thought mistily. His abdomen under the stained tunic was hard and flat, his bare forearms ridged with muscle. He'd make a good meal for the forest scavengers if he died here.

Then at last the riverbed narrowed to a defile and when he scrambled down he caught a glimpse of water ahead. Stumbling over rocks he reached the bank of a pool and kept going, staggering out into the green water and catching cupped handfuls up to his lips. It tasted wonderful. He gasped from the chill of it as he tipped it over his head and the wound on the back of his scalp stung fiercely. Then he scrubbed his face, picking away the coagulated mess of blood and dirt from his eye, giving a moan of relief as he was finally able to open both of them together. He spun round in a circle, glimpsing a trickle of water coming down high rocks at the far end of the pool and the spindly structure of a bamboo pier on the far bank. Signs of some sort of settlement – thank the gods.

His stomach contracted around the cold water and a wave of dizziness washed over him for a moment. Then he stared down at himself as the ripples flattened about his waist. From the water the face reflected up at him was dark-eyed and badly needed a shave, the hair which hung loose down to his jawline greying despite the fact that he didn't look old enough to warrant it. Funny, he thought; his hair should have been longer than that, and tied back.

There was a splash from the other bank and he looked up sharply. That movement sent a spike of pain

3

and nausea running through his head, and as he blinked it away he became aware of two things in turn: the first that there was a girl on the opposite bank crouched over her bronze water-pots but staring at him with wide eyes; the second that the warm caress on his right shoulder was fresh blood running down to mingle with the pool.

He tried to take a breath but the air had thickened in his lungs. He took one step back towards the bank and the green water swung up to meet him and closed over his head; cold as steel, dark as death.

He awoke in hell. That was the only way he could account for the burning, and for the smell of smoke. His skin was on fire and he was sweating acid, pain lancing through every muscle as he tried to move. His throat was raw. Then a face drifted through the gloom to stare down at him.

Maybe there was some clemency in the infernal regions after all, because the face seemed to belong to quite a pretty demon. She had dark eyes and plaited black hair tied up on top of her head with red thread. He tried to lift his hands up to her but they were too heavy and fresh pain tightened across his back. Panic swelled within him at his helplessness and only weakness stopped him thrashing with fear. He croaked wordlessly. The girl-demon turned aside and he tried to follow her movement, but his head felt like a block of stone, too heavy to lift.

The girl's face returned and brought with it a hand holding a bowl. It glinted in the dim light and he remembered some pots among ferns by the pool. Maybe it was her. He tried to focus on her face, on her plump lips, on the breasts straining under the red cotton of her dress. The allure of her figure was like a light in the dark cavern of his pain.

'Drink,' she said, tilting the cup towards him. Most of it went down his cheek on the first attempt and when he did sip some the water tasted bitter, but then there was a bitter smell everywhere; something burning that seemed to be an acrid mixture of feathers and herbs by the stink. He wanted to look down at his body to see if it was his own flesh on fire, but he couldn't even raise his head that far.

The girl reached away again and this time brought out a cloth that she squeezed until the water ran down her bare forearms. There was far too much water here for it to be hell, he thought. Unless this was a special realm reserved for soldiers who'd betrayed the Empire.

The thought was like a knife: it slid in and out leaving a wound so clean that for a moment he didn't realise he'd been stabbed. But the room spun.

Was he a traitor?

She wiped the cloth across his face and when it had passed it left an ephemeral sensation of coolness. He moaned with relief and was startled when the demon smiled nervously. She continued to wipe away the sweat, rinsing the cloth every so often to cool it again. She worked her way down from his face and across his shoulders and chest, her touch gentle and cautious. Not a demon after all, he thought. But at the point she reached his belly she stopped and withdrew into the gloom. He tried to crane after her but the smoke was too thick and it filled his mind.

When it cleared away he realised that some time must have passed. The light had changed. He looked again for the girl, but the face he discovered was much older; still female but this time extravagantly filthy, the skin grey where hers had been golden-brown and the eyes black stars gleaming from deep pits. This one truly looked like a demon, if you believed in such things.

'The fever is down,' said the woman, jabbing him with one finger. 'But it hasn't broken. It will return.'

She'd rubbed herself over with ash, he realised, and darkened the hollows of her eyes with charcoal dust. Black ropes of hair framed her ghostly face, and where the ash had been licked away her lips were red.

'He's lost a part of his soul,' the woman continued, 'and a fever spirit has taken its place. I'll ask my spirits how it's to be called out.'

He must have been somewhat better because he now managed to watch her even when she stood and walked away from him. He could make out the walls of the room too, the close-set bamboo poles outlined in light. The younger woman was squatting a little way off, the red dress pulled tight over her thighs, her gaze fixed on her elder. He was even aware that he was covered to the waist by a cotton sheet that was plastered to his skin. But he saw it all as from far away.

The woman stood back, shrugged her dress from her shoulders and let it hang from her waist as she reached for a drum. He noticed that she'd rubbed ash down her breasts too, so that they seemed luminous against the darker skin of her torso and her broad nipples were only outlines against each orb. He tried to swallow, unable to take his eyes off those breasts. Big enough to fill my hands, he thought. Then the ash-witch struck her drum with the heel of her hand and the sound went through his skull like a mallet-blow. She struck it again and cried out in a harsh voice, her head thrown back, before launching into an insistent driving rhythm that thudded in his breastbone. He could feel the skin on his belly jumping to the drumbeat. The noise was horrible; it felt like an assault. He realised the younger woman was drumming along too. But the girl kept her seat by the wall while the older woman began to dance, her body twisting to the heartbeat of the drum, her matted locks swinging about her head, her breasts bouncing and swaying as her feet stamped.

No, he groaned silently. What's happening?

Then the panther walked into the room. It came through the wall, passing through the bamboo poles as if they were smoke, and for a moment he could not believe that it was real. But then he saw the gleam of moisture on its nose and tongue and teeth, saw the silky darkness of its black fur and smelled the carrion stink of its breath, for it came straight to his bed and stared down at him, its golden eyes more beautiful and more terrible than any nightmare could ever be. He stared helplessly into the black mask of his death. Then the cat turned away with feline contempt. Sweat ran into his eyes.

The panther went over to the witch and she flung her arms about its neck, her bare breasts leaving ash-streaks upon its jet pelt. It rubbed its face ecstatically against hers.

He had to shut his eyes against the salt sting. The drumbeat pounded in his head, the darkness spun in a circle around him – but when he opened his eyes again there was silence. And he and the women were alone in the room.

The witch came over and knelt by his pallet, her breasts still heaving from the exertion of her dance and little streaks of moisture tracked through the ash. Her nipples were hard under their grey dusting. She patted her thigh, signalling to the girl, who laid aside her drum and joined her.

'My spirits tell me,' said the witch, 'that the fever spirit is a red centipede. It must be sucked out of him. With his seed.' She looked slyly at her companion. 'They said that you should do it.'

The girl made an 'o' with her mouth and shook her head, her eyes suddenly unable to fix upon the supine body before her.

'Tch,' clicked the witch with her tongue; 'you're too old to be afraid of men, Mehetchi. If you weren't my apprentice you'd have been married by now.'

'I'm not afraid – I just don't want to,' the girl said, wriggling. 'He's a foreigner.'

'A man is a man. There's no difference to speak of. Anyway, his hands are tied: what are you worried about?'

He then realised that the pressure he'd felt across his back was a length of cord attached to either wrist. A cold stab of fear ran up his belly.

The girl hissed between her teeth. 'I don't ... I'm not ready for this,' she muttered.

'Don't give me that, girl. You're training to be a spirit-talker, so don't tell me you're squeamish. You do what the spirits instruct.'

The girl stuck out her lower lip but didn't reply. Her colour was high. He wasn't capable of imagining what she was feeling, but he knew he didn't want this at all. He was too weak to protest, but his muscles clenched in painful cramp. This wasn't how he wanted it; not tied down and helpless, picked over by two witches like a couple of vultures on a corpse. He tried to protest, but it came out as a groan.

The witch poked his right nipple sharply. 'Don't be impatient, you,' she admonished. 'Now Mehetchi, pull that down. Take a look. It won't bite; this serpent has no teeth.'

He felt a cooler flutter of air as the girl reluctantly

turned down the sheet over his thighs. Thin trickles of sweat crawled over his hips and down to the small of his back.

'It's not so bad, is it, girl?'

The younger witch made a face. 'It's ugly. Not sweet and smooth like a woman's.'

This drew a bark of laughter from her elder. 'It's sweet enough, girl! And soft and smooth most of the time, the tenderest part of a man until he starts to imagine somewhere even more tender to put it. Now this one though, he's already thinking on your plump lips, Mehetchi.' She flicked his cock with one long nail; he couldn't see his own reaction but he could certainly feel it. 'Hee! Look at it jump! The fish are biting tonight!' Mehetchi's eyes widened. 'These are things you have to learn, to be a spirit-talker,' the other told her. 'Now go on; put your hand on it.'

Mehetchi obeyed slowly, her cool fingers circling his cock. He squeezed his eyes shut but it made no matter.

'How is it?'

'Hot. Every bit of him is fevered.'

'Not so soft now?'

Her hand hefted his flesh uncertainly. 'It's getting heavier. It moves in my hand like an animal,' she observed.

'Ah; you must pet it like an animal then. Stroke it gently. Yes; like that.'

Her apprentice was wary. 'What will it do?'

'It'll get harder still.'

'I don't like it hard. It was nicer before. Look: it's too big and ugly already.'

'But it must get as hard as it can before it'll spill its seed. Harder than a length of mahogany. See how much bigger it is now? He may be weak with fever, but his flesh is still charged with life.' She raised a finger.

9

'Listen, child; you must understand that a man feels desire just as a woman does, but there's more than one spirit in his flesh. The prick of a man has a spirit of its own that moves it without his intention. It brings flesh into being from the spirit-world. It makes him rise even when he has no thought of lust in his heart. When he sleeps, the prick-spirit stirs. When he wants to piss, it won't let him. It can be very strong, very cunning. More cunning than the man's own spirit. Look at that serpent – has it any eyes?'

'No. Only a mouth.'

'There, you see; a prick-spirit is blind. To it all women are the same. Old and young, pretty and ugly. A prick is as happy with the arse of a goat as with that of a girl. Heh! – a man will fuck mud when his prick is in charge. He'll do anything to obey it. That's why they are dangerous.'

Mehetchi made a face and squeezed him savagely until his spine arched.

'This spirit is treacherous, child. It can trick a man into believing he desires a woman, when really he finds her repulsive. Only when the prick-spirit has had its way will he realise that he never wanted her. And then, when he approaches the girl he lusts after the most, the prick-spirit may abandon him, and for all his desire he then will be unable to stiffen for her. When you're a full spirit-talker, you'll find that many men, or their wives, will come to you to complain that their prick-spirit has fled. It'll be your job to search out the spirit wherever it has hidden and bring it back to his body.'

'Where do they go?'

'Into the Underworld. I'll show you the place later. I'll teach you a song to call them, and another to send them back, should you ever need to.'

'And what about those below?'

'Go on; touch them. They're nothing to fear. They're soft like ripe fruits.'

Mehetchi knelt forwards. 'They're wrinkled like they've hung on the stem too long then! Ugh!' She giggled, her eyes flashing.

He felt the humiliation writhe in his belly.

'Those are the source of all his seed. The spirits of all his descendants wait there, anxious to see the light of life. Often they're too eager and they pour out when there is no womb to receive them. That is your task now. You must draw his seed out and hold it in your mouth; the fever will come with it.'

The girl licked her lips nervously, and even that sight sent a spasm through his helpless flesh.

'The serpent's mouth is wet! Is that his seed?'

'Hah!' the older woman snorted. 'No – he's just impatient, child. His prick drools like a toothless old man before his dinner. Suck it.'

No, he said, but his voice went unheard.

There was a moment's pause, a flutter of breath and then Mehetchi's mouth – cool and soft and liquid – wrapped itself around the burning head of his cock. He groaned, and the embrace became a sucking before it was then cruelly withdrawn.

'It tastes salty,' she murmured. 'Not so bad. Not as bitter as the vision-beer.'

'Keep sucking. Lick him,' her mentor instructed. 'He likes that. See; his muscles are like stone.'

She obeyed. He felt the fever rip through his bones, a grinding ache that became a fire as it mounted to his skull.

'When his snake spits into your mouth you must catch it. Whatever you do, don't swallow, or you'll take the fever into your own body. I have a pot here. You must spit the centipede into that.'

The girl mumbled agreement, her lips wrapped around his erection. He could have screamed for frustration at the teasing, infuriating gentleness of her touch, without rhythm or expertise. Her tongue lapped and slithered but to no purpose; she didn't command his cock, only played with it. He wanted to catch her head and thrust deep into her throat but he didn't have the strength or the reach and could only strain uselessly against his weakened frame, his teeth bared.

'It's not working,' Mehetchi moaned, after long waves of glorious torment had rolled over his shaking body for what seemed like forever. 'I can't do it.'

He managed to pull one deep gasp into his lungs and then let the breath out in a moan of frustration. 'You are at the wrong angle,' said the witch shrewdly. 'Turn around. Straddle his chest.' She guided the girl until she was kneeling astride him, her feet tucked under his shoulders, the tight red cloth of her skirt filling his view. He got one glance down between their bodies as her mouth closed about his monolithic cock again, but then that vision was eclipsed by the scarlet curves of thighs and buttocks. The witch was right; this was a better angle for him, he would have been able to push further into her throat if only his thighs had been able to obey him, or his spine had been more than a limp rope of hot pain, or the pressure in his skull wasn't threatening to split the bone. This is going to kill me, he thought.

Then an ash-pale hand descended from the shadows onto Mehetchi's scarlet up-thrust rump. The girl quivered. The hand gripped and stroked and ran smoothly up the tight fabric of the skirt in a confident, soothing, commanding caress that seemed to release the girl from uncertainty. Then it slid down and caught the edge of the material, pulling the skirt up to reveal to him the golden-brown skin of splayed thighs. He could not look away. Higher and higher the skirt was rucked, until it slipped up over the curves of the girl's beautiful bottom and left them entirely naked, framing the dusky pear-shaped glory of her sex.

Mehetchi gasped; he felt the cold inhalation up the length of his cock.

The young witch was possessed of a powerful charm that had nothing to do with spirits. Her plump mons was fluffed with the darkest, downiest hair and her rosy inner lips peeped from behind this curtain, hinting at a deeper cleft hidden within. Her anus was like a velvet flower. He felt the fevered blood boil in his veins at the sight. And he could feel something else rising within him too: not just the bubble of orgasm but something harder, more compact, like a pebble forcing its way up his throat.

Then the older woman's filthy hands slid down from above, parting the buttocks, stroking the soft fur. Mehetchi moaned in shame and jerked as if about to tear herself away. The hands restrained her, gentle but strong, patting the soft mound, soothing that quivering sex.

It was a name, that pebble. A name.

'Mata!' the girl whimpered, her voice all but unintelligible around the thickening shaft of his cock. But the older witch was merciless. Her ash-stained fingers parted those innermost lips, laying bare the mysteries of her maiden sex to his eyes. He could see the pink pearl of her clitoris and the tender, vulnerable mouth of her hole. He could see the moisture, slippery as oil, clear as water, welling up to slick the swelling tissues. He could smell the sharp perfume of her arousal and see the wetness gleaming on the witch's fingers, no longer dusty-pale. Those fingertips closed now on the exposed bud of her clit and stirred her beyond endurance.

The name was his own. It rode the swelling tide of his fervour, a black and jagged rock borne on the flood, and he leapt to catch it.

Mehetchi squealed with pleasure and shame, and at the cry and the sight Veraine erupted at last.

He was sitting at the edge of the pool between the buttressed roots of a fig tree when the witch Chu came to him, many days later. He was wearing only the loose fouta pants he'd been given and his bare feet were trailing in the green water with a fishing line running out between them. Half dreaming, his head propped against his curled fist, his thoughts skipped among fragments of the broken past. Clean and fed now, rested, even newly shaven, his memory was still as opaque as the algaed pond. If he glanced down he could see the pale scars traced across his torso by a history of which he had no recollection.

'Catch fish?' Chu asked.

Veraine indicated two fat leaf-wrapped bundles beside him.

'Good,' she said. Her coating of ash was looking thin today, no longer quite disguising the golden brown of her skin or the birdlike delicacy of her bones. A necklace of pig teeth tapped her breastbone as she squatted down. She showed him a small gourd she was carrying, the top tightly sealed with leaves. 'This your sickness. I trap it. I keep it – you stay strong.'

It had turned out after some experimentation that they did have one language in common, one she called Yamani, though she had only a clumsy grasp of it. That was still better than Mehetchi, who couldn't understand a word he said; the two women spoke only their own tribal tongue between themselves. There was, Veraine was quite aware, absolutely no way he could have really followed their conversation when he was ill. But then after all, he told himself, he had hallucinated the panther.

'Thank you,' he said cautiously, considering the little pot with some distaste. He did have a fever-memory of a tiny scarlet centipede trying to climb out of a gourd and being flicked back in by ashy fingers, but he didn't trust that memory. And even if the invertebrate had existed, he told himself, it had been palmed by the witch and had never originated in him.

The woman leaned forwards and regarded him from an alarmingly slight distance. 'You still miss piece of spirit. I go look, but it not in world down there,' she said, pointing at the soil, 'or up there.' Her filthy fingernail waved at the dense tree canopy. 'Your spirit in this world. I not look in this world. You maybe look.'

Veraine nodded. 'There's a woman,' he said, his voice still hoarse from his illness. That was all he had recalled during his convalescence. 'I was with her. If I could find her again maybe I'd remember. Maybe she could tell me.'

'She your spirit,' the witch said impenetrably.

Veraine shrugged.

'You be careful. While you missing piece of spirit, it easy for malia to get inside you.'

He caught his breath as if the unknown word had stung, but recognition turned into doubt and confusion at once. Chu had noticed and paused, but when he frowned and shook his head she continued. 'They make you sick again.'

He nodded to stop her talking. 'I need to find people. Lots of people. A place where there are travellers; foreigners. Is there a city anywhere round here?'

She shook her head slowly. 'City, yes. Maybe not lots people.'

'Huh?'

'Summer city in hills,' she said, pointing across the pool. 'But one year, lots men . . .' She mimed hacking at something. 'Men not from here.'

'They cut the forest?'

'Kill people.'

'Ah. Soldiers?'

'Mm. Came here. We run into forest, hide away. Soldiers take food, take everything. Burn village. Then go to summer city. Maybe they burn city. Maybe they kill everyone.'

Shit, he thought to himself. Was that my army? 'How long ago?'

'One year.'

Maybe that's how I got here, he wondered: a pillaging army. Maybe I was one of those murdering soldiers. But not a year ago, surely. Oh – I'm lucky they didn't just cut my throat, if this has been a war-zone. He felt the nausea of frustration. 'So, is the city empty? Is there anyone left?'

'Maybe. No one come here. I not go.'

Perhaps the soldiers are holed up there. Perhaps we met a scouting party. Perhaps that's where my . . . where she was taken. The woman who knows me. 'How far away is it?'

She shrugged. He suspected anything further than the little village downstream was beyond her reckoning. 'You are kind to me,' he told her wearily. 'I thank you. But I have to go to the city.'

She looked dubious. 'You walk good?'

'Yes.'

'You look for your spirit,' she agreed, as if it were inevitable.

Veraine cracked a little smile. 'Then before I go, is there anything I can do, to help you?' He looked back towards the hut, wondering if they needed the roof patching or something. He really didn't know what this sort of life involved. I'm from a city myself, he thought, seizing upon the new information with satisfaction.

The witch stared at him narrowly then said, 'Big tree up river, fall down. You cut it up, you please Mehetchi. She not like hard work.' Her eyes glittered: around here woodcutting was counted as women's work.

Veraine shrugged one shoulder. 'Fine.'

He went back to the hut for the axe; a length of wood with a head of bronze embedded in one end. Mehetchi was husking rice in the yard, squatted on her haunches and tossing the grains in the wide basket with an indolent rhythm. She cast him a quick, sidelong glance and he smiled at her. He took the whetstone from its bag by the door, glancing around the interior one last time. The simple hut that he'd shared with the two women these last days was green with shadow, sweet with the smell of smoke and dried herbs. He had nothing of his own either to leave or to collect.

Jumping the narrow end of the pond, he walked back up the dry course of the stream, retracing the route of his arrival until he found the fallen tree. Snapped-off branches showed that the girl had made some attempt at gathering the dry wood, but she'd made no mark on the bulk of the trunk. Veraine checked the bole for bees' nests and rapped it hard to warn off snakes before starting work. He'd learned more than one survival trick in the last few days.

Cutting the wood was hard work even in the comparative cool of the morning. He still felt a little dizzy from his illness and he grimaced in frustration; I should be stronger than this, he thought. Whatever body fat he'd been carrying before he'd been attacked was now melted away by fever, and his muscles stood out like ripples sculpted on damp sand. He shook the loose hair from his eyes and gradually began to enjoy the pull and stretch across his torso, the sight of the wood flying into chunks, the slow beat of the axe-blows. For the first time that he could remember, he felt good.

He didn't see Mehetchi arrive. As he lowered the axe and turned to find the whetstone he was startled to find her there behind him, poised against a tumbled boulder. He didn't like that – the thought that he'd been watched, unknowing. He preferred to be in control. His breath, already burning shallow and fast in his throat, seemed to catch under his ribs. Her red dress looked faded and a little shabby in the direct light; she needed a new one. Perhaps one that was a little less tight, he thought distractedly as he wiped his forehead.

Mehetchi smiled, then looked away quickly. She'd avoided him ever since he'd been on his feet, always shy in his presence. Veraine was still not sure how much he'd dreamed and how much had really happened between them, and up till now he'd tried not to embarrass her further. In pulling him out of the pond the girl had saved his life; he was well aware of that. But now instead of shunning him she had sought him out. She was carrying a tall jar of beaten copper in one hand, and a cotton package secured with jute in the other. She put this latter object carefully down and then lifted the vessel towards him, taking a hesitant step.

He sniffed the contents of the jar and then tilted it, letting the thin village beer wash down his throat. He hardly meant to, but he'd drained the jug dry before he lowered it again. He'd been more parched than he'd realised. As he handed it back her fingers grazed his and she flashed him a glance like a startled deer, all dark liquid eyes and parted lips, turning her face swiftly away with decent maidenly modesty. He was amused.

When he'd borrowed a knife to shave that morning she'd been torn between her curiosity – the men of their village didn't need to shave – and a clear horror of being caught watching him. It took an effort of will now not to reach a hand up to her burning cheek, but some instinctive honour made him restrain himself. It didn't stop him watching her as she turned away though, or prevent his gaze from wandering over her waist and hips and buttocks, thinking that she had a fine round arse that the dress was doing little to conceal; and that as she walked away that arse twitched from side to side in a manner calculated to tease the coolest of men.

His cock stirred uncomfortably under the cotton folds of his fouta and he laid one hand on it, intending to tuck it away. But he didn't take his eyes off the girl.

She stopped, quite still in the middle of the stream-bed, one hip hooked up, her dirty feet sunk in the warm sand. She looked back over her shoulder, as if nervous of facing him full on. The skin on her nape was golden brown, and the copper jar dangling from one hand glinted like fire. Veraine felt his blood, already running hot in his veins from his labours, thicken with fiercer heat.

The gods save us from pretty girls, he thought insincerely.

Mehetchi's free hand took hold of the fabric of her skirt and gathered it, raising the hem right up her dark amber thighs to expose the curve of one cheek.

Veraine let the axe fall and in a few strides he was behind her. When he put one hand on the bare skin of her neck he felt her tremble and the warm spice of her scent made him shiver too. He tilted her head back to expose her throat before slipping his arm round her, pulling her softness up tight against him. Her whole body went taut with instinctive alarm. He ran his hand over her breasts, squeezing them through her dress, and she let out a kittenish wail.

You started this, he thought, cupping her plump mons. She arched against him, pushing her breasts up into his hand. Then she gave a gasp as he sank to his knees in the sand, drawing her tight into his lap. She was so slight, for all her girlish roundness, that he took her weight without even noticing it. He could feel her heart rocketing. She whimpered, her thighs splayed and quivering on his own. Lowering his lips to her hair, Veraine smiled and he let out a growling sigh.

They said nothing; they had no words in common. But he understood the language of her skin, and the little breathy gasps that escaped her parted lips. And, however inexperienced, she couldn't have failed to interpret his erection pressing up into her through their clothing. She laid her head back against his shoulder, her wide eyes staring into the forest, her pulse beating against his palm as it pressed her mound. They didn't need words. Flesh spoke to flesh in a primeval interchange that carried its own message and worked towards an inexorable conclusion.

With one hand he undid the twist of cloth that held up her dress, pulling it down to reveal girlish breasts without a hint of sag, as if they were somehow weightless. He played his hand across them, wondering at the sight of his callused fingers on the flawless mounds, at the scar on the thumb that teased the fragile points of her nipples. There was little darker pigmentation to those nipples at all, but they hardened under his touch like any older woman's. Mehetchi whimpered and wriggled, grinding down harder on his imprisoned erection. Veraine smiled again. Still caressing her breasts, he released his grip with the other hand long enough to pull up the cloth of her skirt, fingerful by fingerful, to bare the black fuzz beneath.

Now that was a fine sight, he thought, looking down over her shoulder at the whole length of her body. That pathetic dress, always more provocative than modest, now draped no more than her hips and waist, a scarlet signpost to her shocking exposure. Her thighs were parted wide for all the forest to see and she made no attempt to close them – even her hands were reaching back to clasp his thighs. He laid his palm back where it belonged on her mound, stroking it as if it were some small, timid animal. She had a soft fleece. And she was wet; her hot folds awash with the juices of desire. He could smell her now, musky and sweet – a girl more than ready to become a woman, just needing a little assistance over the threshold.

He found her clitoris and teased it softly, rubbing it in circles. The strange thing was that he couldn't even remember having sex with a woman, but his hands knew exactly what to do. Mehetchi's whole body responded to that touch, jerking then flattening against him, simultaneously tense and yielding, demanding and surrendered. His hand was a shameless pillager, coaxing more and more moisture from her sex, sliding one finger into her tight hole as the heel of his thumb massaged her higher and higher. But it still took him by surprise when she came – mewing and jiggling, his hand suddenly drenched.

For a moment Veraine was taken aback; he hadn't expected anyone so inexperienced to have such a talent for pleasure. Then, while the girl was still in the half-swoon of orgasm, he seized the chance to lift her hips and release his own member. It stood up from the damp cotton folds like a cobra from a basket. He was almost appalled by its appearance, by the thought of trying to fit anything so big into that neat bit of a girl.

Perhaps best not to let her see.

He settled her back down into his lap, letting the hard length of his cock ride the length of her wet slot, cushioned by her swollen labia. Mehetchi stirred uneasily in his clasp, coming down from her first peak, a note of dismay in her soft moan. He wasn't having that. His hands went back to work and in moments she was helpless again, abandoned to the pleasure, climbing towards another plateau. Despite his own need he was ruthlessly patient, stoking the flames of her passion, sliding his thickened cock up and down the furrow of her sex, bathing it in her juice – working her to such a state of urgency that this time when the first trembles of her crisis rippled under his fingertips, he was able to push inside her.

Mehetchi cried out then and tried to pull away, but he took no notice. He made her accept the whole length of his cock and then, just as brutally, made her love it. With fingers and nails he sent her spilling over the edge, her orgasm swallowing the pain of penetration. Her cry was the choking call of a netted bird. Tears streaked her cheeks as she finished, glazing her smile.

He gave her only a moment to catch her breath and then pushed her forwards onto hands and knees, their bodies still joined by the tumescent length of his cock. Bunching the red dress up onto the small of her back, he looked down at her ripe buttocks and at the thick rod buried in the cleft between them with profound satisfaction. He gripped her hips and took his own pleasure without hurry, her rump slapping his groin with every thrust and quivering with each muffled blow. She buried her hands up to the wrists in the sand and kept her rear high until he came with a breathy grunt.

When he withdrew he wiped himself clean with the hem of her skirt: the spots of blood wouldn't show up on her scarlet dress. He wiped his forearm across his brow.

'I hope it was what you expected,' he said softly.

Mehetchi stared at him, uncomprehending. There was shock written large on her face, but also a secretive, knowing glee.

He touched her cheek. 'It takes getting used to,' he said, 'just like anything else.'

She got to her feet, adjusted her dress and hair, and then with a brief smile she turned and disappeared downstream.

Veraine sat back until his breath returned, feeling quite dizzy though he was not pleased to admit it. You must be getting old, he told himself, sifting the sand through his fingers – then wondered how old he was. He turned his attention to the bundle she had brought, picking open the coarse knots. The cloth turned out to be a large piece of cotton big enough to wrap right round him. It contained a fishing line, two fistfuls of rice and a clay firepot guarding a tiny glowing ember. Enough to get him on his way, he thought, pulling a wry face. Chu had been more than generous to him, he was quite aware. He just wished he had some sort of weapon to take, but at the moment he possessed not even so much as a knife.

Knotting his clothes back around his waist, he gathered up the bundle and – after a moment's painful hesitation – hid the axe away out of sight under the tree before setting off in the direction of the promised city.

2 **Stolen Treasure**

Myrna realised, as she came to, that the coarse stuff on her tongue was horsehair. She jerked her head back, opened her eyes on a bright and lurching world, then shut them again in dismay. Her cheek sagged back against the horse's mane. Her stomach felt like one great bruise.

The bandit walking next to her laughed, said, 'Awake again?' and slapped the horse's neck right next to her face. Myrna didn't need the gesture in order to remember him; she'd passed out after he'd punched her in the stomach. She pushed herself upright, catching her breath as the swinging, emerald world resolved into the leaves and shadows of the dense forest all around. They were following a narrow path. She could see the other horse ahead and two more of the bandits leading it. Others were walking behind, she guessed, but she didn't feel steady enough to turn and check.

They're our horses, she thought. She was tied to this one like a piece of baggage and could feel the cord biting into her ankles. She'd ridden this animal hundreds of miles over the previous months, and yet now she was mere saddle-baggage and Veraine was –

At the thought of Veraine lying face down in the sand she felt a bubble of fear swell in her breast. She saw again the glint of blood in his hair and the gleam of the teak club in the hands of the man who'd struck him from behind. And she felt again the pain of that moment; he had folded onto the earth like a sacrificial bull, and she who'd seen so many lives poured away in crimson abandon had screamed with despair. For a moment her only wish had been for them to kill her too.

Staring into the trees, she sent her soul crying into the forest. *Are you really dead? I saw you fall. I saw your hands claw at the sand and then relax. Relax just as when you sleep, your fingers crooked into curves as if you were cupping some unseen breast. But this was no sweet sleep with your breath warm on my hair. I saw the blood. And no matter how I screamed you didn't wake up.*

Fear is like a blade cutting its way inch by inch through my belly. It is a physical pain, a raw and burning agony. I'm not used to fear. I didn't know until now that it has a taste: coppery like blood.

I cannot believe that you're dead. It wouldn't be so simple. If you were dead, the sky would blacken and the earth would crack. I've seen you struck down and I still don't believe it. You will live. I will it that you live. You will wake and find me, even here.

How could I live – without your touch, your voice, your smile? You cannot be dead. You cannot.

She took the bubble of panic and released it silently in to the hot sunlight, feeling her pulse steady and her breath slow. He couldn't be dead, or she would know it. Her heart would have stopped beating. And if he were alive then he'd come looking for her. He would free her again.

Myrna glanced down at the cords twisted around her wrists, then at the smiling upturned face of the bandit beside her. He wore a square cotton cap and a limp moustache bedecked his upper lip. The rope from her wrists was held quite firmly in his right hand; she was leashed like a bitch. Her captor grinned. He seemed to find the fact that she was conscious of him provocative, and he laid one hand on her bare knee.

A long time ago Myrna had possessed many masks: one for each of her moods and her roles. There had been faces of wood and enamel and gilt, of leather and silver – all shelved in the chamber behind her throne, in a city on the edge of a desert. But the city was far away, and she had been called by a different name then, and she no longer owned any mask, not now. Yet a face is still a mask for the soul. Hers was a perfect blank, devoid of reaction, even when the bandit slid his hand up her thigh beneath her dress. His palm was hot and sweaty. Behind her mask of flesh and bone there ran through Myrna's mind everything that any woman might feel; fear and disgust and outrage, and a myriad lightning speculations. Run? Impossible. Hit back? He'd hit harder. Play along? There was nothing to gain. But beneath the turmoil lay something else, something untroubled and terrible. Some vast implacable presence that felt no fear, because it was fear's source.

I am not just any woman.

She didn't drop her gaze when his fingers reached her crotch. He licked his lips, leering; not from instinct, she saw, but in order to frighten her. His desire was pathetic, she thought, because it was not truly passion except for power over another human.

I am not human.

He scrabbled clumsily at her yoni, unable to get a good grip because of the saddle, then when that roused no reaction he took a fold of the soft skin at her loin and pinched it hard. Myrna felt the pain stab her, liquid fire that made her heart jump. But pain was an old, familiar companion and she knew how to deal with it. She wasn't afraid of pain.

I am pain's own mother. I am the Malia Shai.

She didn't twitch, or flinch, or look away. It was as if he'd never touched her. He withdrew his hand, the smirk on his face pushed aside by a scowl. This was exactly what had happened earlier; having carried her away from the riverbed he had eventually dropped her and demanded that she walk. She'd refused, so he'd slapped her. She'd laughed out loud at that. That was when he'd knocked her out, provoked to fury by her intransigence. No doubt she was provoking him again now, she thought.

The man glanced down the track ahead and seemed to see something he recognised. He leaned in close enough to whisper; 'You're too proud to scream? You'll change your mind soon.'

Their destination turned out to be a rough camp pitched in a clearing; several shelters of cloth and poles with the undergrowth hacked away to make space for cooking fires. Myrna counted only a couple of dozen people, all of them male, and judged this to be a temporary site. It didn't smell bad enough to be a permanent settlement. The men came over to greet the newcomers and one in a blue silk shirt stepped forwards. He seemed to be a leader of some sort, because her own group of bandits all ducked their heads to him.

'Two horses!' he said. 'Not bad, Saji.' He had a round face and his moustache was curled at the ends. He came over to where she was sat. 'Hm. You've found a foreigner I see.' He looked her carefully up and down, frowning. 'She'll do, I suppose.'

'She'll clean up all right,' said her captor.

They were speaking a peculiar western-accented Yamani, and Myrna was fleetingly glad that her ancestors had spread their language so far with their ancient conquests; at least she had no problem following the conversation.

'Is she a virgin?'

The other man laughed. 'No, captain. We killed her man.'

Myrna pushed away the fear clawing at her entrails.

'Well, get her stowed. We're still waiting for the others to get back.'

Saji cut the ankle ropes from her and gripped her wrists. 'Come on then,' he said, pulling her down on top of him, 'let's see if you scream.'

Myrna retreated then, diving back behind the mask, watching from the distant wastes as he sank his fingers into her buttocks and grabbed at her breasts. It was an ugly sight and she shut her eyes. A blow rocked her. She had retreated so far from her body that it took a moment for her to realise that she was lying on the leaves, alone, and that two men were standing above her shouting. Bemused, she realised that the captain was swearing at Saji and jabbing him in the chest.

'What?' cried the other man, his arms wide and innocent. 'What was I doing wrong?'

'You idiot!' the captain snarled. 'Your skull is stuffed with rice, is it, country boy? What did I tell you? Are you trying to get us all killed?'

'She's a worn shoe already – what does it matter?'

The captain's flush of anger was draining away; Myrna was startled to see that he was almost yellow with fear. 'If you touch her,' he explained, slowly and through clenched teeth, 'they will smell it. If they smell you on her they will kill you.'

Saji flailed one hand dismissively. 'They won't –'

'They will, country boy. This is your first job. I've done this for eight years, and I've seen it. You know what they'll do to you? They'll tie your arms to a cattle-post in the marketplace, and they'll open a shallow cut here.' He drew one blunt finger down the younger

28

man's abdomen. 'Then they'll leave you watching your guts spread out all around you like so much rope, not even able to shoo the flies off, until the dogs come to eat their fill. You want that to happen?'

Saji sneered uneasily.

'Then keep your prick to yourself!' There was a ring of men around them by this time. 'That goes for everyone: we bring them back clean. You understand?'

After that Saji took Myrna to one of the shelters and left her there unmolested, though he did it with bad grace. He even brought her a bowl of rice and some water to drink, which she accepted despite feeling little desire to eat. Her belly ached from the bruise, from fear, and from loss. She sat cross-legged on the blanket watching the camp, wondering what was to happen and what she could do.

Where are you, my love? she breathed.

The men didn't seem to be particularly busy; mostly they cooked and ate and smoked water-pipes. She noticed that each wore either a square cap or a waist-sash in contrasting colours of orange and black, and she rejected her earlier assumption that these were bandits; they now appeared much more like a foraging party for an army. There were no women or children here, though a couple were youths not long out of boyhood. One elderly man had been posted as a guard for her some little distance away, though he seemed more intent on the shoe he was repairing. She studied the back of his head, thinking of Veraine until her fingers bit into her ribs, missing with an intensity that was physically painful the little, foolish things like the way he hooked his grizzled hair behind his ears when he was concentrating, the dark curve of his lashes on his cheek when he lay asleep and the scar on his lip. And oh, yes, the way he looked at her when he reached for her, and the touch of his callused fingers soft upon her face, and the heat of his breath on her skin. Spirit and flesh, she yearned for him. Tears burned behind her eyes.

Just before sunset another party of men arrived, stumbling up the hillside. The whole camp gathered round as they slumped wearily into obeisance before the captain. Some were obviously wounded; rusty blooms of blood gleamed on their clothes.

'They saw us coming,' a voice came to Myrna through the jabber of questions and explanations. 'They shot back at us. We lost two men.'

'They'll pay for that,' the captain promised.

One of the newcomers was clasping a girl in a yellow dress.

'We found her milking the water-buffalo in the field. We got a calf too – look, Waso is bringing it in now. We'll eat beef tonight at any rate.'

The men seemed more cheered by the capture of the animal than of the girl and they dragged the beast off enthusiastically. The captain inspected the new captive, who seemed to be almost incapable of standing, and then jerked his head towards where Myrna was sitting. 'Over there. Two will have to do; we'll head back in the morning.'

The young woman was shoved in under the awning, falling to her knees. Myrna saw a sweet face creased with fear – and then the girl grabbed her arm and buried her face in her shoulder. Myrna was shocked, more shocked by this than by anything that had happened since the attack; she had no idea what to do. The girl clung to her neck and began to sob, her whole body shaking, her face hot and wet on Myrna's breast.

'Shush,' she said uncertainly, putting her arm around the girl's shoulders, but her skin jumped with alarm. In all her life she'd never had anyone except Veraine come to her for comfort. She'd never held a baby, she had no memory of her own mother and, she realised with discomfort, she'd never put her arms around another woman, in sympathy or for any other reason. Not in all her life. She felt sick; it was like suddenly realising that she was missing a limb but had never noticed.

'Shush,' she hissed again, feeling stupid and helpless, then simply held the girl without another sound until the sobs slowly wound down into exhaustion. It took a long time. The glow of the camp fires were the only bright points in the twilit forest surrounding their little prison. The men outside moved around, taking no notice of them or their misery. Myrna's back started to cramp. What's your name?' she asked in a whisper.

The girl sniffed. 'Gohlit,' she moaned.

'That's a nice name,' Myrna said, a little bleakly. It meant *Hope*. 'Gohlit, I need to lie down. Come on.' She stretched out until she was reclining on her side and Gohlit lay down with her, never loosening her clasp. Her body was soft and warm and comforting. 'Where do you come from, Gohlit?'

'A village by the Bamboo River. A day from here.' In the indigo shadow of the tent, Gohlit was clearly very pretty indeed despite the puffiness caused by weeping; Myrna guessed she was several years younger than herself.

'Do you know who these people are?'

Gohlit sobbed once. 'Don't you?'

'I'm not from around here. I came travelling from the east.'

For the first time, Gohlit looked up, perplexed, into Myrna's face. 'Did you come from the desert kingdoms?' she sniffed.

'I came across the desert.'

This elicited a disbelieving stare. 'Who are you?'

Oh, that wasn't an easy question to answer, thought Myrna. I was a divine priestess in the greatest temple of the Eternal Empire. I was a slave to a million worshippers. I was a traitor to my people. I was, and I am, the living incarnation of a goddess, the most terrible of goddesses. 'My name's Myrna,' she said softly.

'That's a strange name.'

'Yes ... It's not a Yamani word; it's Irolian. It means *Stolen Treasure*, I'm told.'

'Oh.'

'So who are these people?' Myrna prompted gently. She felt Gohlit tense in her arms.

'They're reivers for the Tiger Lords.'

The title sounded oddly familiar, a name from ancient myth. 'And who are they?'

'You've never heard of them?' There was a note of panic in her voice. 'The Tiger Lords? They're rakshasa: demons. They send their men out to catch young maidens and then they eat them.'

'Eat them?' Myrna didn't understand.

'They're eaters of human flesh. They hunt people down like deer and eat them – for the sport of it.'

For a moment Myrna couldn't think of any response. It sounded so preposterous compared to the grim probability of rape and enslavement that she almost felt hopeful. 'What do these demons look like?'

Gohlit shuddered and clung closer. 'Sometimes they look like men, and sometimes like tigers,' she whispered. 'They can change their shape. They're stronger than ten men and faster than a horse at a run, and they have claws like daggers. You can't fight them.'

'Your villagers did, I heard.'

'They fought the reivers! That was different – those are only men. And it was stupid anyway, because the Tiger Lords will send soldiers to punish my village now.'

Myrna stroked her hand across Gohlit's braids while the girl sobbed again. Her hair smelled of jasmine. 'Don't cry for them yet,' she said at length. 'You don't know what might happen. Things change.'

The girl's laugh was bitter. 'You don't know what it's like. Your family don't live in terror of the rakshasas all their lives, do they?'

'I don't have a family.'

Gohlit's sniffing ceased. 'Were you on your own?' she asked incredulously.

'No. I was travelling with a man.'

She could see Gohlit's eyes widen in the gloom. 'Your husband?' she said, reaching up to touch the cloth that bound Myrna's hair. 'Is he dead?'

'No, to both.' Myrna's voice felt rough, as if it were scraping her throat. 'He was hurt, but he'll survive. I know.'

'Your brother?'

'My . . .' Myrna paused and shook her head. 'We wouldn't have been permitted to marry.'

'Oh.' Gohlit bit her lip. 'That's why you're travelling. You've run away from your village with a man, haven't you?'

Close enough, she thought, nodding.

'Were you married to someone else?'

'I was a priestess. In a great temple.' She heard a slow hiss of wonder and doubt.

'What's he like then?' Gohlit's breath was warm on Myrna's neck. 'Your man.'

'Well; he's strong.' Myrna stared at the roof of the tent and let her inner vision drift. 'He used to be a soldier.'

'Go on.'

She let her breath out slowly. 'There are pale scars all over his arms and chest from fighting. He has funny

33

hair. It started off dark, but it has these streaks of grey in, though he isn't that old. I mean that he's older than me, but not an elderly man. Just grey. When he was in the army he grew it long, right down his back. That was the soldiers' fashion where he came from. But when he left the army he cut it off. It's still too long, but I don't mind.' She smiled.

'Is he handsome?'

'Oh.' She considered this. 'I think so. He's nothing like the men I grew up with. The first time I set eyes on him I thought he was so strange ... but I also felt that this was someone I'd been waiting for all my life. As if I knew him, somehow.'

'You're lucky.' A sigh warmed Myrna's cheek.

'Am I?' The idea made her frown.

'To have someone your heart knows.'

'Ah.'

'Is he kind to you?'

'He's gentle like the stillness in the heart of the storm. He's very quiet; he doesn't talk a lot. I don't think he trusts people easily. He's quiet until there is danger and then suddenly you see the fire.'

'So he's brave too?' Gohlit snuggled in closer, seeming to find comfort in her description.

'Very. Braver than anything in stories.'

'What does that mean?'

'He gave up everything. Heroes in stories don't do that; they just keep gaining more and more acclaim. But he sacrificed everything – his rank, his home – for me.' She stopped, her voice breaking.

Gohlit reached up and touched the tears running down her cheeks. Then she kissed her on the lips and Myrna trembled. For a moment neither of them moved. Myrna thought what a comfort it was to have a warm and living person to hold, for all that the contours were unfamiliar and the lips too plump and soft when she was used to hard muscles and the mouth of a man. Just having a body pressed against hers was enough to kindle a warmth in her breast and belly.

'Don't cry,' Gohlit begged. Myrna reached out and stroked her cheek. Though she was feeling warm, little tremors were running down her limbs. 'Hold me tight,' whispered Gohlit and kissed her again, long and soft and lingering.

Heat bloomed in Myrna's belly and thighs; she returned the kiss with fearful sweetness, and both women opened to each other, their tongues dipping with the cautious grace of deer stooping to drink. Then they broke away and lay face-to-face in the dark, breathing as one, feeling each other's heartbeat.

It was Myrna who moved first to put her hand on the younger woman's breast. She felt the soft weight of the orb, warm in her hand through the thin cotton, and discovered the little nut of the nipple by running her thumb over it. Gohlit gasped with pleasure as her nipple was rolled and teased into full erection. Myrna was surprised by the unbridled reaction. She kissed the girl again and they clung to one another, fondling each other's breasts until both of them were sighing. Their thighs were pressed together, feet entangled, but it wasn't enough to satisfy Myrna. The whole of her pelvis felt like boiling butter.

She was shocked by the feral urgency of her need and by the fact that it was another woman arousing her, not Veraine. She knew this was an illicit pleasure, that it shouldn't be happening, though it undeniably was. She longed to feel Gohlit pressed between her legs, into her wet and burning sex, yet their long skirts frustrated every attempt to interlock. At last Myrna simply pulled both garments up. Silky skins met and kissed. Gohlit whimpered and Myrna pressed her fingers to her lips, holding the hot and anxious breath back. 'Shush. It's good,' she reassured the younger woman.

Then it was easy for her to slide her left thigh in until their limbs were enmeshed to the hilt, Gohlit's pelt rubbing on her hip, her left hand on the girl's soft and rounded rump. She couldn't believe how strange another human could feel to the touch: it was the slenderness and the fragility of her frame compared to Veraine's solid bulk, the smoothness of her skin, the perfume of her heat. She felt tiny like a child, like something that would break under the pressure of lust. Was this how she felt to Veraine? Was this how any man felt when he lay with a woman – this mix of power and wonder and anxiety?

Gripping her tightly at the small of the back, Myrna pressed into the younger girl. She could feel the incredible heat of the young woman's sex on her thigh, smell the musk of the wetness that was leaking upon her upper leg. They were lying mouth to mouth, breath interlaced, Gohlit's hands framing her face. Myrna slowly moved upon her, straddling her thigh, aching for the friction that would bring release even though she was scared she was crushing the breath from Gohlit's lungs. A burning need was taking control of her body. Her tongue lapped on the girl's soft throat and she arched under her, lithe as a snake, cruel as a kitten, her nails scoring Myrna's hips.

'Shit. Take a look at this,' said a voice.

Myrna jerked her head up at the sound, her face flushed and her hair falling out from under her dishevelled headcloth. Out at the front of the tent a cluster of men stood watching. It was far too late to hide what they were doing; with a yelp of shock Gohlit brought her leg up hard between Myrna's thighs, and on that firm surface Myrna came, staring straight into their avid faces. She couldn't bite back her cry. The rush of orgasm was like light in the depths of the darkness; it was like sanctuary.

'Sweet fuck,' Saji groaned. She recognised his voice in the gloom, though there were nearly a dozen men there and more arriving by the moment. She knelt up as straight as she could, her dress clinging to her damp frame. Gohlit whimpered, trying to push her skirt down to hide her glossy jet bush. Myrna looked down at where her frightened face glimmered in the dusk.

They were all watching, all enthralled, all unable to look away. And yet they didn't dare come nearer. Myrna watched Saji reach down inside his loose cotton trousers and fumble at himself.

'Don't stop, you bitch,' another man pleaded harshly.

If they touched her, they would die.

Gohlit whimpered again. Myrna reached forwards to press a finger on the girl's lips, then laid a gentle hand upon a full, heaving breast before bending to kiss her again.

The men seemed to stop breathing.

'Don't worry about them,' she whispered. 'There's nothing to be afraid of.' Gohlit's lips were irresistible. Myrna kissed them until she felt the other girl melt once more. She was aware of the men watching them, masturbating their cocks in sweaty hands, hypnotised and helpless. They meant nothing to her, enclosed with Gohlit in a sacred space where nothing else mattered but the giving and receiving of solace.

Gohlit seemed to taste her confidence and to take it from her tongue. They sank back into the breathy exchange of caresses, Myrna stooping to mouth the other's breasts, feeling the stiff points of nipples thrusting against her tongue through the wet cotton. She reached to stir the wet curls of her fleece and soaked her fingers in the honeydew that welled there. Gohlit mewed, all need for discretion now gone, her sex pulsing around Myrna's hand like a flower opening up to the morning sun.

They coupled without haste, with the deliberate enduring pace that women work to everywhere in the world, not rushing to any finish because they know that every ending is the start of another cycle. Outside the tent the men squatted and raced each other to their prize, battering their stiff cocks until their semen leapt in the moonlight and clotted in the dust. The two prisoners outlasted every one of them, even the grizzled old men; and when the women fell asleep, drunk with comfort, they were still intertwined, still throbbing with the beat of their orgasms, still tracing the paths of pleasure across each other's drowsy flesh.

The next day the reivers' party rendezvoused with others on the banks of a sluggish river. There were rafts drawn up on the dirt beach, and dozens of captives of both sexes huddled in the shade, though the male captives were much outnumbered. All were guarded closely by scores of reivers. Gohlit joined the other young women eagerly, thirsty for familiar accents, weeping and whispering with them. Myrna was a foreigner not possessing the currency of a common life to trade with and remained at the margin of the group; inscrutable and aloof, it seemed to the others.

Some of the guards kept keen watch that night, but there was no show for them.

They embarked on the rafts at dawn, the reivers singing charms to placate the river spirits as they poled the unwieldy craft downstream. It was a two-day journey by raft down the Green Snake River, which emptied into the sea by Siya Ran Thu, the city of the Tiger Lords. Myrna talked in whispers with the other prisoners but she learned almost nothing of their destination. They were farmers and villagers who knew little of the world beyond their fields and had barely imagined that their lives could change, until a few days ago when they'd been captured or given up in tithe or sold by desperate parents. There were, between the tears, rumours shared of the cruelty of their demon captors; lurid tales that she found hard to believe. Nobody spoke of any hope that they might be rescued, or that escape was possible.

At least they were fed well enough, and nobody tried to assault or hurt her further.

On the third morning the river widened, winding its way in labyrinthine passages between steep green islands that rose out of the water more like craggy pillars than hills. They beached on the left bank and the captives were marched over a shoulder of rock to a cove where a waterfall splashed down rocks into a deep beachside pool. There were buildings here of bamboo and wood and many boats drawn up on the water-side, clearly some sort of permanent base. And there were more people waiting. These were not reivers; they were dressed in far richer clothing, and those that bore weapons also wore lacquered armour.

These men and women came over to inspect the prisoners. At first Myrna assumed these were the pur-chasers, the famed demon lords, and she was confused to find them so mundane with no whiff of horror about them, only the dull evil common everywhere of those who traffic in human misery. A portly woman with a drooping left eye pulled down the front of Myrna's dress and pinched her breasts with all the passion of a cook plucking a chicken.

It became apparent that the prisoners were being

sorted into lots. Some, those that met with little approval under inspection, were marched away to one of the huts. The others were batched into three groups; men, younger women and a small group of slightly older women among whom Myrna was shoved. She saw that Gohlit was in the other, larger, female grouping. The girl, like most of her companions, looked sick with fear.

The reivers, their job done, settled down on the beach to smoke and relax.

Then the captives were ordered, a group at a time, into the pools at the base of the waterfall. The young men were sent first, but when they waded in fully dressed their guards shouted, 'No, No – Get those clothes off. You don't need those.' The youths shed their crumpled foutas, hot-eyed and clumsy, while the guards laughed and the other prisoners sat and stared. Only some of the older women looked away out of respect.

Myrna didn't look away. She saw that she had come to a place where modesty was as worthless as fallen flowers, where the rules of society which she'd struggled to assimilate so recently had broken and dissolved. She watched the young men and took pleasure in their golden beauty; all narrow hips and angular shoulders, their torsos hairless, their legs long and toned. They scrubbed themselves down with brutal, angry strokes as if they intended to punish the pretty flesh that had brought them to this end.

Myrna closed her eyes, her head filled with the gleam of hard muscle and the arch of proud backs. She never prayed, but she could and did talk to the gods. Among the solid thighs and the smouldering eyes in her mind she sought out a face she remembered from her dreams, the bright and laughing visage of the Sun Lord. When she called his name he turned to her and grinned.

Brother, she said.

Sister, he replied, mocking a little, for their relations had hardly been so formal or familial in the past.

I want you to bring me back Veraine. He's a warrior and so one of yours, though he doesn't acknowledge it. *Bring him back to me safely and you'll have my gratitude beyond all time.*

What's that worth, my Sister?

She wasn't surprised. Where every act is significant, nothing is given for free. And every action of the gods echoes on through mortal history.

He'll serve you. He'll do a great deed to your glory. I'll see to it.

You promise?

I promise.

She was awoken by a slap on her shoulder, and for a moment had no idea where she was – she had as always sunk further into her trance than she'd realised. The woman with the slack eye glared.

'Come on, get them off!'

3 **The Rani**

Veraine stood in the thickening morning mist, uncertain whether to give in to dread or to despair. Beneath the shroud of fog lay the remains of Chu's 'city': a jumble of houses and outbuildings whose stone foundations and blackened spars were being rapidly overrun by the forest. The settlement had been destroyed by fire and only the wild had attempted to reclaim it. The one building left standing was the palace at its centre, whose façade bulked darkly above him through the mist.

He'd climbed to this place over three days, through increasingly strange forest where the ferns grew taller than he did and the trees were festooned in grey swatches of hanging moss, and he'd approached it after finding a weed-grown road whose flanking statues of sensual tree-nymphs had been mutilated, their faces and breasts smashed off. The wantonness of that vandalism had been unnerving – Veraine could sense the presence of war as surely as if he could taste it – and the first glimpse of the palace on the hilltop had been worse. It had loomed over the tree canopies, a great multi-storied stone house with balconied windows rising in tiers. As Veraine stepped from under cover a flock of crows had gone rocketting up, their harsh voices cawing an alarm that could be heard for miles. But there'd been no response from the palace: no movement at all.

Now he stood before the gate, soaked to the skin by

mist and only too aware that he was down to his last reserves of strength and that his sole weapon was a length of branch. Water droplets were pearled in his hair. Not a sound was audible except for his own breathing; even the crows were silent now. It was as if he had stepped into a world that was only half made.

By now he was convinced that the palace had no guards. The building was formed as a great hollow rectangle around a courtyard, with the arched gateway standing wide open and the ancient timber doors hanging awry on their hinges. He could see the grass growing thick about their bases. Somehow that didn't detract from the menace of the entrance passageway.

Veraine took the chance of cover offered by the fog and crept into the darkness of the tunnel. The enclosed place smelled damp, with no scent of wood-smoke such as should betray an inhabited place, and there were no side-passages that he could discern. The only exit was the pale gap of the inner arch, and he slipped out through that into the palace courtyard.

Here, he anticipated, was where he would be most vulnerable, and he paused for a long time looking and listening. The mist and the shadow of the four enclosing walls hid almost all details. He could make out the blank dark patches of windows and something like a wide stone dais in the centre of the yard, but little else. Weeds had heaved up the flagstones around his feet. An absolute silence held sway. He made his way, stepping carefully across the cracked stones on his bare feet, to the structure in the middle of the courtyard. As he got closer he saw that he'd been mistaken: this was no solid platform but a rectangular marble tank, filled to the brim with rainwater. The sight of the pool tugged at his memory like a hooked line, threatening for a moment to bring something wriggling into the light, but then slipped free and left him empty-handed and stung by the loss. He took another step forwards and then all the anguish of forgetting was thrown aside, as he saw that someone was lying on the wide rim at the far side of the pool.

For a long time he hung on that moment, frozen. But the figure didn't move, and slowly the conviction grew in him that it would not. He stepped cautiously around the pool until he stood within arm's length and confirmed his grim suspicion that this other was a corpse.

She lay on the marble kerb, nearly as white under the long drape of her veil as the stone itself. The edge of the silk trailed in the pool and had wicked up the water, so that the translucent cloth covering her from head to toe clung to her slender frame. She wore some sort of thin dress beneath that veil, though the material did nothing to disguise the ashen pallor of her dead flesh. The colourless nipples stood up against the cloth like pebbles, but no breath moved that breast. She'd been beautiful in life and the vestiges of it still clung to her, as delicate as the silk, with no obvious marks of violence or decay upon her. Veraine stared down, his mouth tight with dismay, strung between wanting to recognise that still face and dreading the consequences.

The woman opened her eyes.

Veraine jumped back, cold with shock, and stared in horror as she sat up on the kerb and raised a long, thin arm from under the wet shroud, reaching towards him. He couldn't make a sound. She stood, still draped, and took a step. He retreated but she matched his pace, closing, her dark eyes like pits under the cobweb-cover of her veil. He thought his heart was going to rip itself apart, but as she laid her cold fingertips on his chest he at last found the courage to reach out and grab her throat. It was courage born out of desperation. The revenant shuddered under his grasp, her fingers scrabbling at his wrists, a rasping sound issuing from her gaping lips. Her saw her eyes roll back in her head, and for a moment relief was like a flame in his belly. Then he realised: he was choking her.

He let go and the woman fell to her knees on the cold stones, her lungs heaving. 'I'm sorry,' he gasped.

She pulled the long veil from her head, revealing smooth black hair, and then when she'd composed herself looked up at him. He saw a delicate face with sharp cheekbones barely padded by flesh and arched brows over large, dark eyes rimmed with kohl. It was the look in those eyes that struck him dumb. He had expected fear or rage, and had been about to apologise again, but what he saw made his stomach twist. They were the eyes of a starving wolf bitch, looking upon a fresh carcass. He took another step back.

'There was a time,' she said, 'when to see the Rani Mirabai unveiled would be to suffer the most terrible torture and execution.' Her voice was hoarse.

'Lady,' he said weakly, then dropped his branch and held out his hands to help her up.

She stared at his palms. He wondered if he'd made another insulting error. Then she laughed and slid her hands into his. Her skin was cool, and he had to thrust aside the question of how long she had been lying there in the cold and the mist, and why.

'Do you know me?' he asked.

She tilted her head, eyes bright, smiling a little. 'I've known so many people, and forgotten them. Their faces fly round in my mind like little birds, too swift to catch. Do you have a name?' Now that he could see her bare face, he could reassess her pallor and recognise it as the blanched ivory of a wealthy woman who'd never been exposed to the sun. He tried to release her hands but she held him lightly, looking up into his face.

'Veraine,' he told her.

'Of what land? You're not one of my subjects.'

'Of no land. I don't even know where I am now.'

She opened her eyes wider. 'Then you must have fallen from the sky. Come with me, Veraine,' she commanded, turning away.

'Where to?' he asked, a little more roughly than he intended. 'What is this place?'

She made no reply, only turning upon him eyes whose smouldering challenge made the hair rise on his neck. He took hesitant steps after her, frustrated and afraid. She drew him to a doorway and they entered the body of the palace.

He wouldn't have willingly followed her into that place, except that his head felt as hollow as if he were walking in a dream. The interior was unlit, the ceilings high, their route a path through shadowed rooms that he could barely see. She glimmered before him, her progress unimpeded by the darkness. His skin was tight with gooseflesh, not simply from the cold but from a crawling sensation of unease. The smell of damp was pervasive.

'Keep up.'

'I can't see my way. Tell me where we are.'

'This is the Summer Palace of the Kingdom of Lhanghar.' Her voice was clear now, and it sent little echoes fluttering away into the darkness. 'Here I held my court, and all of Lhanghar attended me. Forty virgins of the purest blood served at my feet, and the elite of the warrior-nobles stood guard. Here there was music which never grew silent and the chime of bells to wake me and to soothe me to sleep. Can you hear them now?

Here were perfumes and spices and peacocks in the gardens, and the milk of a hundred pure white cows brought in golden dishes every day for my bathing. Garlands of orchids crowned the black hair of my maidens and nested among their little breasts, and no man wore the same silken garment twice. My gems were like the stars in the sky for number, and I the pale moon that outshone them. I ate the flesh of hinds and doves and milk-fed lambs, sugared flowers and fruits brought a hundred leagues. Naked children danced for me in the courtyard when I crossed it, and singers charmed the clouds and the winds from the rooftops. It was my summer refuge from the heat of the lowlands. But no refuge from anything else. Lhanghar lies in the heart of the Twenty Kingdoms. Do you know where you are now?'

He did not: the names meant nothing to him. 'What happened then?'

'The Horse-eaters came.'

They were climbing a stair. The banister was an invisible riot of carving under his hand. 'And the Horse-eaters,' he asked, when it became clear that she wasn't going to explain further; 'who are they?'

'They are barbarians,' she offered, her voice thin. 'A great horde of barbarians who came riding from the north-west. They defeated my generals at the river crossing and then they came here, laying waste to every village and settlement in their path.' She paused in front of a door, turning to look down on him, and in her pall of drifting silk she looked like she had coalesced out of mist that had seeped inside. 'They took this house and slew everyone they could find. Then they left, and rode east.' Light bloomed around her as she pushed the door open, and they stepped through into a large room with many windows.

Veraine blinked only for a moment. The shutters in here were open, but the room was still protected from the direct rays of the rising sun by carved sandalwood screens and long silken drapes. In the diffuse light he could see that he was in a chamber opulently furnished with many chests, low tables and couches, though the fabrics were faded and grimy. A large bed dominated one wall, gold leaf glinting on the accents of its ebony frame. A suit of armour slouched on a rack. Veraine went over to this and touched the lacquered breastplate gingerly, but the design looked alien and uncomfortable.

'That belonged to my husband,' Mirabai said, watching him.

'Is he alive?'

'No. He died long before the invasion.'

Veraine stepped away sideways to the next object along the wall; a mirror of polished obsidian as tall as he was, framed in silver, a thing of extraordinary opulence. He looked at his own reflection in its sinister depths and saw a tall man, athletic in build, slabs of muscle chevroned down his bare torso to the cloth slung low from his hips, his eyes darkly shadowed and made even more intense by the volcanic glass, his mouth a hard line amid the beginnings of a black beard. He ran his fingers down an old scar that crossed his ribs on his left side. An event that brutal, he thought, ought to have left some inkling of memory.

'Am I a Horse-eater?' he asked at last.

Mirabai laughed and was suddenly behind him, sliding cool hands about his waist. Veraine jumped and turned quickly to face her, disliking the clamminess of the wet silk. He pulled the veil off her shoulders and dropped it to the floor. She shivered and bit her lip, looking up into his face with a flash of the avidity she had revealed before. The clothes she wore under the veil were equally wet, but they clung to her body in a manner entirely more appealing, the fabric transparent where it touched the ivory skin.

Veraine said nothing, but his grim expression demanded an answer. She smiled again. 'No, of course not. Why do you have to ask?'

'I was hurt – in a fight, I think,' he admitted. 'When I woke up I couldn't remember anything. My history is ... lost.'

Her eyebrows lifted even further. 'You remember nothing at all?'

'I have fragments, pictures, but they carry no meaning.' He hesitated, trying to put it into words. 'And there are things which have meaning to me, but I don't know why.' The pool, he thought. Something about a raised pool of water.

She laughed down her nose, the delicate arches of her nostrils quivering. 'How strange a stranger! Maybe you did drip-drop down with the morning mist, on the breath of the mountain.'

'Maybe,' he said, uneasy.

'But you're not a Horse-eater, I can tell you that. I think you're an Irolian.'

He tasted the word. 'What does that mean?'

'That you're months distant from home. The Irolian Empire lies across the desert to the east. The only reason I know that is that I once gave an audience to some of their ambassadors. They looked a little like you.'

'What were they like?'

She smiled at the memory and he realised she enjoyed playing with him. 'Arrogant.' She put her palm on his bare chest and he let it lie there. 'Beautiful men, with their fine armour and their long legs. But arrogant as peacocks, ignorant of every other nation and proud of it too. They didn't like dealing with a queen. They value women very little.' She traced the length of his breastbone with her polished nail. 'It's rumoured that their preference is for other men in everything.' She emphasised that last word and raised her eyes questioningly to his face.

She might have been trying to provoke him, but Veraine felt no sting. He felt nothing at all for these putative Irolians. 'I've come a long way then,' he said.

Mirabai's eyes lowered modestly. She had very long lashes that lay on her pale cheek like smudges of soot. Her hair too was charcoal-black, hanging in a single thick braid down to the small of her back, though she was no young girl – he could see the tiny lines feathered about her eyes. In every way she was the opposite of the robust Mehetchi, and yet in her slender, almost sickly, fragility she was still desirable.

'Are you hungry?'

'Starving,' he said without exaggeration.

She stepped away and struck a small gong near the foot of the bed. 'I've been inhospitable. I'll order you food.' At the thought, his stomach cramped painfully and he could only nod. 'Sit,' she offered, waving him to a divan. As he was settling himself a door opened in the corner of the room and in came a figure who knelt and bowed her forehead to the floor.

'Ah; Jodha,' said the Rani. 'We have a guest; bring him a good meal.'

The servant and the stranger stared at each other, and their surprise was equally matched. Veraine had assumed that Jodha, in her dirty dress, was an aged serving maid. He tried to hide his shock upon realising that the person in the dress although aged was clearly male; a skinny, bearded man with a damning glare. Brass bracelets were stacked up his wiry wrists.

Mirabai didn't seem to notice anything amiss. When the servant had bowed out again she went to a table and poured a cup of liquid. She sat close beside Veraine and pressed it into his hand. He looked into the cup doubtfully; the liquid was murky and the silver of the cup tarnished.

'It's fermented tamarind. Flavoured with rose-petals, pepper, almonds and poppy seed. It's very strong – some prefer to drink it with water.' She took a sip and pressed the cup to his lips. He could think of no reason to refuse the drink, though something deep in his mind twisted away, fearful. The spirit burnt his throat, and though the taste was too sweet to be pleasant he was grateful for the warmth.

'There were things the Horse-eaters didn't find,' Mirabai said, kneeling up at his side with a rosewood box of sweetmeats. He ate two, ravenous even for the sickly almond and aniseed paste. But even in his hunger he couldn't forget what had brought him to this house.

'I need your help, Rani. I came here to find a woman.'

'You've succeeded, then.' Her smile was as sweet as the confectionery, her pale lips moist from the tamarind drink.

'No,' he reprimanded gently. 'I mean one I was travelling with when I was hurt. I think she knows me. I'd hoped she'd been brought here.'

'And who is this lucky woman? Your wife? Your mother?' Mirabai's hand came to rest on his thigh, making the muscle there jump.

'I don't know.'

'Do you remember what she looks like?'

He shook his head, and with the movement felt the rush in his skull. 'What's in these?' he demanded, suddenly angry, pushing the box aside.

'Only bhang. Nothing to be afraid of.' She popped one of the crusted, sweaty morsels between her lips and then leant forwards to kiss him. He could taste the anise on her tongue and the hunger behind the sweetness. Despite his state of deprivation he lost all interest in food. 'Are they not to your taste?' she asked, her lips sticky on his.

'I'd prefer something a little more satisfying,' he admitted. His scrotum felt heavy.

'I'll try my best,' she breathed, and delved between his lips with her cool tongue. Instinct and his better judgement warred briefly, but the demands of the flesh were stronger than any sense of unease. She slipped open the wet knots of his fouta with practised expertise as they kissed, and wrapped her fingers around the girth of his cock. His cold, aching muscles thrilled with new heat. When their lips parted they both looked down to enjoy the sight of her pale hand playing up and down on his erection. He'd come to full hardness almost at once. Mirabai smiled hungrily, showing pearly teeth. He moved his hips, relishing each exquisite stroke, knowing that a very few more minutes would see him spending irrevocably.

'Come here,' he chided, lifting her into his lap, ignoring the flash of frustration in her eyes. She straddled him but didn't sit. Her body was slight, her breasts small, but the nipples under the rough silk were stiff in anticipation of his hands and her lithe spine descended to a trim and surprisingly rounded bottom. He ran his hand up her leg, searching under her skirt, so intent upon her sex that he found but didn't really register the ridges of scar tissue on the skin of her inner thigh. He cupped her mons, finding the little mound hard in his palm. There was no lush padding of flesh on her bones and only the rough silk of her fleece told his fingers that he didn't have hold of some skinny child. She was dry to the touch. And even though her lips were fierce on his own, her sex recoiled from his exploring fingertips. Her sharp little teeth bit at his tongue, and as she slid her hands up his shoulders to the nape of his neck her nails bit too, scoring tracks. He didn't think fast enough to stop her, but when the pain roared through his skull his hands moved faster than thought, flying up to capture her wrists and jerk her away, not gently.

'No,' he gasped, sweat standing up on his temples. 'Not there.'

She stared at him, lips parted, until he slowly reduced the pressure of his grasp. It occurred to him that that porcelain flesh would bruise very easily, that he'd already left marks upon her.

'Your head?' she asked.

'Where I was injured.' He didn't want to think about the missing patch of hair or the still-raw scab.

'Poor lamb,' she whispered, her face as expressionless as a doll's. She reached for his cup. 'You ought to drink more,' she suggested, taking a full sip. Her lips glistened as she moved in. She insinuated her tongue softly and let the spirit pass from her mouth to his, and he felt its bite in his throat. Then as they kissed she lowered herself upon his crotch. His ardour had been cooled by his pain, but he stiffened anew to find her now, at last, slick and wet. She rubbed herself upon his thickening length. He wondered what it was that had thawed her so, but was too busy manoeuvring his cock into her to spare it much attention. She took him easily, her interior grasp cool and firm, and he let fall a little noise of satisfaction as he slid in to the hilt.

'That's good,' she whispered, stirring her hips.

He reached out to clasp her breasts, kneading their small softness through her clothes. If there'd been some means of entrance he would have freed them, but he couldn't find laces or tags and his questing seemed to irritate Mirabai. She squirmed, losing focus, and then took his hands and wrapped them around her own neck, squeezing. He tightened his grasp and saw her lashes flutter, heard the rasp of breath in her constricted throat, felt her pelvis buck on his. He understood. He knew what she wanted. His groin jerked to meet her rhythm and the wet grind of their coupling filled the room with an animal musk, but even as he revelled in the sensation filling his prick and felt the growing readiness of his tightening balls, he knew he wouldn't be able to trust his hands in the extremity of his crisis. He tore them away and bore her over backwards instead, leaning over her, one hand bearing down hard on her breast. Her head was nearly brushing the floor, her braid coiled like a snake on the worn carpet. He heard her groan as the blood rushed to her skull and he ground into her, baring his teeth.

At that moment the door opened and Jhoda came back in, bearing a tray. Veraine froze, far more concerned for Mirabai's dignity than his own. He waited for the old man to avert his face and duck out. But Jhoda put the tray down on the table and stood scowling straight at them, his expression a compound of jealousy and disgust impossible to ignore. Veraine felt anger fire his lust like salt on burning driftwood. 'Get out!' he growled.

'Don't stop!' the Rani gasped. She must have been aware that they were being watched, even upside-down she must have been able to see Jhoda, yet she seemed insensible to any shame. 'Fuck me, you shit!'

Jhoda wiped his hands on his dress and left.

Veraine felt the rage sweep his veins, felt his fingers biting into her flesh, and felt the semen come boiling out of him like liquid fury, his thrusts like blows.

* * *

He woke in Mirabai's bed and lay there for some time collecting his thoughts. He didn't feel good. From the colour of the light he must have slept for hours, yet there was no sense of refreshment. His throat was parched and his stomach roiled uncomfortably, and when he turned his head to see if she lay next to him he became aware of a dull and evil throbbing in his skull.

He was alone.

He slowly enumerated the causes of his discontent, obscurely anxious that he understood what was happening. This place made him uneasy, deep in his bones, though any causes he could identify were trivial enough. The meal Jhoda had delivered had been highly spiced, but he'd had nothing to drink all that time except the tamarind liquor and he was now suffering the consequences. He hadn't enjoyed the food, for though the sauce and the bread were good enough and he'd been ravenous, the unidentified meat therein had been little more than gristle and small bones and now it was sitting heavily in his guts. And then, deepest of all, there was Mirabai. Satisfaction had eluded them, for all their rutting.

It wasn't as if she'd complained, or had any cause to. He'd been as attentive as he could, and yet there was clearly something wrong there. She hadn't climaxed. She'd refused to let him undress her and had shrugged away his hands impatiently, almost angrily, when he tried to caress her clitoris or breasts. What she wanted, he didn't know. He'd been too proud to ask her outright. Now he laid back and told himself he was an idiot.

He thought of the Rani's tiny hand, pale on his bare chest, and suddenly was overwhelmed by another image, another hand – this one cinnamon-dark, splayed across his flat stomach under flickering firelight, a mound of ruddy curls heavy on his ribs and tangled under his fingers. For a moment the scene flared bright in his memory, and then it faded away. He stared at the cracked ceiling with eyes wide, but saw nothing except stains.

Come back, he mouthed.

The bedding smelled bad, he became aware; not just the mustiness of sex-sodden sheets but a mildewy dampness that eventually prompted him to roll over and sit up. His skull thumped and he reached for the cup beside the bed, judging it best to stave off the hangover with more alcohol since he had no water. But he found a cockroach nearly as long as his thumb floating drowned in the liquid, and when he looked over at the dishes that they'd abandoned on the rug he saw the shiny brown carapaces of dozens of roaches in lively motion. Veraine grimaced and flung the cup across the room at the diners, finding grim satisfaction in seeing them scurry away lightning-fast under the furniture. The spirit made a new stain on the carpet.

Rising, he moved gingerly around until he found his clothes and the stoppered jug of liquor. He drank straight from its neck, and when he lowered the pitcher he found he was facing one of the window screens. It was intricately carved with a scene of an elephant hunt, the figures inlaid in ivory into the fragrant sandalwood. Feeling a strong desire to reconnect with the clean air and the living landscape, and to see his surroundings by good strong daylight, Veraine moved the screen carefully to the side and turned towards the window beyond, but was blocked by bars. The area between the screen and the drapes was filled with a tall birdcage. There was no movement from within. A dozen tiny, sad clusters of dusty feathers and clenched claws lay scattered across the floor. He rubbed his hands across his brow, shaking his head but somehow not surprised.

When he turned back for the bottle Mirabai was standing behind him.

'You're up,' she said, and giggled. She'd combed out her hair and it fell about her shoulders like a black veil. She was all black and white, her hair and brows and eyes in uncompromising contrast to her dress and face and bare, slender arms. No jewellery adorned her but she still shone like the moon; and like the moon gave off a pallid, bloodless, uncanny light. He felt his cock twitch and knew that both the pity and the unease he felt were tainted by a far more primal lust.

'I need to go soon,' he said hoarsely. 'I have to find this woman.'

The Rani cocked her head slightly, like a bird. 'Find her, bind her.'

'Are you sure no one has brought a woman here? I remember – I think I've some idea what she looks like. She'd be very dark.' He thought of Mehetchi with her clear skin like boiled butter. 'Not like the people round here – a foreign woman. She has red hair, I think.'

'Then she isn't your wife,' the Rani announced sharply. 'Your concubine or your whore, perhaps.'

Veraine frowned. 'What do you mean by that?'

'She's not an Irolian, is she? She's a Yamani.'

The word meant nothing to him except the name of the language they spoke. 'And?'

'And the Irolians made their Empire by conquering the Yamani kingdoms and enslaving the people. That woman is most likely your slave.'

He didn't know what to say to that. She might be lying; he didn't trust the slyness in her eyes. He pictured the dark red hair wrapped around his fingers and thought, she beds with me, but said nothing.

'You're wasting your time looking for her here, anyway. She hasn't come here.'

'Are you sure?'

'You're the first stranger I've seen in a year.'

He nodded. 'But the servants might have seen someone . . . ?'

'What servants?' She gestured around her. 'There's only Jhoda, the silly old bitch. Everyone else is dead or has run away.' She smiled, mirthlessly. 'The Horse-eaters were quite thorough.'

Veraine digested this. Somehow he'd assumed that there were other people around, that the Rani wasn't simply alone with an old man. 'I'm sorry.'

Mirabai's eyes were huge and black. 'And why do you need your past back anyway? What if it's full of pain and shame?'

'I need to know who I am,' he said softly.

'You might regret that.'

She sleeps with me; she lay with her head against my chest. 'And she might need me.'

There was a cold smile at that. 'Don't you think you'll be a bit late?'

A tiny bubble of pain burst in Veraine's chest and he turned away to rake his fingers across the bars. Why did she have to state such a vicious, undeniable truth?

'Is she beautiful?' the Rani asked, after a long silence.

'I don't know.'

'You said you remembered her.'

'I remember her hair. Her hands.' He clenched his fists.

'And you lost her in this fight?'

'Yes.'

'Who did you fight with?'

He shook his head, defeated. 'I don't know that.'

'If she was taken by professional slavers, not just villagers, then they'll have already shipped her down to the coast. There is a big slave market at Siya Ran Thu.

She could be taken anywhere in the world. You can't find her now.'

He turned a cold, grim gaze on her and she shrank back from him, hands moving to her throat. 'I can go to Siya Ran Thu though,' he said. 'Do you have weapons here?'

'Weapons?'

'I need something I can fight with.'

'Come this way.'

She led him from her chamber, down another dark corridor and through another door. Stepping into the circular room beyond, Veraine was taken aback. The floor and walls were covered right up to the roof in blue and white tiles, so that his first thought was that this was some sort of bathhouse. But there was no bath. The roof was a white-plastered dome, and set into the plaster were large pieces of thick glass which allowed the daylight to sift in. There were no other windows, though there was a door in the far wall. Four tiled pillars, joined in a horseshoe shape by a curved marble balustrade, supported the ceiling. It was much cooler in here.

'What is this?'

'My husband's pride and joy.' She gestured him over to one wall, and as he approached he saw that there were racks protruding from the tiles. 'His collection. The Horse-eaters took all the bows, but were less interested in the others.' She indicated the empty spaces, then let him see for himself what remained, and Veraine felt his heart lift. Despite the gaps on the racks there were plenty of weapons left in the royal collection: beautiful weapons designed for show as well as use, mostly bronze but some steel ones too. There were halberds and scimitars, thrusting knives with triangular blades, axes, elephant goads and ebony clubs and daggers of twisted buck-horn, maces with heads cast in the shape of clenched fists; weapons familiar and unfamiliar, inlaid with silver or chased with gilt, draped with scarlet tassels, hafted on ivory or studded with semiprecious stones. Veraine ran his hands over them, lifted them, swung them, tested the edges and raised his eyebrows at the workmanship.

'What are these?' he asked, touching the savage spikes set into a pair of metal cuffs clearly intended to fit around the hands.

'Waghnakh,' she replied: 'tiger-claws.' She was leaning against the wall by a full set of intricately etched silver darts. 'Do you know how to use them?'

Veraine let them drop back onto their hook. 'Not my thing. Now this – this is more like it.' He had spotted a steel blade with a long handle and a wicked point. Taking it down he hefted it for balance. The handle, inset with silver wire, was longer than he was used to and it had only a single edge, but the broad back to the steel and the two-handed grip suggested a parrying style too. Interesting. He felt he could get used to that.

'I like it in here,' Mirabai's dreamy voice said behind him. 'We used to play so many amusing games.'

The skin of his lower back contracted around an icy point.

He reacted without hesitation, spinning round and knocking the knife from her hand with the hard edge of his fist. The weapon landed in a puddle of refracted light and the rubies in its hilt seemed to catch fire. 'That was a stupid trick, Rani,' he said through clenched teeth. His head thumped and he had to struggle to swallow his anger

'You're fast!' she gasped. She was clutching her sore fingers, but there was no anger or panic in her wide eyes, only delight. 'You're good at this.'

He took a step towards her and she shrank away, but

her lips trembled into a smile. 'Games like that will get you hurt,' he said.

'What's the point of a game where nobody does?' Her shoulder knocked against a rack and she turned her head. Following her glance he saw that she was backed against a collection of whips. The flush on her pale cheeks was visible even in this dim light as she whispered, 'We played in here often.'

'Oh I see,' he said contemptuously. 'That sort of game, was it? Little amusements for your husband and yourself?'

She took a dreamy pace forwards and laid her cheek on his bare breastbone, light as a sparrow, cool as deep water. He was too proud to retreat from her. 'It was a necessary pleasure,' she said. 'If a slave had displeased my husband, then she had to be punished.'

The light pressure of her body against his was maddening. 'And you enjoyed that, did you?'

Her hands fluttered across his ribs and she turned her face up to his. 'Wouldn't you? Don't tell me you've never wielded a whip. I know better than that.'

He could feel the ache in his clenched jaw. 'You've no idea about me.'

'No?' Her eyes were like jet. 'I know more than you do, my poor lost lover. There's a darkness in your heart, and I can see it even if you deny it. Dark like the night. You –' she placed her cold fingers on his nipple '– would have a talent for that sort of game.'

'It's not a game, though, is it?' His flesh made a hard point between her fingers and he could smell the fragrance of her hair, like flowers left to rot in the rain. 'Not for the poor slave whose life depends on your whim.'

She pulled back a little, pouting. 'We didn't kill them. Executions were carried out in the courtyard. In here they only danced under the lash. Beautifully.'

He stared at her, stony-faced. He was aroused despite his anger by her proximity and her touch. But that only angered him more.

'Besides, they were only slaves.'

And the anger boiling inside him took fire in his belly, burning with a blue alcoholic flame. He dropped his falchion and grabbed her shoulders, nearly lifting her slight frame from the floor. 'How dare you?' he hissed into her face. 'You bathed in milk and wiped your arse on silk and had total power over those poor bastards, and you have no idea what real pain and fear are like.'

'Teach me then,' she whispered. Her eyes burned. 'Teach me pain. Hit me. That's what you want to do, isn't it? '

'Hit you?'

Her pale lips writhed into a sneer; 'Can't you do it, you coward?'

Without another word he thrust her over to the low balustrade and shoved her face-down over the rail so that her head almost touched the floor and her rump was thrust high, and then while still keeping the pressure on her back he scooped up her skirts and flung them over her head. Her narrow hips writhed and she scrabbled at the tiles but she couldn't right herself. Her moon-pale cheeks, each small globe tight and pert, quivered as he dug his fingers into her flesh.

'Like it now?' he asked, and struck her hard. Mirabai shrieked aloud. Her whole arse bounced from the blow and a red palm-print bloomed upon her paleness. 'Again?' he demanded, and landed the next strike on the other cheek. Her thighs thrashed helplessly and her buttocks heaved, the dark cleft between them exposed to view, its soft fur no protection. He retreated to arm's length to get a better swing; there was no need to hold her down. And he walloped her hard, not listening to the shrieks that almost drowned the slap of flesh on flesh and not pausing for rest until his arm ached and his hand was numb and her arse was a burning rosy mound seemingly swollen to twice its original size. He stopped and wiped the sweat from his eyes, breathing hard. His head was in a muddy, throbbing haze and his erection was like an iron spike. He laid one hand roughly on the Rani's rump, feeling the heat. There wasn't one patch of untouched skin on either buttock. She moaned and twisted her hips as he squeezed a quivering handful, spreading her cheeks wide as she tried to escape his harsh fingers. He could smell her sex, sharp and musky. He could see the dark puckered hole above the shadowed valley of her cleft. He could see the pink lips of her labia thrusting out through the dark pubic pelt, and the glisten of moisture on the folds. Without thinking he clapped his hand to her pudenda and found them soft and swollen, as full of juice as a peach left in the sun. He squeezed her hard and to his utter shock she screamed and came in his hand – there was no mistaking it; his palm was soaked, his fingers running with her juices. Her vulva clenched and sucked at his hand.

'You dirty bitch,' he breathed.

'Oh please,' she begged, beating her fists on the tiles: 'Fuck me now!'

Left-handed, he ripped the flimsy silk of her dress right up her back. He pulled out his stiff prick and dragged the engorged head up and down her cleft, soaking it in her juices. Then he plunged his tool right into her overflowing well.

'No!' she gasped: 'sodomise me!'

'Shut up, slut.' He pulled out. The head of his cock was purple with pumped blood and slick with her juices. The shaft felt as hard as bone under his hand. He steered the weapon to her other orifice, to the tight and pulsing iris of her anus; it was dry but he made no attempt to lubricate it. He had no intention of being gentle. Without mercy he rammed into her. For a moment the ring of muscle resisted him, but it couldn't hold out under such attack and he forced entry, hearing with cold joy the perfect, musical accompaniment of her scream. He climaxed in a few thrusts. The pleasure almost blanked out the white streak of pain in his pounding skull.

As he recovered, still buried in her arse, his surroundings came only slowly back into focus. He saw the sweep of her spine before him and heard her gasping brokenly. A drop of sweat fell from his brow to the small of her back and he moved automatically to wipe it away. Under his thumb he felt a smooth, unnatural undulation, a polished ripple too hard for flesh. He blinked several times and had to use his hands as much as his eyes to work out that he had found, in the whorls and ridges of shining scar tissue left upon her skin by fire, incontestable proof that the Rani, despite his accusations, was more than familiar with genuine pain.

Doubt and a creeping horror at his actions started to eat into the orgasmic glow. He pulled out of her with far more care than he had shown in penetration, then leaned against one of the pillars, watching as she hauled herself back over the balustrade.

'Don't stop,' she moaned as she turned to face him. Her ruined dress hung loosely off her shoulder, revealing a breast puckered with ancient wounds. She slid to her knees in a pool of white silk. 'Please, keep going. Don't stop. Don't leave me.' She lurched forwards, grabbing him around the thighs and trying to seize his cock in her mouth, but he intercepted her with frantic hands, pushing her aside so that he could tighten the knots of his fouta. She fell to the floor then, kissing his ankles and licking at his dirty feet. He cringed, but she couldn't see. 'I'll do anything you want,' she promised, gasping; 'anything at all. I'm not afraid. You can do what you want with me. You can hurt me as much as you like. Just stay.'

He couldn't respond for a long moment and he couldn't move, because what he wanted to do was kick her. Her abjection roused in him a churning revulsion, her weakness made him want to be cruel, and the small brutality of what he'd done already cried out to be vindicated by committing worse. He realised that she wasn't lying; that he could stay and wreak any atrocity he liked upon her body, and that nothing would stop her begging for more except death. Maybe she would welcome even that. Maybe it was what she wanted.

The thought made him dizzy.

He bent and seized her shoulders. 'Stop it!' he ordered, knotting his hands around her fragile arms. 'Get up!' When she only clung tighter and sobbed louder he picked her up bodily and thrust her away from him so that she staggered against the far wall and collapsed there. 'What the hell are you doing to yourself?' he demanded. He scrubbed his hands across his face, trying to rub off the filth he felt encrusting him, but they reeked of sex and he stopped at once, nauseated. 'What are you doing to *me*?'

'You're too weak,' she moaned in a broken voice. 'You're a coward. Useless. Useless.'

'Why?' he whispered. 'Why are you doing this?'

She tilted her face up to his horrified gaze, her white skin glazed with sweat, her dark eyes blank, not like eyes at all but like holes into some terrible interior darkness. 'The pain,' she breathed. 'The pain reminds me of what it was like to be alive.'

4 **Tiger, Tiger**

Myrna looked around her and realised that the younger women had already been in the pools and were out again, dripping in huddles, while the supervisors handed out bundles of new clothes. Had it really been that long? The men were already dressed. Her own group were struggling out of the grubby clothes that they'd travelled in for days. She got to her feet and tugged at her headcloth, letting the heavy plume of her hair fall free. She dropped the scarf without regret, feeling pleasure in the cool touch of the air on her scalp. Then her glance fell on Gohlit through the clustered crowd and her heart cramped.

Gohlit, wet and gleaming, was clutching a bundle of clothing to her as if too ashamed of her nakedness to get through the ordeal of putting the garments on. Her pretty face was warped by misery into something intolerable. Myrna knew there was nothing she could do to save the girl, but that didn't stop the dismay twisting under her ribs. She strode out of her group, past the guard who had turned away to make a ribald comment to his friend and through the scattering of wet and stumbling girls to Gohlit. She put her hands gently around her face and turned it so that they were eye to eye. The younger woman's were raw from crying.

'Gohlit, please remember,' Myrna said, speaking softly and as clearly as she could. 'Whatever happens to you – whatever – it will not last forever. The pain will end. And after that, it won't matter to you any more.

You'll be made anew.' She took a deep breath. 'Did you ever hurt yourself when you were a little girl? Did you cry?'

Gohlit nodded, frightened beyond speech.

'Does that pain matter to you now? Do you even remember what you cried about when you were a baby? Gohlit, in your next life, the pains in this won't mean a thing to you.'

A heavy hand descended on her arm and she was wrenched away. 'Get back in line!' the guard snapped, but though he lifted his fist it didn't fall. They were, Myrna guessed, trying not to bruise the merchandise now. She seized one more look back at Gohlit, trying to cast her strength with that glance, as she was hauled back to the pool edge.

'Rags off,' said the woman standing with the scrubbing brush.

Obediently she let her dress fall, stepping down the bank into the pool. The water was cool round her calves. She heard the woman splashing up behind her. 'Deeper in, girl. Get that hair clean. No one will want you if you stink.'

She waded in to her waist among the other women and as she bent and sluiced her hair the supervisor scoured her back. It stung, but it was good to get clean. When the woman abandoned her and waded off to administer to others, her dress billowing around her in the water, Myrna kept ducking and scrubbing, using a handful of grass snatched from the margin to cleanse herself. She was aware of the guards and the overseers and captives watching them, aware of eyes all around, but it didn't detract from the simple pleasure of bathing. When she straightened the sun shone on her bare breasts, clasping her upper body in tender warmth. Her nipples were hard as pebbles from the chill, her torso gleamed and her hair slopped heavily on her back and shoulders. Sun sparkled in the droplets that fell from her fingers. She rubbed her fingers through her scalp, feeling the warmth of the light on her belly and inside it too.

When the order came to leave the pool she obeyed and stood wringing out her hair, making no attempt as the others did to hide her body. It wasn't that she was unselfconscious: far from it. She could feel the sun and the breeze on every particle of her flesh and she revelled in it. The gaze of others seemed to enhance that sensation.

A horn sounded across the bay.

In that moment the place changed. Everyone in authority turned towards the water, and following their gaze Myrna saw it too: a single vessel emerging from behind one of the steep islands, a silk banner flying from its stern. One of the guards nearby swore. Then suddenly the whole place was in motion like a broken nest of ants; guards and supervisors were grabbing prisoners and hustling them down to the beach. A pile of folded cloth was thrust into Myrna's hands by a frantic woman: 'Get them on, get them on!'

'What's happening?' someone next to her said fearfully.

'It's them!' the nearest guard rasped. 'Get moving!'

Myrna managed to disentangle the clothes but struggled to pull them on over her wet skin. They were a dull white and she identified the fabric as raw silk. A long skirt with a wide neck settled eventually just below her hips, cloaking her to the ankle but leaving her navel exposed. The other piece she had been given was a tight sleeveless choli bodice that laced up at the front. This covered her breasts, just about, but the whole ensemble left her midriff naked, emphasising the curve of her waist and the overhang of her breasts. She looked around and saw that all the female captives were in similar dress. Damp was making the silk cling to her, turning the thin fabric into a second, paler, skin through which the warm tones of her flesh seemed to glow.

'Hurry up!' the harsh command came again, and she was pushed with the other captives down to the beach with its strip of white sand and shoved into line with the rest of her group. The younger girls occupied the far wing and the men were stationed in the middle. As they reached their places the gilded boat drew into the shallows and men with ropes jumped from the prow to make it fast. Myrna squinted into the bright light flashing off the water, trying to make out who commanded the vessel.

The woman on her right was praying rapidly under her breath.

'Rao Dhammazhedi himself,' said the overseer hurrying past down the line, in a tight voice. 'That's just what we need.' He paused to yank someone's rucked skirt into place, then scuttled on. Myrna could see the fear in his eyes.

A gangplank was lowered over the side of the boat and a man stepped up from the deck onto it. Even from this distance Myrna could see that he was very tall. In two swift strides he was down on the shore and in another moment he was joined by a woman, equally nimble, who needed no helping hand to keep her balance down the incline.

'On your knees!' shouted one of the guards, and the cry was repeated all across the beach. Everyone – prisoners and soldiers, reivers and overseers – folded to the floor and pressed their foreheads to the backs of their hands flat on the ground. Myrna started to follow suit, but she got no further than her knees. She couldn't tear her eyes away from the couple on the foreshore who so clearly demanded her fullest attention. She remained straight-backed, the only figure still upright in the whole line, as they stepped away from the boat. The man, resplendent in a coat that seemed to reflect the sunlight like gold, paused to speak to one of the sailors but his companion didn't want to wait; she strode up the beach straight towards Myrna's group, and she felt her heart turn over within her as she watched the woman advance.

This woman was nothing like any other she'd seen. In the sunlight she seemed to burn and even as she entered the shadow of the cliff she still gleamed. She was immensely tall, her bared head sported hair cut short enough to display the nape of her neck – extraordinary for a woman – and she moved like a leopard on the prowl. As she drew closer Myrna realised she must be fully as tall as Veraine and that the bare stomach between her blouse and skirt was taut with shadowy blocks of abdominal muscle clearly visible about a slender waist. Gold bracelets were entwined around her arms, but didn't hide the hard slabs of muscle under the flawless skin. Her shoulders were broad, her hips lithe, her breasts high like a girl's though she was clearly no child. She didn't look mortal. She was like a woman cast from gold and she carried the gleam of fire.

Myrna felt the sand shift under her knees, and everything solid in the world crumbled with it.

The woman strode along the line of prostrated bodies, her gaze slipping over them with apparent indifference. She stopped a pace away from Myrna, who lowered her own gaze, searching inwardly for equanimity and trying to order her thoughts, seeing only dimly the woman's skirt with its heavy layers of maroon silk smothered in embroidery worked with gold thread and carnelians.

'Overseer; tell me why this one doesn't bow.' The Tiger Lady's voice was simultaneously the softest of purrs and as hard as diamond.

A supervisor climbed to his feet and gawped at the sight confronting him. Myrna was facing the wrong way to see him go red, then pale, but she could hear the stammer in his voice; 'Great lady – this one is simple. Born witless, the reivers told me. She doesn't understand what goes on.'

The lady lifted a hand towards Myrna's chin. She could see the long fingers, the gilded nails that had been filed to wicked points. 'So you're bringing me idiots now, are you?'

'She has other virtues, great lady,' the overseer squeaked.

'Really?' The hand tightened under her jaw and with careless, terrible strength jerked her to her feet before releasing her. 'Novelty value perhaps.'

The captives on either side were shrinking away from her. Myrna stood under that merciless gaze, knowing that her damp and clinging clothes were no more concealing than the milky bloom on the curves of a ripe plum. She could feel the warmth of the taller woman like the glow of a furnace on her face, could smell the scent of her – like heated cloves – and it was making her head spin. The Tiger Lady had a curved, sardonic mouth, arched brows and eyes like polished amber; Myrna had to tip her head back to meet them.

'Is he right then?' she enquired. 'Are you a simpleton?'

'You judge,' Myrna said, her voice hoarse.

She quirked one brow. Then she reached out and dragged her long fingers through Myrna's wet and tangled hair, pulling her head back with one hand while she stroked her exposed neck with the other. Myrna could feel her pulse slamming in her throat and knew that the lady could feel it under her fingertips. 'Well, have you the wit to be afraid, little mouse?'

Myrna swallowed. 'I'm not afraid,' she answered obliquely.

'Idiot,' she murmured softly. 'I'm going to kill you now.' Her nails bit into neck and scalp.

'Is that supposed to frighten me?' She saw the lady hesitate, the tip of her tongue peeking out between her lips. 'I've lived a thousand lifetimes,' Myrna said. 'I will live a thousand more, if necessary, until my purpose is complete. You can't stop me.'

A cold smile answered her. 'But I can certainly affect the conditions under which you leave this one.' Hot fingertips closed on her earlobe. 'Doesn't that worry you, Mouse?'

'Pain is nothing,' Myrna told her, knowing she wouldn't understand. 'Fear is less than nothing.'

'Truly? Is it nothing if I turn you over to the palace guard for their sport? Is it nothing if I take a knife and pare you raw, inch by inch? Is this pain nothing?'

Hot lips brushed her own, the sharpened nails sliced into her earlobe, and pain poured across her skull like water and flooded her veins. She blinked and stepped away from her body on the soul's swift feet, and didn't cry out or wince. A lifetime and more's training in the art of Sunyata, of Not Feeling, of Emptiness, was at her command. Flesh is dust, she thought; I am immortal.

'Maybe it's not enough,' the great lady admitted, easing off the pressure. Blood was running freely down her captive's neck. She stooped to lick the crimson runnels, nuzzling at the torn lobe. 'Ah. You taste of the desert sands,' she whispered. 'And incense. Sandalwood and smoke. Parchment. Dust.'

Myrna's eyes opened wide in shock.

The Tiger Lady pulled back, her lips smeared. 'I smell betrayal on you,' she said thoughtfully. 'Broken vows. And...' Without finishing her sentence she reached down and clasped Myrna's mons, and the slight woman gave a gasp then that the pain had never been able to wrench from her. Her legs almost gave way and she sagged forwards against the other woman's arm.

This wasn't what she'd been trained for. This wasn't pain. It was a wet heat low down in her belly and a tingling ache in her breasts. It was a scent of musk and a leaking moisture that even human senses would not have been able to miss. And weakness, not just in her limbs but a helplessness spreading like spilt wine through her every part, staining her red.

'Oh Mouse,' said the great lady.

'What do you have there, Shinsawbu?' said a lazy masculine voice, as deep and dark as the forest itself.

Myrna managed to focus a wild glance upon the newcomer, and the remnant of strength left in her seemed to shrivel like leaves in hot oil. It was the man from the boat – if 'man' was an adequate term. Two average men together wouldn't have matched him for bulk. He was taller even than an Irolian, broad with it, and yet he carried the weight lightly. There was a sinuosity to his muscle and a grace to his carriage that made the hairs on her neck stand up. His arms were folded across a torso clothed in a turmeric-yellow coat that hung open to the waist, where it was bound by a broad orange sash, and from there over tight trousers down to his knees. The bare chest framed by the satin gleamed with the sheen of polished bronze. His hair hung in black, oiled ringlets, matched by a dark moustache. His face was handsome, but brutally hard.

He had the same amber eyes as his sister. And the same scent of cloves and hot leather.

Myrna was swamped by the memory of her first glimpse of Veraine and his officers. It had been a shock to her then; the tall soldiers in their white tunics with their long hair and their bare legs, their loud voices and harsh accents, the gleam and clash of bronze armour and the horse-stink they'd brought with them into the cool antechamber of the temple. They'd seemed impossibly alien – barely human. Now she was going through that again, though it was a year later and she had far more experience of the wide world. Her pulse was thumping against the invading knuckles.

'I have a mouse, brother,' Shinsawbu said, smiling. 'A pretty little mouse.' Rao Dhammazhedi lifted one corner of his mouth in a sneer, as if anything further were too much effort. 'But she hasn't the wit to fear the cat, it seems.'

'That can soon be fixed. I've never met any creature that couldn't be taught to fear.'

'Don't you fear even him?' the Tiger Lady wondered, stroking Myrna's face and squeezing her sex, long and firm. Myrna bit her lip. She knew from one glance at him that any woman would be a fool not to fear this man. She had seen that cold, dead look before; it was the gaze of a man in whom pity and imagination and compromise had long been eaten away by the gnawing acid of power. It was the look of a man who could not remember a time when there was any will but his own in play. She shook her head, wishing the roaring in her skull would still.

'Go on, Mouse,' said Shinsawbu; 'say something clever.' She rippled her fingers in the swollen swamp of her sex and Myrna felt her spine turn to mush. She bit back a moan.

'I'm unimpressed,' the great lord remarked.

It took all her willpower to frame her words. 'I am a goddess,' she said thickly. 'What do I have to fear from a little forest demon like you?' Then she watched as he raised his fist, thinking in the moments that passed, slow as falling honey, that there was no change of expression on his face at all and that he was certainly going to break her jaw and probably her neck with that one blow. Then there was a wrench, and Shinsawbu had thrust her to the side and stepped in front of her. Myrna slid to her knees.

'Now brother,' said the Tiger Lady; 'you said you wanted the maids and you promised me the pick of the other women. I want this one.'

'Her?' His derision was palpable. 'You want the idiot-girl?'

'She's not an idiot, Dhammaz. She's mad. Didn't you hear what she said?'

He snorted down his nostrils. 'I see your taste is running to freaks and lunatics this season.'

'What does that matter to you, so long as your own preferences are unimpeded?' Crouched behind Shinsawbu's skirts, Myrna could hear no trace of cajolery or petulance in the lady's words. Her challenge was languid and filled with the flirtatious amusement of one who relishes the confrontation.

'My preference is to scratch out an irritation,' he growled.

'And mine to tease it.'

She's not his toy, Myrna thought, reassessing her earlier judgement. She might not be able to stand against him, but she can turn him aside.

'We'll not argue over a mouse, sister. Keep her if it amuses you. Only see that she doesn't run between my feet.' He stalked off across the sand, shining like the sun itself.

'This one, overseer,' said the Lady Shinsawbu carelessly, before she walked away to inspect the rest of the line.

Myrna felt the pulse bubbling in her cut ear, felt the sand coarse and yielding under her hands and her splayed thighs. She wanted to raise her head, but her bones felt like they were melting. Her limbs wouldn't obey her. She was accustomed to a body that did as she commanded and this rebellion filled her with confusion and alarm. Her flesh had turned traitor, responding to a usurping power. Power was precisely what the two Tiger Lords embodied; not just the dry authority of rank but the visceral pump of physical energy, vital and untrammelled. They breathed it and they walked it; it oozed from their pores. They stank of it. They were not human. And it made her wet.

The chosen captives were separated out. Myrna was loaded into a small boat with a single sail along with two other women who'd been picked out by the Lady Shinsawbu, and the sailors pushed off from the beach. Myrna cast one long look back at the shore for Gohlit, wondering if she had been chosen by Dhammazhedi or rejected altogether. She couldn't see her among the multitude. 'What happens to the people not chosen?' she asked a sailor.

'They're sold in the city. There's a big market for slaves.'

It was the first time anyone had used the word *slave* to her face. Myrna shivered inwardly. She had fallen a long way, from divine priestess to traitor, from refugee to slave. She wondered if she was strong enough to carry that burden.

As the sail was unfurled and the boat surged forwards she looked covertly at her fellow captives. Both were beautiful; one tall and willowy with delicate cheekbones and a look of taut determination about her mouth; the other with heart-stopping eyes and the longest hair she'd ever seen, now lying coiled in her lap to prevent it trailing in the bilge. Myrna felt dowdy in comparison, a moth companioned with butterflies. There was a bloodstain on her bodice. A pulse still throbbed in her earlobe, and was answered by the one in her yoni. She looked away over the swell at the emerald islands and the sapphire-glinting waves, and wondered how long it would take the gods to lead Veraine to her.

The water was startlingly clear, she realised, and bright shoals of fish darted beneath their keel. But when she dipped her hand in the pellucid liquid and scooped it to her lips the taste was foul beyond words and she spat it out, shocked. The boatmen whooped with laughter.

'Why is it salty?' she asked in consternation.

'This is the sea! Didn't you know?'

Her stomach tightened with unease. She'd never seen the sea and had hardly been able to picture it. Born in a desert city, she'd never laid eyes on so much as a river until this last year. She felt suddenly appalled at the inadequacy of her human experience, realising how much she had relied upon Veraine to make sense of the world for her. He was the one who'd known how to ride, how to light a fire, where to find shelter or food and what was the way to talk to a stranger. He'd hunted and cooked their food, cared for the horses and faced down the dangerous attentions of other men; he was her guide and her protector and her teacher. What had she ever known except sacred dances and chants and the sprawling web of stories that made up the history of the gods? Without him she was hopelessly unprepared for the wide world.

Siya Ran Thu was a shock too. She had expected a larger version of the villages she and Veraine had passed through over these last months, but as the shore came in view between two of the islands she realised that this place was as big as her own city of Mulhanabin and bigger. Perched on a limestone outcrop, the buildings spilled down to a broad quay and a bay crowded with boats, while behind them the hills were striped with lines of terraced fields. The blue glazed roof-tiles of the great house at the apex of the city seemed to rival the sea for colour. As they pulled in closer the smells and the sounds of the city came to them across the waves; the aromas of smoke and dung and fish, the squabble of voices, the mewing of gulls hovering over the unloading boats, the clatter of wheels. On the vessels they passed men were casting out nets and ragged black birds sat with wings outstretched, waiting to retrieve fish from the depths for their owners. Stood on the quay were three elephants with foreheads painted in bright colours, patient as the cormorants, waiting to unload heavy cargo.

This is a rich city, she thought.

She didn't change her mind as they were disembarked and loaded into an ox-cart with a silken awning. She peeked out through a gap between the pieces of stretched fabric as they lurched away up the street, unwilling to tear her eyes from such splendour. It was a beautiful city too. She was used to the monotone of desert sandstone from her old home, but here they clearly loved colour. Pots of blossoming plants stood on every balcony. The houses were made from wood and each building was a wonder of interlocked carved timber, the tiled eaves spread wide to protect the painted walls between the beams. They passed a woman who was retracing a faded but intricate design on the plaster, her careful strokes of new paint bringing the vermilion spirals back into strong relief. Perhaps Myrna's stare was tactile; the painter turned her head and looked at the cart. But she dropped her gaze straight away and Myrna didn't miss the look on her face, or the pitying shake of her head.

She turned away from the bright outside world. There were no guards in the cart with them, although she could see some trailing the vehicle on foot. 'My name's Myrna,' she told the other two.

'I'm Anada,' said the one with the long hair.

The taller woman seemed reluctant to speak. 'Harzu,' she said at last.

There was nothing else to say: their past had been erased and their future was beyond speculation. They sat in silence until the cart thumped to a halt and they knew they'd arrived at the palace of Rao Dhammazhedi. They stepped down into a paved courtyard shaded by a mulberry tree, and after glancing around Myrna decided this must be some inferior entrance; there was only one guard leaning upon a halberd. On a long veranda a man stood waiting to meet them. He was no Tiger Lord, this one, and in fact it would have been hard to imagine a greater contrast to the masculine furnace of Dhammazhedi than his spare frame and his quick, fussy movements. He held himself stiffly and tilted his head when he inspected them, clicking his tongue and patting a fan of peacock-feathers against his chest. His mannerisms put her in mind of a bird and his plumage seemed to match; his long open-fronted wrap was turquoise, his tight trousers aquamarine and his eyelids coloured a sea-blue. They suffered his scrutiny only for a moment before he nodded and said, 'Go in. You'll be prepared.'

They ascended into the building, and into the care of a cluster of silent women in plain cotton dresses who led them through courtyards and corridors to an interior room containing only a huge bronze laving-bowl and a scattering of benches with padded leather seats. Bowls of soap as thick as cream were laid by and steam rose from the water. Once more they were inspected, muttered over and prodded. Teeth and nails and feet were scrubbed clean, as was the blood on Myrna's throat. Then they were instructed to undress.

Myrna was surprised to think that they were to be washed again, but even more taken aback by what actually happened: each of them was lathered with soap and then servants took up razor-sharp slivers of obsidian and, laying them down upon the benches, shaved them from throat to toe. Not an inch of flesh was spared. The process was terrifying: to flinch from the glassy blade, even when it was drawn tickling up the most intimate paths between splayed cheeks, would have been to risk a savage cut. The result was almost more alarming. Denuded of even the slightest fuzz, a whole new territory of soft and tender flesh was exposed to air and view. Myrna saw the looks of shame on the faces of Harzu and Anada. Nothing was hidden now; the pubic fleece that clothes even the naked had been taken away, exposing the cleft between their thighs as if they had been reduced to childhood again, revealed to lascivious eyes for the first time. To lose the veil of hair was to be stripped of the very last vestiges of modesty. Myrna rubbed her legs together and felt a smoothness that was almost slippery, skin upon skin in unnatural, provocative closeness. She ran her hand over her thigh and it felt like satin.

Finally they were smoothed all over with fragrant oils to soothe the burning sting of their sensitised flesh. All this time, the peacock man had watched, his eyes devoid of passion. 'Stand,' he said when they were finished, signing them forwards with a flick of his fan.

They obeyed, and waited while he circled them slowly. Myrna felt a trickle of oil sliding down between her flushing breasts. He didn't touch them, but he used his folded fan to heft Anada's breast briefly as if judging it for weight and firmness. Walking behind Myrna he tapped the taut muscle of her buttock. Under the feathers the fan had a rigid frame and the slap made her flesh quiver.

'Right,' said the man, returning to face them. 'Green for her, I think.' He pointed the fan at Myrna first. 'Red for that one. Saffron for her.'

The women in their respectable cotton dresses hurried forwards, brandishing what Myrna saw to be short lengths of leather. They were collars. Hers was dyed green and stitched with a pattern of malachite beads, but it was still a collar just like you'd put on a dog; it had laces at the back and a thick bronze ring passed through the leatherwork at the front. A hard lump of unarticulated protest rose in her throat as nimble fingers tightened and knotted the device at her nape. When that was done she was dressed in a silk skirt of the same emerald hue that cinched low about her hips. It was heavily pleated and long enough to brush the tops of her feet as she stood, but she quickly realised that the generous folds of material concealed two slits, one up the front of each thigh, from hem to belt. Every time she took a step her legs would be revealed, and if she moved too fast or bent without care so would her shaven mound.

'Good,' said the man when the three slaves were attired in their chosen colours and the servants stood back. Myrna looked down at the sweep of her skirt past her bare and jutting breasts and imagined fleetingly what Veraine would think of her dressed like this. She could picture the avid delight of his smile and it somehow gave her comfort. She fingered the stiff leather of her slave-collar and brushed the solid knot at the back.

'My name is Sao Mor,' said the man, after waiting while the servant-women retired from the room. 'I am the Lady Shinsawbu's steward, and if you listen to what I have to tell you now, it might just prolong your lives.'

5 The Storytellers

Veraine felt the Rani's words smack into his skull like sling-stones; it was as if they tore him new eyes and he saw her clearly for the first time. Her eerie beauty suddenly seemed to be little more than dust and cob-webs, and what lay beneath that was something he couldn't bear to see. He recoiled several steps, fighting the urge to flee, then crouched to pick up his weapon, but he was unable to take his gaze from her broken body and her ravaged face. Her hands twitched across her scarred breasts like dying spiders.

It was like taking a misstep and seeing for the first time that he'd been balanced on the edge of an abyss, oblivious to the darkness yawning below. He could not even feel pity for her, so great was his horror. He had to leave.

He chose the wrong door. In his haste to get out he lurched not into the corridor which he'd expected but into a much bigger room, one which faced out the back of the palace onto the forest; he knew that as soon as he saw the treetops through the gaping hole which had once been a row of windows, past the rotted remnants of the curtains. The whole room was open to the ele-ments and the rains had been in here, soaking the furnishings. His feet slithered on floorboards that were green with mildew.

There was an unearthly scream from the slumped remains of a pillared bed and Veraine ducked, his fal-chion flying instinctively to a guard position, his heart

83

slamming in his chest. But it was only monkeys; they poured from the stinking heaps of cloth and fled towards the window, their feet thumping on the charred timbers – though the biggest male, as large as a dog, rushed at him with bared teeth and eyes rolled back in its skull. Veraine raised his weapon and the animal scrabbled to a halt, shrieking with rage, but it was too canny to attack and leaped out through the gap in the wall behind the rest of its troop. Veraine stared around the room with mounting disquiet, breathing the smell of decayed fabric and sodden wood, until his eye fell on the huddled piles in the centre of the mouldy carpet. With a grimace he turned back to the armoury, his heart cold and his stomach nauseous.

He didn't want to look at Mirabai as he passed her. The part of him that hadn't grown old and cynical of such stories was afraid that the Rani would have dissolved to green bones too.

But she spoke to him. 'There's something else you don't know.' Her voice was breathy and taut. He had to turn and look at her, and he saw that she had her hand buried in her rumpled skirts and was masturbating with the thick stock of a whip. Its braided leather tails lay across her spread thighs. Her face was slick with sweat and ghastly pale. 'There are scars on your back, my noble love,' she sneered, her head weaving from side to side. 'They're quite faint now, but they are there. You've been whipped to the bone yourself – and why do you think that might be?'

He couldn't answer. She and her words filled him with a sick fear. Finding the far door he pressed through it at a pace that was only barely less than a run, but he couldn't stop his ears to her whooping, choking laughter. He strode swiftly back through their grimy bedchamber, down the stairs beyond and through the dark belly of the palace. This journey was nightmarish; he had only a vague recollection of the path and he tripped and floundered among the hidden furnishings as he sought a door to the courtyard, trying not to breath the thick miasma of wet rot that his blind passage knocked from unseen and unidentifiable obstacles. When he at last found a door out into the sunlight he kicked out a sagging plank and fell through the gap with something approaching desperation.

But not all nightmares take place in the dark. As he turned around to survey the courtyard for the first time without its cloak of fog he thought his heart would stop altogether. Chill raked his spine. He understood how he could have missed the signs of fire on the towering walls, the scorched plaster and the gaping window-sockets of the upper floors. But how could he have failed to see the bones? They littered the flagstones in disartic-ulated drifts, white and clean out here where the sun and the animals of the forest had been able to work upon them, lolling jawless skulls staring at him from empty sockets. There'd been a massacre here and he hadn't seen the signs that were now so obvious. He clenched his fists; although his back was running with sweat he felt so cold that his muscles were threatening to tear.

He moved to the pool, his steps slower now. He needed to drink, to wash his aching head clear in rainwater. But when he reached the stone lip he saw that it was sundered by a wide crack, and that the interior was empty and dry except for the rotted litter of a year's fallen leaves and black crusts of ash. He shut his eyes briefly, passing his hand over them, but when he looked again the cistern was still ruined, just as it had been since the Horse-eaters sacked this place. Faintly he thought he heard a cry from within the palace, but whether it was human or animal, laughter or screaming, it was impossible to tell from this distance.

He turned and left the courtyard, out through the gateway and away from that house of the damned.

He walked through what was left of the afternoon and when the sun set he kept walking. His way was quite clear; the paved road wound down into the valley and he stuck to it even in the growing darkness. When the moon rose he stopped and made a makeshift sword-hanger from a strip torn off his clothes, and when he crossed a stream he paused to drink deeply, but he didn't make camp that night. It would have been pointless; he had no food and no fire-pot anymore and he didn't think he was capable of sleep. After a while he didn't think at all. He ceased to look out for danger, ceased to wonder where the road would lead him, ceased even to feel hunger. He was faintly aware of the pain in his feet and the heaviness of his limbs, and of the shadows cast across his path by the moon on the stones, but mostly there was nothing in his head but a gnawing, empty horror. His only goal was to get as far away from that ruined palace as he could.

He stopped when it slowly entered his consciousness that dawn had risen over the tree-tops, turning their veils of mist to gold. Birds were shrieking their loud praises to the sun god, and faintly he could hear the barking of dogs. He thought too that he could smell smoke. That probably meant a village nearby. Veraine knew he needed to find a settlement and that he'd have to risk the dogs and the men who guarded it. He was sick with exhaustion.

That was what made him unwary. He was on top of the confrontation before he knew it and stopped only at the last moment, blinking and bewildered at the sight.

A brightly painted high-sided cart with two white oxen hitched to the front stood by the road, a woman holding the lead rope. Behind the cart, where a rough track plunged away among land which had had been cleared of trees, was a group of men. Five of them seemed to be facing a sixth, who was holding on to the back of the cart. A few dogs were nosing round.

'It's too late,' insisted the sixth man, the one dressed in dark blue. 'The gift has already been given.' In one hand was a stick but he wasn't brandishing it with any confidence.

One of the other men laughed. 'That's all right. It can be given again,' he said, and the others joined his jeering. All the men looked young, and Veraine knew well enough that a group of youths gathered together like that meant trouble. He glanced at the woman, who was watching the others intently, and saw the fear on her face. No one had noticed his arrival, so focused were they on their quarrel. He took another few steps forwards before one of the dogs looked up sharply and barked at him.

Everyone turned and stared. The quintet shifted their casual slouches to something more defensive, though there were no weapons in evidence beyond a few sticks. Veraine raised one hand to his side, fingers spread in what he intended as a peaceable gesture. All the dogs were growling now.

'Please,' said the woman impulsively, then bit off her words as she took in his appearance.

'Road-trash,' said the leader of the little pack of youths with contempt. He jerked his head. 'Get him.' At his command the dogs snarled and sprang forwards. Veraine's hand leapt to his sword-hilt and suddenly everything blurred and reeling about the world came into sharp and bitter focus; the bunched muscles and the exposed fangs of the lead animal, the drag of fabric on the blade as it shore through the makeshift scabbard, the weapon like an extension of his own arm. He followed the swing of the blade, stepping sideways and sweeping it in an underarm curve which connected with the first dog just as it made its leap. Its head flew past his left shoulder. The body spun and rolled, kicking in the dust.

Veraine recovered and turned in readiness but the other dogs, no fools, were already scrambling out of reach, ears flattened and necks low. The humans stared. He straightened and pointed the blade at the man who'd ordered the attack. The youth grunted an obscenity, and suddenly all five of them were backing off down the track; stiff-limbed and growling like their dogs, spitting in the dirt but unwilling to stand their ground. Veraine watched them disappear and then he sat down rather abruptly. He cast a wary glance at the sixth man, but he didn't move at all. It was the woman who came running from behind the cart; she went straight to her companion and clasped his neck.

Veraine looked away to the corpse of the dog and then at his bloodied blade. He wiped it carefully on the grass. It had felt like the falchion had come alive in his hands, and that he had come alive with it, but now that the combat was over all that fire and strength had drained away down the steel. His legs were all but incapable of bearing him and he could actually see his wrist trembling.

A shadow blocked the sun and he looked up unsteadily into the face of the young woman. He could see little of her features, but her head was framed by a blue aura. I've gone mad, he thought with despair.

'Thank you,' she said, touching her forehead and bowing. 'We're grateful.'

Veraine shook his head.

'If we stay here, they'll come back,' she said. She cast a glance behind her at the man in blue. 'They'll bring men from the village. We should go now. Do you want to come with us?'

Veraine, staring at his feet, realised that the stuff caked between the toes was blood. He didn't want to look at the soles. 'I don't think I can walk any further,' he admitted.

She puffed out her cheeks and blew out a breath. 'Will you ride in the cart?'

He nodded. Getting himself to his feet was not easy; it had been a mistake to sit down. He limped to the back of the bullock cart and the young man gave him a hand up onto the tailgate; he looked shaken but his smile was warm. 'You bless us!' he said. Veraine lay back among a heap of painted cloths, let his feet dangle over the edge and despite the lurching of the axle on the stones was asleep before he could even wonder where they were going.

'These are a mess,' Teihli said, plastering the herbal poultice onto his soles. Her expression was appalled, but her hands were gentle. 'You were intending to walk all the way to Siya Ran Thu like this, were you?'

'I didn't know how far it was,' replied Veraine, reclining on his elbows as he watched her.

'Well, you'd be hobbling on your bare bones before you got there. You need shoes.' She looked at her husband, who was laying wood on the fire. He was a handsome young man, probably a couple of years younger than his wife, Veraine guessed.

'You can have mine,' Rahul said promptly.

'Don't bother.'

'No problem. I can make another pair easily enough.'

'You're very kind.' He was quite uncomfortable with their gratitude. They'd carried him all day, fed him, cleaned his wounds and now Teihli was binding his feet with clean bandages, her hand firm on his calf. 'I only killed a dog.'

'You know what you did,' Teihli admonished, managing to frown and smile at him simultaneously. She had an open, mobile face that could dart through a hundred vivid emotions. When she smiled, which she did often, she showed the gap between her front teeth. Her large breasts were firmly held by her tight choli blouse. And her hair really was blue-black, as was Rahul's; they washed it with indigo, the same dye that dominated their clothing. A long orhni shawl, tucked in at her waist, was draped over her head and right shoulder to frame her face becomingly. She was, he thought, charming. 'The gods,' she said happily, 'sent you to us.'

Veraine smiled just enough to be polite. They thought a great deal about the gods, these two. Twice during the journey he'd woken when the cart stopped and seen them lighting incense at a wayside shrine. When they made camp both had gone into the stream – fully clothed – and washed before making an offering of flowers and burning butter under a nearby tree. And the cart was covered in the multi-coloured, multi-limbed pictures of what seemed to be hundreds of deities. The gods, after all, were their business. They were, he'd found out, travelling storytellers; he the bhopa and she the bhopi. They related their tales of divinities and heroes, princes and monsters as well as more mundane and up-to-date tidings, in countless villages spread throughout the forest all through the dry seasons, before returning to their tribal village for the rains.

Veraine realised he'd been looking at Teihli for too

long, that his crotch was growing warm, and he tilted his head back to gaze at the stars instead. Rahul seemed a man of unusual good-nature, perfectly willing to let a strange man into the close company of his wife and grateful rather than upset that someone else had come to her defence in a crisis. Veraine found this attitude slightly surprising but had no intention of testing his good humour.

'Does this road go to Siya Ran Thu?' he asked.

'No; to Lhanghar City,' said Rahul. 'But we don't go there anymore; we'll be leaving the road tomorrow and heading across country.'

'Why's that?'

'Since the barbarians invaded there's been no king or queen. Lhanghar City is in ruins, and the area around the rubble is fought over by rival sardars – well, they call themselves chieftains but they are nothing more than bandits. It's a bad place. No one wants to hear the old stories there.'

'But you've still an audience in the villages?'

'Oh yes. We're welcomed. Many villages were burned out, but in this forest the barbarians missed many more, and people were able to hide in the hills. Life is hard, but it always was for them. They look for a sign of peace and stability, and they welcome us. They are poor, but they still pay what they can. What you saw this morning wasn't typical, you understand. We'd spent a good night in their village ... It was just troublemakers who followed us out.'

'It would be hard for you to find a welcome around here, though,' Teihli commented. 'People are distrusting of strangers nowadays. There are no royal soldiers left, just bandits. We two travel under the protection of the gods, but even we're afraid when we meet people on the road.'

'It's an evil time,' Rahul agreed. 'But better than when the Horse-eaters invaded. And we must thank the gods that they left quickly, that they didn't stay.'

Right, thought Veraine. 'They'll have left because this is bad country for cavalry: too hilly and the forests too dense. You need open land if you have a mounted war-force. Do you know where they went?'

'We heard,' Rahul said, 'that they crossed the Great Desert and were destroyed by the Empire Beyond the Sands.'

Veraine digested this, trying to piece the fragments together in his head. 'That's the Irolian Empire?'

'I think so. There are stories that the gods sent down a curse of fire and plague on the Horse-eaters, that their army was swallowed up by the earth.'

'You believe that?' He himself did not. Armies weren't destroyed by divine intervention.

'Who am I to say what the gods can and can't do? I listen for the stories travellers bring, and try to make sense of them, and pass them on.'

'I worry that the Empire Beyond the Sands might choose to march this way, now that their enemies are dead and we have no queen,' said Teihli.

'No,' said Veraine decisively. 'If the desert is as big as you all make it out to be then its strategic value is as a border. It might be crossed by someone trying to found an empire, but not by someone trying to expand one.'

They looked at him a little strangely.

'Your real problem is going to be your close neighbours among the Twenty Kingdoms,' he added, 'if any of them are still standing.'

Rahul nodded slowly. 'The raids from Siya Ran Thu are getting more frequent,' he said. 'The Harimau reivers used to buy slaves from Lhanghar; now they take them by force.'

'The Harimau?'

'The present rulers of Siya Ran Thu. They're said to have come out of the hills decades ago and taken the port for their own. The word Harimau means *Tiger* in their own language. There are stories about them . . .' He glanced around at the night pressing in on their camp-site. 'But they're not the right stories to tell just now.'

After that they spoke of inconsequential things and of their planned route, while tasks were finished and they prepared to sleep. The names and directions meant nothing to Veraine and their itinerary was not his concern. He was going to Siya Ran Thu, to the Harimau's city, because there was no other path that he could see before him. Teihli gave him a reed mat to lie on and an indigo-dyed sheet to cover himself against the night insects, then the three of them stretched out around the fire. Veraine pulled the cloth right over his head and watched the firelight through the coarse dark weave. He couldn't stop the dark, sickening memories of the recent past crawling to the surface of his mind now that he was quiescent; they made him squirm inwardly.

What was he? And how could he trust himself now? Since his awakening in the dried streambed he'd known he couldn't rely upon his past, that he might have been anyone and done anything, great or low, fair or foul. He had guesses to go by, fragments of habit and memory that suggested a pattern, but none of them made sense. A soldier without an army. A foreigner a thousand miles from home. A lover without a name or a face for the woman he sought. What did that add up to? When Mirabai called into doubt his assumption that he was a free man – well, he should have been ready for that. Perhaps he was someone's slave. It made as much sense as anything else that he should be an escaped slave, maybe someone's bodyguard. He hated the thought, but that didn't make it untrue. But he'd had a faith in himself that didn't suggest servitude, an instinctive trust in his own strength and dignity and purpose. Now the encounter with the Rani had shattered all that. He no longer trusted his courage or his actions. It appalled him beyond words how he'd behaved, how close he'd stepped to the edge of an abyss he hadn't even seen. In addition it seemed he couldn't believe the evidence of his own eyes. It frightened him that he could no longer tell the difference between shadows and sunlight, between sanity and madness, between that which was and that which was gone. Lying there on the hard mat, listening to the night insects, he felt his chest ache with a howl of frustration and terror that he could never utter.

In the end he dozed, though he only knew it when he woke. Something was moving very close by, actually tugging at the sheet that covered him. He rolled and grabbed blindly, felt soft flesh crushed beneath his grip and then heard a tiny, muffled squeak of pain.

'Shush!' Teihli whispered, her breath hot on his ear. 'It's all right!' The moment his grip relaxed she wriggled further under the sheet, pressing herself along his right side. Her hand, still smelling of the butter and spices of their evening meal, fluttered up to his lips. 'Who did you think it was?'

Veraine swallowed hard, willing his heart to stop pounding. Then he threw back the cloth, not so that he could see her but in order to look across to where she should be lying. The fire was still glowing brightly so he couldn't have been unconscious for long, and Rahul's sleeping form lay motionless. Teihli swept the cloth back over their heads, returning them to the warm darkness.

'This isn't a good idea,' he breathed, wondering how

she thought she'd get away with it so close to her sleeping husband, and how he was going to defuse the situation without destroying every gain of the last day.

'No?' she giggled, low in her throat, and laid her hand on his groin. That ruined everything. The cloth was thin and loose, no armour against a confident grope, and she could plainly discern the thickening curve of his cock under her palm. She wrapped her hand around it with a little breathy noise of discovery.

Veraine watched all his good intentions flare up and fly away. 'No,' he whispered, but her body was warm and firm against him, her leg already sliding up to hook over his thigh. Her lips, clumsy in the dark, found his, her kiss hot and wet and greedy. His penis reared in her grip. You've been far too kind, he thought. I am grateful.

Teihli let go of his crotch and sought his hand, laying it on the curve of her right breast. Her blouse had a lace-up front. He could feel her nipple straining against the cotton, as hard as an unground kernel in the midst of soft flour. Her hand returned to its task and his shameless member leapt to meet her. 'What about that?' she asked.

That was good. How was he supposed to deny it? She had a full, curvy body, nothing out of the ordinary but young and healthy and it was stirring him now to the depths. He squeezed her breast and pinched the precocious nipple through the blouse, feeling his stones tighten and fill. Her hand was stroking up and down his shaft, not hurrying him but letting him know what she had to offer. She chuckled again provocatively, forcing him to find her mouth again and enter it, his tongue dancing on hers, tasting the sweet spicy flavour of her, finding her yielding and eager. He snagged the dangling bow of her laces and drew it out, loosening them so that he could slide his hand up and fill it with her bare breasts.

They were heavy in his hand and he was hard in hers, fully erect now, making a tent-pole for his fouta. He pinched her nipple and felt her gasp, stealing his breath.

Suddenly he was ferociously glad of her big breasts, her broad hips, and the generosity and heat and solidity of her body, so vital and so unlike Mirabai's. He wanted her big tits – the bigger the better. He wanted them pouring over his face and filling his mouth and his hands. He yanked impatiently at the laces so that he could wrench her blouse open and, no longer concerned even that she keep on pulling him off, hefted her over to straddle his torso and pulled her down so that her heavy orbs were dangling on his face. He rubbed himself against them, sucking in great mouthfuls of firm flesh, tugging her nipples with his teeth and licking the warm, peachy skin, burying his face in the suffocating bliss of her cleft. He found he could squeeze her breasts together and take both teats into his mouth at once. Teihli moaned and wriggled, gripping his waist with her thighs, trying to thrust her rump backwards so that his stiff cock could poke it. She cradled his head in her hands, dragging her fingers through his hair as he nuzzled and nursed on her.

She was everything the Rani was not, and he washed himself clean in her.

Putting his hand under her skirts he found her pulsing with heat. He took the juices that greased his hand and painted her nipples, then sucked the wanton flavour of her from them, dipping from breast to breast. Teihli's whispers were incoherent, her limbs heavy. He ran both hands up her thighs as she sagged forwards weakly over his chest. Her loins were soft as apricot-flesh and her arse was as plump and round and voluptuous as her breasts.

'Let's get this off,' he said and she wriggled out of her

skirt with a literally indecent haste. He settled her back on his stomach, feeling her sex squash hot and wet on his belly, sure that his navel must be filled now with her milky nectar, that it would soon overflow and run down around his waist. He kissed her again as he groped for his own clothes under her splayed thighs. She gasped and giggled and bit at his nose. Then he drew her down, sheathing himself inside her with one push. There was no need to search for entry; she was agape and ready for him. He felt her body grip him in a sliding, lubricious embrace that made him arch underneath her even as she arched above. Her hands drummed on his chest. 'Oh yes!' she gasped.

He couldn't brace his feet to thrust but he used his hips, grinding in tight circles as she plunged above him. He knew he wouldn't have to stir her pot for long. She was losing her rhythm now, submitting to his, clinging to his body through the storm mounting in her flesh. She straightened her back and light billowed in under the edge of the sheet, gleaming on her great dugs hanging over him. He drank in the sight. 'Yes; come on,' he whispered.

What he wasn't ready for was her sitting back and throwing the sheet aside. He nearly spent at once in shock and in wonder at the sight. In the firelight she was magnificent; her head thrown back, her belly stretched tight, her large breasts – each round and gold and seemingly as huge as an autumn moon – shuddering and quivering. He could hear the liquid sound of her quim working on his pole. He buried his thumb in her pubes, stirring until he saw the climax overwhelm her and he heard her stifled cry. He had to grab her hips to steady her as she swayed. Her whimpers were quite audible. He looked across the fireplace to check that Rahul hadn't heard, and his fingers bit into Teihli's flesh.

Rahul had heard all right. Rahul was already awake. The bhopa was sat up on his mat, leaning on one arm, his smooth chest gleaming in the dim light. He was stroking with his right hand the shaft of a long, slender erection, strumming it like a musician playing a sitar, his face a mask of concentration and lust.

Veraine, deep in the trance of his own approaching crisis, stared at Rahul's jerking hands and his quivering, muscular shoulders, and when he spoke it was without thought, as if his voice issued from elsewhere. 'Rahul,' he said thickly, 'come here.'

The younger man, eyes widening, grew still. Then he obeyed, crawling on all fours, his stiff prod hanging like a ploughshare below him as if he would cut a furrow in the dirt. 'Get in behind her,' Veraine said. 'There's room.'

Teihli stared. But when her husband knelt up behind her between Veraine's legs and slid one hand over her stomach she tipped forwards to allow him access.

'That's right.' Veraine could feel Rahul. He could feel the man's knees brushing his own legs, feel his fingers collecting the spilt lubrication of her orgasm from her stretched lips and from where it had dribbled over the root of his own penis. And when Rahul pushed the swollen plum of his prick into her anus and bore down into her – oh then Veraine felt that prick because it was separated from his own by only the thickness of a wall of skin and they were cock against cock, ridged hardness sliding against ridged hardness within the yielding feminine container of Teihli's body. She let out a liquid moan and her eyes fluttered closed as she was pressed down onto Veraine, spreading her legs as wide as she could. He put one hand on her breastbone, supporting her.

Her husband went to work now, leaning forwards on her more and more. He was careful, making no savage movements, but his rocking penetration was inexorable. Veraine could see his face over her shoulder, his eyes closed, his expression filled with awe. He saw Rahul's hand come round and across her ribs and cup her left breast, squeezing, the nipple poking out between his fingers, while the young man's cock rubbed up against his own through her vaginal wall. The two of them were moving together, Teihli imprisoned between them, turning her inside out with sensation. She climaxed first, crying out, and then Rahul quickened, riding her arsehole until he filled it with his cream. Only then did Veraine let go, and he fucked watching their dazed, ecstatic faces, fucked with Rahul's semen leaking out onto his balls, fucked until Teihli was overflowing above and below, drenched in their come.

They detached slowly, breaking apart to lie back. Teihli was quivering with the aftershock of her pleasure as Rahul wrapped his arms around her, reclining with his belly against her back. But Veraine didn't stay lying down. He rose and crossed to the firewood stack, dropping sticks onto the embers until sparks swirled into the sky.

He was disturbed by what had taken place and by his suspicion that he had walked into a trap prepared for him. When there was enough light to see by he stood and turned to them, impervious to the fact that he was naked and gleaming with their mingled sweat and looked in the firelight like bronze just come out of the furnace; ignoring the cock that was still pumped with blood and hung distended and threatening; unaware that the black look on his face was accentuated by the leaping shadows.

'Now you tell me,' he said, 'what game you two are playing at.'

6 Shinsawbu

'You've been chosen by the Lady Shinsawbu,' said Sao Mor, focusing somewhere above their heads, 'as her personal slaves, and your purpose is to please her in any way she chooses. You'll be taken to her chambers shortly, and confine any future movement to the palace and the gardens unless instructed otherwise. There are guards to see to that. Every day you'll be washed and shaved and oiled just as you were today. When your clothes becomes dirty there will be clean ones provided, and I'll see to it that you are fed at least daily. I have full charge of all her slaves and my job is to keep you in good health and looking your best. If you need anything, ask me. Do you all understand?'

They nodded.

'The Lady Shinsawbu is only one of the great Harimau family that reigns in this kingdom, but she is a most powerful and exalted personage. You'll find that she is only overridden in her decisions by the Rao Dhammazhedi, of whom she is the favoured eldest sister. All other members of the family – there are nineteen of them, including children – are of lower status. You will address Shinsawbu as 'my queen' and the Rao as 'my king'. You may address the other Harimau as 'great lord' or 'great lady'. Servants and persons of free status such as myself must bow when family members are encountered but, being slaves, you do not. In theory you must obey the commands of lesser Harimau; however, in practice you'll find that it's highly improbable that anyone will give you instructions, for fear of annoying your mistress. The one exception is the Rao himself. I suggest you keep out of his way if you can.'

He paused and they waited. Then he cleared his throat. 'I used to tell new slaves that if they were loyal and obedient then they'd be safe. I no longer do so; I find lying becomes more burdensome as I grow older. You're not safe, and nothing you do will make you so. There are no rules that will keep you alive.' There was no gloating or amusement in his voice, only an old, dried-up weariness. 'However, you are lucky. Luckier than most of the other captives, in that you've been chosen by Shinsawbu; I've known some of her slaves last for several years. The Rao himself, in contrast, has a taste for novelty and acquires slaves specifically for the sake of discarding them. And certain other family members deem it a necessity of fashion to try and outdo one another in their excesses. Do you understand?'

No one moved this time.

'You will remain alive only so long as you amuse your mistress. That is the sum of the advice I can give you. That, and don't draw the Rao's attention. Have you any questions?'

The women stared back, wide-eyed. Myrna was surprised to feel a touch of pity for him.

'What does she like?' Anada asked.

'You mean this week? Or today?' His mouth twisted. 'What she appreciates in one drives her to rage in another. She's a possessive woman, quick to jealousy. Apart from that, I can't help you.'

'If I wanted to find out what had happened to another one of the slaves . . .?' Myrna said.

He shook his head. 'No. Haven't you been listening? You don't want to find out. Now, follow.' Motioning them behind him, he led the way from the ablutions room and they proceeded through the corridors of the palace. There seemed to be no alternative to obedience. Guards in lacquered armour stood watchfully at doorways and intersections and Myrna felt their eyes upon her and the others; her nipples prickled with the awareness of their gaze.

'Here,' said Sao Mor. 'Her quarters. She isn't in at the moment; I understand she has gone hunting with the Rao.' He indicated double doors of ebony patterned with sheet silver in the form of leaping deer. Two men were standing outside; one was a young soldier braced rigidly at attention, the other much older, his bare head silver-haired, his armour more ornate. He seemed to be in the process of instructing the junior man, but he turned at their approach.

'Narathu Min.' Their mentor inclined his head politely.

'Sao Mor.'

'This is the captain of the royal household's guards,' the steward explained. The captain looked them over, his expression unreadable. Unusually, he sported a small, close-cut beard. 'These are the lady's new slaves.'

The young guard was gawping over his superior's shoulder, his gaze snatching at their breasts. Harzu shrank back behind the other women.

'I see.' There was nothing elderly about the officer's hard glance, or the firmness of his voice.

'Is everything well?'

'Fine. The cubs are out in the orchard.'

Sao Mor blinked, as if remembering something he should never have forgotten. 'Ah. The cubs.' He turned again to his slaves. 'There are tiger kittens resident in the palace. You're not to interfere with them or thwart them in any way.' He pushed open a door and waved them within.

As she passed the soldiers Myrna heard Narathu Min murmur, 'What a waste.'

The room inside was apparently an audience-chamber but they didn't linger to look around; he led them through a succession of rooms, throwing open more doors to point out a bathing chamber, a wardrobe full of hanging dresses, a dining hall and others which Myrna hardly registered. They were all beautiful, with polished wooden floors and intricately slotted beams carved and painted with foliage designs. The last one they entered was a bedchamber dominated by a vast bed, and the screen doors that made up the far wall were folded back to show what must be a garden beyond. From outside came the sound of trickling water and tinkling windchimes. The sunlight was bright; it must be afternoon by now, she realised. In here it was cool and shaded, perfumed and calm. The only sign of disorder was a bowl of rambutans upon the floor, in which peel and pits were mixed up with still intact fruit. Sao Mor tutted.

'On the bed,' he told them. They climbed up, cautiously, onto the white coverlet. The mattress was soft under Myrna's knees. To their distress, Sao Mor retrieved from beneath the bed three long lengths of thin chain, each attached to the frame at one end and dangling a tiny lock at the other. He snapped the first lock shut on Myrna's collar, his fingers fastidious and quick. He was careful not to touch her skin as he leaned over her. The chain grazed her nipple as it hung, the cool touch making her skin contract. She shivered, though not from the cold. The chain was delicate and perhaps not strong enough to restrain a real dog, but it was enough. She was doubly captive now; enslaved and chained to her owner's bed. She looked at the other two women, abject and cowed, their eyes filled with unease, their chains gleaming against their skins, and she wondered if she looked as submissive as they, or as lovely.

'There,' he said without warmth, stepping back to get the full picture; 'you couldn't present a more perfect sight.' Harzu stifled a sob, her eyes brimming. 'Don't,' he warned. 'You'll spoil your prettiness. Tomorrow you'll get a full meal, and I will find you cosmetics to make you look even more beautiful.'

If we survive the night, you mean, Myrna thought. That crucial first test.

'Here,' he added, passing them the bowl of fruit; 'you can finish these if you want. Tidy the bowl away under the bed when you've finished.'

'Won't that make her angry?' Anada asked.

He twitched his head awkwardly. 'How should I know?' Then he left them. The three women, half-naked and enchained, were left upon the bed with nothing to distract them from their mutual plight.

In the end they ate the rambutans because they'd not been given anything else since dawn. Their fingers became sticky and sweet and they had to lick them clean. 'This isn't so bad,' Anada said, though her voice was not entirely steady. 'It doesn't look like they expect us to cook or draw water or do laundry. Sex-slaves have it easy. If all we have to do is keep some hungry pussy well licked, then I can manage that.'

Harzu flashed her a startled look.

'I was concubine to a village sardar,' Anada explained. 'I could satisfy him and his men too, when he got drunk enough to let me try. One Tiger Lady is no big deal.' She smiled a little, wobbly smile. Then, spying a dribble of the sweet juice fallen upon her breast, she cupped the orb and licked it clean with a pink and dextrous tongue.

'How did you end up here?' Myrna asked, trying to look away.

'Oh. The reivers started muscling in on his territory, demanding a tribute. To show his loyalty, they said. He included me, along with three other girls . . . the bastard. The reivers are always more interested in slaves than anything else. What about you, Harzu?'

'I'm a widow,' she said. 'Because I was barren his other two wives sent me back to my father's house after the funeral, so that they'd have more of the estate to split between their children.' She paused, eyes shining with unspilt tears, while Anada sighed and shook her head sympathetically. 'Well, they said they were sending me back home; but the sons who were supposed to escort me took me to the reivers and sold me.'

'The world's full of bastards,' Anada observed.

'I won't be a slave,' said Harzu. They looked at her in consternation as she shook out her hair and continued, 'I was a respectable woman. This is shameful. I can't last like this.'

Anada was alarmed. 'No, don't think like that! You're alive – that's what matters.'

'If my father could see me he would die of the shame.'

Myrna listened to them talk but took no part herself. She knew nothing of family honour; it had never applied to her even back in her homeland where she'd always been a woman set apart. Such things as maternal ambition and filial duty were only stories to her. I am not a respectable woman, she told herself, listening to their dialogue. Anada was pragmatic and clung fiercely to hope, trying to counter Harzu's shame and despair.

Myrna shared neither point of view. *I am She without mercy and without regret*, she said to herself, as she'd said every day to the rows of priests bowing low before her. *I am the broken vessel, the dusty well, the motionless millstone. In Me is every hope brought to despair. I am She who reminds thee that thy hands are empty. Hold not fast to wealth or joy or life, for those things of the world are illusion and thou art free of them.*

And what about Veraine – was he illusion? She turned the question aside as she had done every time it arose. She knew her passion for Veraine was something that – however inexplicably – had arisen, inexorable, from somewhere deep in her nature. And her nature was divine, and it could not be denied or questioned any more than the storm or the earthquake.

What dismayed her now was the Tiger Lords. The ancient hero Gidindhi had warred against them. She remembered, because she had been there on the battle-field all those millennia ago. She remembered all the goddess Malia's history. Yet it seemed wrong now; in her mind's eye the Tiger Lords had been far more beast than human: nothing like those she'd met today. Had she been mistaken? Veraine would have said that she was remembering only a story she'd been told from childhood; for the first time she wondered if that were true. Veraine didn't believe in past incarnations, nor did he place any faith in any gods whether Yamani or Irolian. He thought he loved a mortal woman, but she'd never let his unbelief trouble her before now.

The argument between Harzu and Anada died away. All three were exhausted by uncertainty and fear and once they'd finished eating they lay down. The mattress was far softer than the straw pallet and the hard earth that Myrna had known all her life. She rolled onto her back in a foam of green silk and tumbled hair and stared up at the ceiling. It was deeply carved, she saw, with the lithe forms of nymphs and heroes intertwined in a vast orgy: a hundred erotic contortions and a thousand variations of male and female, male and male, female and female in frantic, gymnastic copulation. It was a catalogue of sexual technique and a peon to erotic pleasure.

'Look at the roof,' she said in wonder, but the other two were already asleep and a moment later so was she.

She awoke confused and adrift but aware that it was a noise that had roused her. The light was golden now so she knew she must have slept for hours. Raising herself to her elbows she blinked and stared just in time to see the Lady Shinsawbu ascend the steps from the garden. For a moment the tiger queen was outlined in gold by the light, as effulgent as a goddess. No clothes obscured that outline. Two tiger cubs danced and leapt at her heels. 'Well; such sleepy puppies,' said Shinsawbu.

No; she was not quite naked, there was a thick belt round her hips. And she carried something heavy and large in one hand, dangling against her thigh. Harzu and Anada were awake now, getting to their knees, tangled in the long chains. Myrna felt hers bite into her breast as she tried to sit up.

Then Shinsawbu stepped forwards out of the evening glare and suddenly became visible. Harzu cringed; Anada put her hand over her mouth in disgust. The object dangling in her grasp by one of its long spiral horns was the severed head of a large antelope, tongue lolling and eyes blank. Its neck was a ragged stump and the tiger cubs were working themselves into a frenzy batting and chewing at it.

'All right, kittens,' said Shinsawbu indulgently, and

she threw the head across the polished boards as if it were no weight at all, leaving a broad streak of blood. The cubs chased after, shoving and squalling at each other. Then Shinsawbu turned her attention back to the bed. Her smile was lazy. 'A good hunt, though I had to let Dhammaz take the best prize. Come here, puppies; let me look at you.'

They crawled across the width of the bed to her. She surveyed them with satisfaction, moving to Harzu first and taking her delicate face in one hand, forcing her chin up. Harzu looked sick, shutting her eyes for fear. There was blood on Shinsawbu's hands, blood down her leg too from carrying her trophy, and her whole tawny length was beaded with sweat. Myrna, kneeling up on the edge of the bed, couldn't wrench her eyes from that long, muscular figure, those hard curves and those shameless breasts, her nipples large and well defined and almost black in colour.

The lady dropped Harzu, patted Anada's face with a slap that was only just short of a blow and finally stopped in front of Myrna. 'Mouse,' she smiled, hands on hips, her voice a throaty purr that made the smaller woman quiver. Myrna could feel the heat rising up her breasts and throat and she dropped her gaze, seeing then that a flimsy strip of pale silk stretched down from the woven belt between Shinsawbu's thighs. It was so damp that it was completely transparent and the dark curls beneath were quite visible. 'Are you pleased to see me again, Mouse?'

What answer could there be to that? The wet heat was gathering in Myrna's sex just from the sight of her. She could see tiny freckles of blood spattered on Shin-sawbu's throat and torso, and the dewy beads of sweat hanging from the undercurve of each small and perfect breast. She could smell the musk of excitement and violence and it was making her own poor, exposed nipples harden to painful points, her breasts tingling. 'Yes, my queen,' she admitted hoarsely, because it was partly true.

Shinsawbu chuckled, low and throaty, then grabbed Myrna's chain and pulled her off the bed, onto her knees. 'Then welcome me properly,' she said, shoving her face to the taut skin of her hip. 'I need cleaning off.'

Myrna pressed her open mouth to the wet skin and tasted the salt sweat on her tongue. Her own heart was pounding hard. She licked, finding the skin far hotter than her mouth, as if Shinsawbu burnt with fever. Her tongue burst a hundred tiny beads of sweat. The lady wore the droplets like seed pearls.

'Yes,' Shinsawbu purred. Myrna felt the word vibrate through muscle and bone and she swallowed it gratefully. She tasted the metallic tang of blood too; the filth of the hunt sprayed across velvet skin. She shut her eyes. I've tasted blood before, she reminded herself, and not just in this lifetime.

She could feel her own thighs splaying as if the wet pressure between them was forcing them open. Then fingers were knotted in her hair and she was jerked up and her face pressed into Shinsawbu's crotch. Beneath the thick weave of the belt the wisp of silk was soaked through. Myrna kissed it, smelling her musk, but her tongue couldn't work through the taut cloth. Shinsawbu let her struggle a while, then cuffed her away. The slaves shrank back before her. Her amber eyes could burn your soul, Myrna thought, her ear ringing from the blow.

'Time for my bath,' Shinsawbu announced, uncinching her belt and shedding her sole item of clothing. Carelessly she snapped the three chains and wrapped the dangling ends around her fist. However soft the metal, her strength was clearly beyond the normal. 'Follow,' she commanded. 'Good girls. On your knees.'

They were forced to crawl behind her on hands and knees as she led the way. Looking up, Myrna could see only the Tiger Lady's long legs retreating before her, and the tight backside that swung bewitchingly above them as if powered by some sultry pendulum. A glance to either side permitted her to share the shame and the trepidation on the faces of her fellow slaves as they crawled, rumps thrust out and hair in dishevelled tresses about their flushed cheeks. The wilful contempt of Shinsawbu stung her hard. It was not her pride that was hurt, she reasoned; it was her sense of righteousness. Whichever, it made her face burn.

They crawled all the way to the bathing chamber, their shining leashes swinging before them. The centrepiece of this room was a huge round bath carved out of multicoloured onyx, set into the floor. Myrna had never set eyes on anything so luxurious. It was already filled with water, presumably by servants who knew their mistress' requirements in advance, and set about with tiny lamps that filled the air with the smell of warm butter and flowers. There were several glass and alabaster jars on a tray near the rim of the pool. Shinsawbu selected one of these and when she poured a little oily liquid from it into the water the scent of musk-roses grew at once stronger. Without hurry and with effortless grace the lady descended into the pool, turning over on her back and reclining against the marble lip, stretching out her arms along the stone. Her breasts broke the surface of the water like perfect little islands afloat in a balmy sea. The three chains were still draped loosely in one hand.

'Which one of you will attend me first?' she asked, eyes lambent and wicked.

Anada raised her head swiftly. 'My queen.' Myrna understood from her bright and eager face that she was trying to find favour with the woman who held her life on the end of a chain. Probably an astute move, she admitted. Harzu on the other hand did a bad job of hiding her relief.

'Very well. Soap me.'

A tug on the chain warned her not to waste time undressing, so Anada climbed down into the waist-deep water in a swirl of scarlet silk. It looked uncomfortably like blood billowing through the water. Her long black hair, sheer as a veil, washed about her hips. Anada waded across the pool, searched among the jars on the tray and located some soap. Dribbling the white mess onto her palms she laid them tentatively on Shinsawbu's shoulders and began to massage it into her skin with short, circular strokes, gradually working her way down from firm muscle to the softer curves and peaks. She was trying so hard to please; her kneading and caressing of those small breasts was lavish and quite expert, her fingers manipulating the big black nipples with a firmness that had little to do with cleanliness but was appreciatively received. Shinsawbu arched her back and sighed her contentment at the treatment and Myrna felt her own nipples tingle enviously.

'Not bad,' said Shinsawbu. Her long legs furled around Anada's waist. Now she was anchored at both ends so that her body floated on the surface, within reach of those clever, teasing hands. Anada dribbled more soap between her breasts and squeezed the two islands together, pinching their volcanic tips until the nipples stood up hard and huge. Then she passed her open palm down over Shinsawbu's flat belly, reaching beneath the surface for submerged treasure. Shinsawbu tilted her pelvis, writhing her hips. Her fleece broke the water from below, Anada's hand buried deep in the dark fronds. Shinsawbu was emitting grunt after tiny grunt of concentration and her eyes were narrowed to yellow slits. Clearly something within that sublime body was struggling towards a climax.

Harzu's appalled eyes were lowered, but Myrna couldn't look away. Shinsawbu's legs uncoiled, stretching out rigid as her pelvis thrust forwards. Then, without warning, one leg rose out of the pool with a great wash of scented water and hooked up over Anada's shoulder, pulling her under the surface. She didn't even have time to cry out.

Myrna felt her heart turn over.

The Tiger Lady reached forwards, grabbed the dark mass of Anada's hair and pulled it into her crotch, wrapping her other leg around the slave's neck too. Once she had a good grip with her thighs she didn't need her hand and she leaned back again, neck arching, her breasts bobbing on the water. Only the very crown of Anada's head broke the surface, and that momentarily. There was no way she could breathe. Shinsawbu mewed with pleasure; perhaps the trapped woman was trying to bring her to orgasm by mouth as quick as possible; perhaps that was the only strategy that might work. But it didn't last more than a few moments. There was a sudden flurry of limbs and one hand thrashed above the surface, then that too fell back. Shinsawbu frowned and ground her hips, but in vain. Slowly all movement in the pool ceased.

The soles of Anada's feet drifted limply into view. Her hair filled the pool around her like spilt ink.

'Next one,' gasped Shinsawbu.

Myrna didn't hesitate. She slipped into the water before Harzu could even register terror. The warm liquid clasped her to the waist as she waded through the cloud of clinging hair to where Anada's body floated face down and motionless. Shinsawbu had released her at last, and it took only a moment to scoop her up and raise her head and shoulders from the bath. She was heavy, though. Myrna had no idea that another woman of no great stature could weigh so much, far beyond her capacity to push out of the pool. She dragged her to the edge of the bath and tried to thrust her into Harzu's reaching grasp.

The chain around her neck tightened. One hard pull was all it took to jerk Myrna off her feet. Her soles skidded uselessly on the onyx as the water closed over her head and she was instantly surrounded by roaring silver bubbles, her hands thrashing. It was only Shinsawbu's hands around her face that brought her back to the surface.

'Don't keep me waiting!' the lady hissed. It was a moment sufficient for Myrna to seize a breath. Then she was below the surface again, the smooth weight of muscular legs clamping round her shoulders, perfume stinging her eyes as she tried to make out the dark shape of her target through the haze.

She buried her face in Shinsawbu's muff, seeing the silver bubbles trickle up from her nostrils through the soft fronds of hair, tasting the bitter attar of roses. It was the only tactic she could think of; to concentrate on finding and sucking her torturer's clitoris. She ignored the roaring in her ears and the burning in her lungs. She licked instead; she nibbled; she chased the stray bubbles, stroking and pressing at any opening she could find like a desperate thief trying to pick a lock. She knew Shinsawbu was close to climax, and she also knew she only had moments to get her there. Her own hair was swirling around her face; she could see the ruddy stain in the periphery of her vision. Her lungs were in agony as she breathed out but couldn't breathe in. She ploughed the furrow of Shinsawbu's labia, amazed at how inanimate they seemed here in this world of water where there was no scent, no taste, no body-warmth; they were not like living flesh at all. Some of the bubbles were black now; glowing and pulsing as they swept over her. She pushed her fingers into the dark sea-grotto between those coral petals, but she knew it was too late. Blood was roaring in her ears. Her hair was covering her eyes and she could no longer see any gleam of light above her, only the red abyss through which the black bubbles were rising, and now even the abyss was black and—

And light. And air. And pain in her throat and the roaring of her breath and water running down the back of her nose, burning like acid. The burden on her shoulders was lifted, no longer holding her down. She found her footing and staggered back as she rose, then fell and had to grab the lip of the bath to stop herself drowning anew. Tears were running down her face, but they were invisible among the water drops.

By the time she could see straight Shinsawbu was nonchalantly rinsing her hair. Then the lady rose gleaming from the waters and surveyed her subjects. Myrna clung to the stonework and pushed her own wet hair back from her brow, trying to calm the heaving of her chest. She cast a quick glance across the bath at Harzu, saw that the slave was kneeling over Anada's prone body, and then saw that Anada was moving, that her hands were pawing at the floor and her shoulders shaking as she coughed.

'Feeling better?' Shinsawbu enquired.

At that moment Anada, eyes still closed, began to vomit. It was mostly water, forced in great choking gasps from her lungs, but there was fruit pulp too and it slopped over the onyx lip into the bath.

Shinsawbu flinched. 'Stop that,' she said, but Anada was entirely unconscious of her command. She sprang out of the water with one motion and was standing over the collapsed woman before Myrna had even realised that she was moving. 'I said,' she repeated, grabbing the wet ropes of Anada's extraordinarily long hair and jerking her head back; 'stop that.' And she caught Anada's neck with one solid, economical kick that snapped it with a crunch.

Silence flooded in to the void left by the coughing. Harzu put one hand over her mouth and her eyes above that hand were wild. Myrna stood up in the bath. Shinsawbu felt the weight of her gaze and crouched down over the dead body of the slave like some ravenous carnivore. 'Did that upset you?' she wondered.

Harzu shrank away from her mistress, like wax melting before a furnace.

Myrna thought she might be sick herself. Hot and cold flashes were running through the marrow of her bones. But, looking into those predatory amber eyes, she knew that nothing would delight Shinsawbu more than to discern a point of weakness, and that she wouldn't fail to exploit it. 'No,' she said, letting nothing show in her face.

'I thought from the way you were acting that you might have been fond of her.'

I am the Malia Shai, the incarnate goddess of the Cruel Earth. I am the famine and the plague. I am the forest fire and the locust storm and the flood. I am without mercy or compassion. 'No,' she said again, letting her pity for Anada wither and blow away; 'my queen.' Her pulse was slowing, her breath coming smoothly now. Her eyes were cold and indifferent. She watched Shinsawbu turn away disappointed.

What she didn't let go of, buried deep inside her where it could not be seen and stoked well so that it might not be extinguished, was a single point of white-hot rage.

7 The Gift of the Gods

Rahul was a gentle, good-natured man, conscientious about everything in his care. Every night he would wash the dust from the knobbly legs of his patient oxen and feed them with grass he'd cut on the way. He painted their horns red and green and polished the strings of brass bells that hung around their white necks. He lavished care on the cart and the storytellers' props too, repairing the fragile articulated joints of his shadow-puppets and repainting the decorations scribed on the flat rawhide which gave them expression and identity, even though those details would never be visible through the screen.

Teihli was a singer. She sang to herself as she walked, as she cooked, as she sewed their costumes. She even hummed under her breath when she took a man's prick in her mouth. She laughed more readily and smiled more broadly than Rahul, but she clearly doted upon her young husband. Nor did Veraine's sombre, half-reluctant presence in their lives seem to try her humour. 'You bless us,' she told him. 'The gods have sent you to protect us.'

I'm going to Siya Ran Thu, he'd warned them.

We're heading south too, for the moment, they had replied. You can ride with us.

I'll travel faster alone, he'd argued. You have to stop at every village to earn your living.

But, they'd asked, what will you eat? Where will you sleep to be safe from bandits and wild animals? The land's in chaos and strangers are not treated kindly these days; who else will give you safe passage?

I thought I was to be your protector, he'd pointed out.

You are, Rahul had grinned; the gods arranged for us to meet.

So he had agreed in the end, though he felt far from sure that he was worthy of such trust. Hadn't he screwed Rahul's wife with hardly a moment's hesitation? – and the fact that the young man wasn't jealous, that he took pleasure in sharing her with a stranger, that didn't take away Veraine's unease.

If I had a wife, he thought, I'd not let any other man touch her. Then he could only wonder if he did have a wife and how she might manage without him.

He only came to understand the relationship between bhopa and bhopi when he saw their first full performance before an audience. They had travelled then for several days, dropping down out of the hills into new terrain. This was still forest, but a forest where people hunted and cut firewood, where clearings had been cut for the growing of crops and the groundwater channelled into stone drains that bore the floods of the wet season to ancient storage tanks. They'd met people and even performed for groups of wood-gathering women and for farmers in return for food, but they hadn't unpacked the cart. And at night they'd slept by the road, and Teihli had stretched out between Veraine and Rahul, eager and hot-eyed and seemingly insatiable, and they'd taken her in turns.

But one evening they reached the fields surrounding what was clearly a large village. Farmers shouldering their tools at the end of the day's work made their way through the wheat rows towards them, no less fascinated than the clamouring wide-eyed children and excited dogs who formed an escort to the village gate.

Rahul let the oxen halt on a piece of bare ground before a thick barrier made of dead thorn branches. After the open road the smell of animals and cooking fires, latrines and tanning hides seemed almost overpowering, and the noise a cacophony. Some of the villagers looked apprehensively at Veraine, who stood a head taller than anyone else. He felt out of place, but he watched his two companions smiling and chatting to everyone and assumed that all was well. They had to wait until the children had been shushed and then a small, elderly man waited for Rahul to bow a greeting.

'Welcome, bhopa,' he said. His stubble was as white as his few remaining teeth, and hanging around his neck was a saffron-dyed scarf. 'You bless us.'

'May we play for you tonight, sardar?' Rahul asked.

'Of course. And you will eat at my house.'

They unloaded the cart, tethered the oxen with a pile of fodder and prepared the props for the show before going to eat, while there was still enough light. The villagers went about their evening business too. Veraine and Rahul walked back and forth to the village square with pieces of the stage, bundles of cloth, musical instruments and a metal brazier, while Teihli lashed a framework against the side of the cart that looked as if it was going to be a tent of some kind.

'Why are we camping outside the fence?' Veraine wondered.

She straightened up from throwing a bedroll into the booth. The setting sun made her skin look reddish and the sight caught at his heart. 'Tradition. You'll see.'

Veraine was reaching for one of the flat palm-leaf baskets containing the shadow-puppets when Rahul intercepted him with a hand on his arm. 'No,' he said gently but firmly. 'You shouldn't touch those.'

He looked at Rahul questioningly.

'Only a bhopa or a bhopi may touch them.'

'I see.'

'They're sacred. They're the gods,' Rahul explained, flipping open the lid of one tray to reveal the topmost puppet.

Veraine felt his stomach clench. 'Who's that?'

Rahul snatched the basket beyond his reach. Veraine shivered. The puppet was female, and as voluptuous as all the goddesses were, with jutting breasts and the narrowest of waists. But her skin was a leprous white, her eyes were wide and staring, tusks protruded from her mouth and around her throat dangled a necklace of skulls. Her dress was tattered and over it, low about her hips, was slung a girdle of blackened human arms. She was horrific. Veraine's mouth was dry. It was not one of the ones he'd seen Rahul handling before, yet he knew her. Of all the puppet-gods, this was the one he knew. 'Who is she?' he repeated, his voice hoarse.

Rahul looked worried. 'This is Malia Mata,' he said in a subdued voice: 'Mother of Disease.'

Of course she was. Veraine tried to swallow. He knew her face, and he knew her name. It was as familiar to him as the scar on the back of his thumb. 'Malia . . .'

'We don't tell many stories about her. It's inauspicious.' Rahul squirmed visibly. 'She brings the smallpox and the malaria and the bloody flux. Her demons prowl the forest. She kills children for preference.'

Veraine covered his face with his hands, feeling submerged memories flailing towards the surface. The waters they rose from were dark and very deep. 'Malia. I think . . . the woman I'm looking for . . . she's called Malia.'

'That's not possible,' said Teihli flatly.

'No one would name their daughter that,' agreed Rahul. 'It would be insane.'

The memories sank back down into the darkness, glimmering pale before vanishing. He could not be sure of what he'd glimpsed. 'I don't know,' he whispered.

Rahul covered the puppet and retreated with an armful of baskets. From the look on his face Veraine's words had really rattled him. Teihli looked just as unhappy, but she touched his hand. 'Let's get that awning thrown over there.'

It was after nightfall by the time the three of them had the stage set up and had eaten their evening meal with the sardar and his family, sitting on rugs in their mud-brick courtyard. News was exchanged. The language they used was intelligible to Veraine, being the standard tongue of the region and not some tribal dialect, but they had nothing to say that interested him; merely long accounts of the weather, of the fortunes of farming, of the curse of the reivers and of gossip and rumour from nearby villages. Rahul and Teihli, he presumed, were sifting and committing this to memory, but it meant little to him.

Tiny hot cups of leaf tea were served during the meal, but afterwards a leather flask was passed around. One sniff told Veraine that the contents were raw spirit of some sort and his stomach turned over. He could suddenly smell the Rani's rank, sweet perfume and he had to fight down nausea. He tilted the flask to his closed lips and then quickly passed it on.

As they finished the sardar's wife knelt before Teihli and begged her blessing, which she gave warmly. Then all of the married women of the extended household came in turn to ask her touch upon their foreheads and a murmured word of blessing. Veraine could not begin to guess what this signified, but everyone seemed grateful.

After the meal, they completed the preparations for the night's entertainment. While Teihli filled the brazier with oil and cut the wicks, Rahul turned to Veraine. 'If you sit to the side you'll see everything. Can you drum?'

'Drum?'

Rahul threw him a wooden drum nearly as broad across as his chest, the taut goatskin still hairy in patches. 'Call them in.'

Veraine took the drum into the shadows at the side. When he slapped it the sound echoed off the surrounding walls, and as he set up a beat Rahul joined in, blowing down a short wooden flute with a bulbous gourd to produce a reedy squall. It brought in the dogs first, prancing and frantic, then the rest of the village, men and women and children. As they entered the square each deposited into a basket at Rahul's feet a handful of lentils or rice or millet, or else a clump of radishes or a piece of fruit, until the mixture formed a heap. The audience seated themselves upon the bare earth, propping babies into laps, shooing away dogs that were too nosy. When everyone seemed to be present Rahul ceased the wicked skirling, bowed politely and disappeared behind the draped wings of the screen. Teihli stepped forwards into the expectant silence.

She opened the evening's proceedings with a dance, accompanied only by her own voice and the clash of small brass anklets. Her song about the rainy season was clearly familiar to the audience, who joined in with each refrain. Veraine folded his arms and allowed himself to admire the firelight on her skin, the firm lines of her waist and hips, the generous curves hidden beneath the indigo cloth. Her pliant waist swayed and twisted and her hands described complex gestures. She wore a blouse that exposed the maximum of her midriff and a skirt embroidered with fragments of glass that caught the firelight. Confident, smiling, sensual – she seemed to glow with an inner fire.

After the first song came further parts of the show; Veraine observed with curiosity and respect, appreciating the pair's virtuosity as well as their skill. First Rahul stood to retell the tidings of the year just past, including the invasion of the Horse-eaters and their eventual campaign across the desert. The villagers nodded and murmured and shuddered as he described the massacres, the courage of those who had resisted, the fear of those who fled. They keened at the loss of their Rani but Veraine, hidden in the shadows, shut his eyes and clenched his teeth when he heard how she had been burnt alive in her palace, she and five hundred women perishing in a fiery jauhar of their own devising rather than fall into enemy hands.

Then Rahul described how the Horse-eaters were met in battle by the Emperor Beyond the Sands and the gods themselves had come down to fight; how the Plague Goddess in her tattered robe and the Sun Lord in his gilded armour had waded thigh-deep among the barbarians, slaying hundreds with each blow until they had met in the centre of the field and riven the earth open, casting down into the chasm that dreaded horde and piling upon the top of them a mountain. Veraine listened with furrowed brow, half-amused, half-scornful.

After that Teihli came out again and sang a lament for a beloved lost to the tide of war, accompanying herself on a stringed instrument. Some in the audience wept; everyone in that village knew what loss felt like. As she finished Rahul lit the oil-lamp and the high screen lit up with a golden glow. It was time for the main spectacle of the evening, the puppet-play. The story they told took both of them to manipulate the angular puppets behind the screen and at times Veraine was amazed that it was only four hands and two voices that managed to convey such complex, rapidly shifting scenes. It was a tale of two brothers who gave their sister in marriage to a great king who they realised too late was an evil magician in disguise, and then set off to rescue her. It involved a great deal of magic and many plot-twists before it was resolved to the happiness of all bar the magician-king.

The mood had lightened now and the next turn was a playful one, where Rahul and Teihli came out and sang a comic and rather bawdy love song. Veraine looked over the laughing faces and wondered at their happiness in the midst of such harsh lives. This is not my world, he thought.

When the song had finished with a shout, there was one last puppet show. This was far shorter; a creation-time story, pared down with age. Veraine rested his head against the wall and watched as the gods argued about whether humankind should be created from fire or from earth, and whether they should be mortal or immortal. In the end the great gods moulded men and women from cow-dung mixed with chaff, so that they wouldn't be too proud or too long-lived. Many of these little humans were made and sent off to live in all the earth. But it soon became clear that the dung-people didn't know how to defend themselves from other animals, or to find food, or to protect themselves from the rain and the sun. Some dried up and cracked apart, some dissolved in floods, many starved – and worst of all, they didn't know how to make more of their own kind.

Eventually there were very few people left alive and the gods Chedak and Shadso, brother and sister, unable to watch the last of them perish, came down to teach mankind. Chedak went among women; he taught them stories of the loom and of fire, how to love men, how to mate and how to bear children. Shadso went among men; she taught them stories of the plants and the beasts, how to love women, how to mate and how to sire children. Together they taught human beings the tales of the gods so that they would know how to pray, the stories of kings so that they would know how to rule themselves, and the tales of humankind so that they would know each other.

The light behind the screen flickered and sank. That luminous window into the world of legend grew dim, was suddenly nothing more than a white cloth stretched upon a frame. Rahul and Teihli stepped out from the wings, raised their hands and sang together, no more than a couple of phrases: 'We invoke the blessings of Chedak and Shadso upon this place.'

The performance was over. Clearly the audience knew this; stamping and clapping, they were suddenly on their feet, lifting dozing infants and talking among themselves. Rahul slipped away. Veraine stretched, suddenly feeling the stiffness between his shoulders. Then he realised that it was almost entirely the women among the audience that were leaving. He looked to Teihli, who was standing motionless in front of the dulled screen, hands folded and eyes closed. Was there more to come? Many of the men remained patiently where they were. They didn't talk. The guttering torchlight sent the shadows dancing over their faces. Veraine shifted his stance, uneasy. Teihli's stillness was not the calm of someone at rest; she was holding herself poised. Her breasts were rising and falling visibly with her breath.

Only when the last of their families had withdrawn and the total silence of expectation hung over the men, young and old, who remained, did she lift her head to scan the small crowd. The men sat up straighter. Was she looking for Rahul? Veraine wondered. Or him? Where was Rahul, come to that?

Teihli stepped forwards among the men. Every head turned to follow her progress, some grimacing as if trying to catch her eye. She reached down her hand and touched a man lightly on the shoulder and a murmur licked through the crowd. Quickly the man scrambled to his feet; he was carrying a folded cowskin draped over one arm. She smiled at him. The second man she picked out had a goat kid on a tether. The little animal bleated sleepily and shook its dangling ears. But the third man, younger than the others and dressed very poorly, held nothing in his hands except a little woven basket of berries. As soon as she'd made this choice Teihli turned and walked away.

Suddenly, everyone was on their feet, whether grumbling, laughing, or silent. It took Veraine some time to make his way out between them, following Teihli as best he could. Away from the torchlight it was very dark and he had to grope his way along the walls. Little chinks of light shone from under doors and eaves. The biggest source of light was a fire kindled just outside the thorn hedge, and as Veraine got close enough to make out Rahul squatting over it, Teihli's form emerged out of the dark just ahead of him and the couple moved together to clasp hands, husband and wife smiling at each other. She reached up to touch his face.

'It went well,' she said.

'Veraine?' said Rahul, who had quick ears. His teeth flashed in the firelight. 'What did you think?'

Veraine stepped forwards into the firelight too.

'Did you like it?'

'It was fascinating,' he said awkwardly. Why had

they hurried back to the cart so quickly, abandoning all their equipment?

'It went really well. I wasn't sure whether they'd want all of *Two Brothers* but it just seemed to roll.'

'Well, at least we'll eat for a few days,' said Teihli, smiling, as she indicated the basket at his feet. It contained the food offerings collected from the audience.

'Is that it for the night?' Veraine asked. 'Shouldn't we see to the –'

'Wait a while,' Rahul forestalled him, holding up a hand. Then he nodded past Veraine's shoulder at the village gateway. The scuffle of footsteps in the darkness beyond resolved into the figure of a man with a tanned cowhide draped over one arm.

'Welcome,' said Teihli.

He said nothing but proffered the skin, looking at Rahul and Veraine uncertainly. Rahul took the folded hide out of his hands. Then Teihli took the man by the arm and led him away, into the tent by the cart.

Veraine felt like his face had turned to stone.

'How many did she choose?' Rahul asked, his voice low.

'Uh. Three.'

He rolled his eyes. 'She forgets some of us need to sleep tonight.'

Veraine stared. 'How many does she normally bring?'

Rahul folded the hide. 'It must be at least one. That's the tradition.'

Veraine didn't understand how his tone could be so light. 'This ... doesn't bother you?' he asked, trying to order his thoughts before unconsidered words could escape.

'Why should it?'

He shook his head. 'So. This is how you make your living, then?'

Rahul glanced at him sharply, finally seeming to recognise his dismay. 'She's the vessel of Shadso the storyteller,' he said. 'She teaches men, and brings the gift of the gods to them. That's what our people do. It's how our caste has lived since before the years were counted. It's what my parents did when they were young, and why our families chose us to be married to each other. It is what our children will do when they're grown.'

'You have children?'

'Two, at home. We'll see them when the rains start.'

It was impossible not to be rude. 'And you're sure they're yours?'

Rahul shrugged, complacent. 'Of course. I'm her husband.'

'I see.' He had the bizarre urge to laugh. 'And what about you? Are you the vessel of the gods too?'

Rahul packed the hide away in the cart. 'Sometimes,' he said, 'there are women who can't conceive. Then they can come to me for Chedak's blessing. There's no shame in that.'

Veraine ran his hand across his head, looked at the floor and finally spread his hands in surrender. 'Fine. It makes sense.' He was thinking: It makes sense of the way they've treated me.

'Good. Now look; it helps that you're here. I'm going to go back and bring over the puppets – we can leave the screen up until the morning. You stay here and keep an eye on things.'

'What am I supposed to do?'

'Well. Just make sure you keep order. See off anyone that she hasn't chosen. You can manage that.' He grinned lopsidedly and then suddenly looked serious. 'If there is any trouble in there, if she calls out for help, there has to be someone nearby. Don't worry; she chooses well.'

Veraine watched him slip away into the dark, then sat down by the fire with his blade across his knees. The wood crackled softly, and from the village he could hear the muffled noises of animals in the byres and a distant dog howling. But now that conversation had ceased, he was most aware of the sounds from within the tent; a murmur, a thump, a muffled giggle. It made him feel uncomfortable and he was surprised at himself. He wondered if he should move further off, but decided he ought to be close enough to hear even the most stifled cry of alarm. He cocked his head, catching a few words: '... There, is that ... it feels ...' Teihli, it seemed, was doing quite a lot of talking. A masculine voice growled 'Oh yes!' and after that Veraine listened to a prolonged series of explosive grunts, as regular as the creak of a water wheel. He couldn't help picturing that man pounding into Teihli, face slack with lust, flesh quivering with each jerk.

His mouth was dry.

It seemed a long time before the tent-flap was lifted and the man left, hitching up his fouta. Veraine didn't bother to stand, not even when Teihli emerged and came over to the fire. She was still dressed, except that she'd discarded her respectable shawl and her hair was messed and there was a sheen of perspiration across her bare stomach. She looked at Veraine thoughtfully, without a word – without even her customary smile – and he could think of nothing to say to her. He watched as she lit a small lamp from a burning twig. She sat and wrapped her arms about her knees, looking into the fire, expressionless. Perhaps he would have thought of something to say, but they were only alone for a few moments before the bleating of a kid heralded her second client. She took the payment from his arms, cuddling it for a moment before passing the animal to Veraine. By the time he'd tethered it near the oxen's fodder she had drawn the stranger by the hand into her bower.

This time the tent was lit from within as she'd taken the lamp with her. On returning to his seat Veraine couldn't help catching a glimpse through a gap in the awnings; a lightning flash of Teihli pulling her blouse open, those big breasts bouncing free like twin moons rising, her face luminous. The sight sent a shock through him. He turned away, unable to sit still now, and paced restlessly up the road. His fingers twitched. He looked up at the stars. He rubbed the back of his neck and turned in impatient circles and finally moved back towards the tent. The construction was slipshod; from this angle, even standing at quite a distance, the long slit between two panels of cloth disclosed far too much. Teihli stood with hands clasping lightly the head of the man who knelt before her. He was nursing at her breasts, taking each in turn, suckling until her orbs glistened.

'Beautiful, isn't she?' whispered Rahul.

Veraine jumped, angrier that someone had managed to sneak up on him while he was distracted than that he'd been caught watching the man's wife. But Rahul laid a placating hand on his arm.

'Don't you think so?'

Veraine followed his gaze. 'Yes,' he agreed. All right, maybe not beautiful like some women, but utterly arousing. The way she was standing now, with her shoulders thrust back, her tits in that farmer's face, her lips half-parted as she instructed him – oh, she was loving it.

'She makes me so hot. Watching her makes me hard.'

Veraine swallowed the dry knot in his throat. 'Oh, yes.'

'I love to think of all the men she's had in her. The gallons of spunk she's had poured into her slit. The stuff she's had to swallow.'

'You like that?'

Teihli was rubbing her breasts over the farmer's face and seemed to be trying to blind him with her nipples.

'You know I do. I'd like to spread her cheeks and watch it run out of her like cream.'

'Ah.'

'I'd like to catch her really juiced up and swollen and slimy with come and then pump her with more of my own. I want to see it in gobbets in her hair and on her eyelashes and running down her beautiful bubs.'

Veraine nodded. That made sense too. He was well aware that Rahul hadn't removed his hand. He watched Teihli sink slowly down to the floor of the tent, straddling her consort, and only then detached himself and walked back to the fire. He wasn't pretending to anyone, even himself, that that voyeuristic glimpse hadn't affected him, that it wasn't making his pulse run thick and his cock swell; yet just now this was too new, too unsettling. He reached between his thighs to readjust his uncomfortable testes, felt his prick stir sluggishly against his wrist and gritted his teeth. His tackle felt heavy, far heavier than flesh should be.

When the second man left the tent Veraine saw Rahul step out of the shadows. He caught Teihli in the doorway and pulled her against him for a hot, lingering kiss, his hands groping down to squeeze her arse. She responded eagerly, wrapping one thigh around his leg. His mouth worked on hers, delving deep. He hopes she took it in the mouth too, Veraine thought. He wants to taste it in her.

When he looked away there was another figure at the village gate, dim and self-effacing. His eyes were so confused by the fire and the darkness that he had to stand up and move in before he worked out that it was a woman, wrapped around tightly in her brown orhni and holding it across her face so that only her eyes showed. 'Who are you looking for?' he asked, trying not to sound threatening, though he couldn't keep the rough edge out of his voice.

She didn't reply. There was no way of judging whether she was young or old, pretty or plain.

'Him?' He jerked his head to indicate the tent. She shrank back a little; he could see the whites of her eyes as she looked him up and down. 'Rahul,' he said, louder, turning his back on her. The storytellers disentangled themselves. 'I think you have a customer.'

Rahul came over. Veraine leaned against the side of the cart, looking for the moon as the other man took the newcomer's hand and led her away from the village, up the road, into the dark. Teihli stood quietly in the doorway to the tent, her figure outlined by the lamp-light behind her. Her blouse had been resumed but it hung open, doing less than the gloom to conceal the bounty therein.

Maybe the last one won't turn up, Veraine thought grimly. Maybe I'll be stood here all night with a hard-on.

But the last of her choices, the raggedly dressed man, was quite prompt. Veraine caught a clear view of his face as he passed through the circle of the campfire; a coarse face under a shock of black hair. What had she picked him for? Maybe she just wanted a good hard hammering for her last course, he thought sourly.

And he took forever. Veraine had to force himself to sit still next to the fire and not to watch, not to give in to the base urge to jerk off while spying on their rutting. He couldn't fail to hear what was going on though; the man was loud and rhapsodic. And he kept groaning; big slobbery bass grunts. It was bestial, and it made Veraine's balls tighten like fists.

He wasn't really aware that the man had finished, only that the noises had stopped at last, and that the neglected fire had collapsed into a glowing heap, and that his vision was swimming from staring far into the red distance beyond the embers. Suddenly there she was, standing behind him, wrapped only in her blue cotton orhni which was clinging to her damp skin. This time she did look tired; she was flushed and little locks of hair were plastered to her forehead. She stepped in front of him, shadow and light flowing over her face. The little beads of sweat around her collar bone shone like rubies. 'Have I angered you?' she asked at last, just a bit wary.

He looked at his feet and laughed shortly. 'You hurt my pride,' he said. 'There I was, assuming that I was such an outstanding paragon of manhood that it was perfectly natural that a faithful wife should take one look and throw herself into my arms.'

She waited.

'Well, a fool is soon disillusioned.'

She touched his temple gently and tilted his face. 'I think you are an outstanding man,' she said softly. 'And no fool.'

He could smell the perfume of her hot body. He put his hand on her thigh and drew her forward. 'I'm jealous,' he admitted.

'Don't be,' she whispered, running her fingers through his hair.

He pressed his face to her stomach, feeling the curve of her belly through the damp material. Her hips were firm where they nested snugly in the cups of his hands. He tugged the cotton aside and let his lips brush bare skin, just below her navel, felt the fire within her and tasted the salt on his tongue. His head was filled with the rich tang of her musk, welling up from the altar of her sex – but it was overlaid and intermingled with another scent too; the heady stink of jism. Her lovers. The men who'd paid for her and fucked her and filled her. He trailed his fingers up the inside of her thigh and there – there it was; the wetness, the stickiness of it, drying now to a crust on her satin skin. It had run down her thighs. Her pubic hair was matted in tight coils and ringlets. He thought of everything Rahul had said and he lowered his face to that sodden bush, pressing his lips into it. The salty taste made him shudder. The slipperiness of that which coated his tongue and oiled his lips was almost unbearable. He groaned out loud, his spine on fire, his cock throbbing to full erection in painful jerks, as his fingers joined his mouth in exploring her and discovered she was awash, running over, as formless and unresisting as quicksand. She shook against him, grinding her mound into his face, her hands twisting in his hair. He thrust his fingers up into her pliant quim, spreading her wider, feeling the moisture run down over his wrist. He withdrew his cupped palm filled with pearlescent effluvia, the liquid wash of sperm and her own lubricious pleasure, and he lapped it up, shaking, and plunged his hand in again.

'Veraine,' she gasped; 'take me inside!'

'Haven't you had enough?' he asked, tearing his face away from her delta.

She moaned, but she managed to croak, 'No.'

'What am I supposed to do about it?'

'Oh. Fuck me. Please, Veraine.'

He laughed, bemused. 'If I put you out to the king's own stallion it wouldn't fill you. If I bent you over the cattle-pen and let every bull in the village stuff his pizzle into you, you still wouldn't be satisfied.'

She whimpered. He caught her as her legs gave way, pulling her down to straddle his thighs. His cock stabbed into her through his clothes. She sagged in his grip, dazed and panting. He kissed her hard, letting her taste her own wantoness on his tongue, forcing her mouth wide.

'You want me to fuck you?' he growled, freeing his prick from the folds of cotton. Its swollen head was weeping tears of its own, adding to the lubrication he worked over the shaft. Teihli nodded, then her eyes rolled back as he lifted her and aligned the hard member with her sex until he was poised at her threshold. He felt her muscles contracting, pulsing around him. 'I'm going to fuck you, all right.' He eased her down, a little at a time. 'I'm going to take you so deep I'll be able to drink my own come out of your throat.'

Teihli twisted her hips, fighting to engulf him faster, but he took his time, feasting on her frustration. 'You know what else I'm going to do?'

She whimpered.

'I'm going to make you scream. You took those men with hardly a sound, not from you, though I could hear them all right, the noises they made rutting on you like boars on a sow – but they didn't make you cry out. Not enough for you, were they? You're going to cry out for me, Teihli. You're going to beg for it, you're going to make music for me, you're going to scream when you come. Do you understand?'

'Yes,' she moaned, 'yes.'

He sheathed himself to the hilt and stood, holding her easily with his cock up hard inside her and her legs wrapped around his hips. He carried her into the tent – and most of the promises he'd made, he kept.

8 Transgressions

The Palace of the Harimau was a house of beauty, and of fear. Beauty resided in the carved woodwork and the mirrorwork ceilings, in the paintings upon the walls, the jewelled silks of the inhabitants, the melodies of the musicians, the brightness of fresh flowers, and in the faces and bodies of slaves chosen for their surpassing loveliness. Fear resided, as ever, in human hearts. Myrna saw it every day in the guarded expressions of the servants and the blank downcast looks of slaves. She learned the smell of fear, and the timbre it brings to the voice, and the roar of the silence when no one dares speak.

She saw how people – most often slaves but some-times guards or servants – would be there one day and gone the next, their absence unremarked. And she saw how some of them died. The Tiger Lords were obsessive hunters, and they loved to fight mock gladiatorial battles against wild animals or captives in the Palace Arena. Even when the challenge seemed pitiful they couldn't bring themselves to abstain. It was, thought Myrna, like watching a cat that had spilt a nest of mice and was grown frantic with the slaughter.

Lady Shinsawbu's own preference was for more strenuous hunting in the forest beyond the city. She went out most days alone or in the company of her relatives, and would return bearing trophies of sambar deer and boar and sloth bears. Her other passions, so far as Myrna could tell, were her tiger kittens, bathing, and watching the coupling of slaves. From the avidity with which she watched men rutting, Myrna surmised that her preference was not entirely for women, yet Shinsawbu never touched any man and kept no male slaves for her bed. She teased the younger guards sometimes, flaunting herself wickedly before them, and those men would grow white and sick with terror, because the Rao had forbidden her relations with men of lower status. Once Myrna saw him knock a man across a horse-block, breaking his spine: the stableman's misdemeanour had been in having Shinsawbu lean too intimately upon him as she descended from her palanquin.

If Dhammazhedi was jealous of his sister's honour, she was as protective of her own household. Her personal slaves were not to be touched by anyone else, and were kept out of the reach even of her own brothers and cousins. Myrna's only duties were those involved in pleasuring her mistress, and if that was often punishingly hard work at least she and Harzu came to no serious harm. Shinsawbu seemed quite fond of her mad little Mouse, who claimed to be a goddess and spoke like a mystic but yielded to the touch with a sluttish fervour.

It was not long before Myrna first broke the laws of the palace. She was sitting in the sun on the garden steps, drying the hair which Sao Mor had insisted was hennaed weekly. The treatment had turned her red waves to the colour of glowing embers. Her feet and the pale skin of her hands were hennaed too, in delicate floral designs. Harzu, bruised and exhausted, had crawled back onto the bed behind her to catch some sleep while Shinsawbu was away.

Listening to the song of the caged birds in the magnolias, Myrna was disturbed by a crash and the sound of a girl shrieking outside. She raised her head, sweeping the damp hair back behind her shoulders. The screams didn't stop; they came in short panicky bursts. It didn't sound like an adult. She rose to her feet.

'Don't,' called Harzu, but Myrna stepped out onto the terrace and looked for the source of the noise. A tray of cups lay scattered on the onyx path and a servant girl, no more than a child, was backed up against a pillar screaming as Shinsawbu's two tiger cubs jumped and clawed at her legs. The girl wasn't even trying to defend herself properly, just jerking her feet at the pain and shielding her stomach with her hands. Blood was running down her legs: the kittens were big enough to do real damage.

Myrna walked around the terrace. Between her and the girl stood one of the palace guards, staring into space. 'Stop them,' she hissed as she reached his side.

The guard's face was pasty. 'I can't,' he said through clenched teeth. The girl, trying to sidle away around the pillar, tripped over her own feet and dropped to a crouch, covering her head with her hands. The cubs snarled louder and flung themselves at her again. One jumped onto her back and began raking and biting at her neck.

Myrna looked around once before she moved. The only figures visible were scattered guards, but many chambers backed onto the gardens; if there were Harimau at any window overlooking this enclosure then what was happening here would be quite visible. It was obvious why the soldier was so reluctant. She strode over and grabbed the topmost cub, knotting her fist in the scruff of its neck. The animal squalled as she tore it free, needing the strength of both arms to lift it, and flung it away from her. Then she grabbed the smaller cub and threw it after the first. Both animals regained their feet hissing and shaking their ears. Myrna bared her teeth and hissed back, eyes locked on theirs. They flattened themselves to the ground then tumbled away, spitting, to find amusement somewhere else. The girl's shrieks had quietened to sobs. Myrna pulled her to her feet.

'Get up; go and get those seen to.' The scratches were deep and bloody. Myrna remembered something Veraine had done and added; 'You should put garlic-juice on those cuts. It'll sting, but it cleans them.'

Stifling her sobs with her fist, the girl stumbled away. Myrna turned to find not just the guards staring at her, but also their captain, who'd emerged from a doorway. She took a deep breath, wondering what he would do. Narathu Min gazed at her intently. Then he nodded, just a little. 'Back on patrol,' he told his guard. He waited on the terrace until Myrna had passed and returned to her quarters.

'What happened?' Harzu asked, raising her head from the pillows.

'Nothing.'

For the next few days she waited for retribution to fall, but tiger cubs do not talk. Nor, it seemed, did guards.

'I miss men,' said Shinsawbu, stretching out full length on the carpet. She wriggled from head to toe. 'It's been so long, and there are no men in the palace.' She seemed insensible of the guards who stood around the rooftop pavilion, almost within reach of her naked body and certainly within earshot. The sunlight played across her golden form, picking out the near-invisible down on her skin. The two cubs rolled and cuffed one another. 'Do you miss men?'

'Miss them?'

'Since coming here.'

Myrna, sitting at her side and wafting the breeze over her mistress's body with a fan of crane feathers, was startled. It was the first time the Tiger Lady had ever asked her about herself or alluded to her former life, except in the most self-involved way. But then Shinsawbu had been in a strange mood for a few days, languorous and gentler than usual, almost absent-minded. 'I miss one man, my queen.'

'And why's that one man so special?' Shinsawbu asked, beckoning the fan lower so that its soft tips brushed her torso with each stroke. She shivered pleasurably under its caress.

'He taught me love.'

'Huh. Love is cheap. You can find that anywhere, Mouse.'

'And fear,' she added softly. It was true; she hadn't known what it was to fear until the first time she'd lost Veraine.

Shinsawbu chuckled, eyes closed. 'He must be an extraordinary man to have that effect on you, little Mouse.'

'Yes,' she admitted.

'A tiger of a man.'

'That wouldn't be my choice of words.'

Shinsawbu giggled again, deep in her throat. 'And where is he now, your hero?'

'He's dead.' She had no intention of warning the Harimau.

After a moment Shinsawbu opened her eyes and rolled to look Myrna in the face. Her eyes were golden in the bright light. She snorted. 'You're lying, Mouse. I would be able to smell your grief. You'd taste of burnt limes like Harzu. I think you're waiting for him. You hope he's going to come and find you.'

Myrna, shocked, said nothing.

'What's he going to do, your hero?' the golden woman wondered, mockingly. 'What's he going to do when he finds you like this?' Her question encompassed the palace, the guards in their lacquered armour, the strings of emeralds that were the only covering for Myrna's breasts and the slave-collar about her throat. Myrna made no reply but her gaze, meeting Shinsawbu's, spoke eloquently. After another silence the Tiger Lady threw back her head and laughed out loud. 'Really?' she cried. 'Oh Mouse, you are so funny, you've no idea!'

'No, my queen,' she agreed.

As they descended from the roof an hour later Sao Mor came to greet his mistress and receive her instructions. Shinsawbu had wrapped a red silk orhni several times about her body as her concession to modesty. 'Have me a bath drawn,' she ordered, trailing steward and slaves and tiger kittens in a straggling procession.

'Of course, my queen. And what would you like prepared for your supper tonight?'

'Nothing. I'm not hungry. All the food tastes like mud at the moment anyway; we need a new cook.'

Sao Mor looked distressed. 'My queen? Perhaps some steamed fish with ginger would tempt your palate?'

She turned on him and Sao Mor flinched. But Shinsawbu's shoulders drooped and she only let out a long sigh. They were passing through one of the innumerable inner courtyards at this moment and she paused at the top of the veranda steps, her attention caught by the sight of two workmen up some bamboo scaffolding in one corner. 'Fish, yes,' she muttered over her shoulder, then sauntered down towards the scaffolding. Myrna hesitated by the stairs. The two workmen, both bare-chested, were intent on hammering a wooden pin into a socket overhead and didn't notice the woman approaching.

'What are you doing?' she asked.

They looked down at her open, inquiring face and smiled. Myrna knew with cold certainty at that moment that these men didn't come from Siya Ran Thu and that they wouldn't be returning to wherever they called home.

'We're replacing the beam ... my lady,' said one, giving the head of the peg a last hard smack. 'Hold on.'

He really didn't have a clue who he was talking to, thought Myrna, bracing herself for his death.

'What for?' asked Shinsawbu with wide-eyed innocence.

The man slid down the scaffolding to land in front of her and grinned, a little cheekily, a little deferentially. 'Take a look at the old one, my lady,' he said, pointing at a carved beam that lay on a sheet under the framework. 'It's made of some second-rate local wood and the white ants have got to it. It's like sugar candy now.'

Shinsawbu smiled and bent to look obediently at the old beam, hands on her knees, rear stuck out. The carpenter made a visible but vain effort not to look, and wiped his hands hard on his hips. He was middle-aged and sported a round gut that sagged over his fouta. His younger companion, still on the scaffolding but looking down at the Tiger Lady with keen interest, had a broad face that looked like it had been in a fight more than once. They were coarse and rough, the antithesis of the handsome slaves of the palace, but both men had thick muscles in their arms and shoulders that made up for their lack of beauty.

'I see,' said Shinsawbu: 'All those little holes.'

Myrna let her pent breath out, confused. She'd never seen her mistress behave like this.

'No strength left in the wood. What we're doing, my lady, is replacing it with teak.'

'That's better, is it? It's a good, hard, wood?' Her emphasis on the last few words was just ambiguous enough to make the carpenter blink.

'It's ... hard enough. We had to bring it down the river from the deep forest, but it'll be worth it.' He put his hands on his hips. 'Bit of a bugger to carve, mind you.'

'It's not carved at all,' Shinsawbu said, looking up and clasping her hands behind her, and in the process pushing her breasts out.

'Ah well, we'll do that now that it's up and we can see what pattern we have to match.'

'It's a nice one,' said his companion from on high, waving at the woodwork close at hand. 'Nymphs.'

'Yes, they're always a pleasure to carve.'

Shinsawbu smiled kittenishly. 'Are they difficult to do?'

'Not so long as you've got the right inspiration,' the first one said, grinning back and taking an undisguised look at her figure.

'My queen!' said Sao Mor sharply. Myrna could see the concern etched on his face.

She swivelled on her hip and pouted at him with a flash of her old fire. 'I said I'd have fish!' she snapped. 'Go and get it sorted, old man!'

The carpenters looked momentarily nonplussed. The steward bowed, his stiff posture proclaiming his alarm and disapproval. 'My queen,' he muttered to the flag-stones. As he backed out of her presence Myrna saw him whisper to one of the guards that stood by the far doorway, and both men disappeared from the courtyard.

Shinsawbu turned her attention back to the artisans.

'Do you think I'd make a good model for a nymph?' she asked, raising her arms over her head and striking a coquettish pose. Her scarlet wrap covered her only from breast to mid-thigh, and it left no doubt as to the shape beneath.

'Oh, I should think so.' The carpenter clearly couldn't believe his luck. The second man slid down to ground level to join him, grinning. Myrna looked around the courtyard, but the two guards visible were steadfastly not watching.

'Do you think I have the figure for it?' She stretched languorously against a column.

'Well, nymphs tend to be . . . How would you put it?'

'Heavily built,' said his friend. 'In certain dimensions.'

'Heavily built?' Shinsawbu pouted and traced a finger across her breasts. 'You mean here?'

'Yes.' His voice was getting husky. 'Big, you know.' He reached over her shoulder to lay a hand upon the carved wooden breast of the tree-spirit draped about the pillar. He cupped the pouting orb with practised appreciation and thumbed the nipple.

'You think I'm not big enough?' she asked, looking wounded.

Myrna's skin was jumping. She had no idea what, if anything, she should do.

'Not at all. I think yours are . . . just right.'

'Very nice,' added the other.

'You sure? You're not just being polite?'

This elicited a chuckle. 'No need for politeness here, my lady.' His wrist was almost in contact with the bare skin of her shoulder. All he had to do was drop his arm to grasp her.

'It's not just the size anyway,' said the younger one. 'The nipples have got to be right, for a nymph.'

'Nipples?'

'Big, bold nips, that's what you need. Like roasted nuts. Stiff enough to put your eyes out.'

She obligingly traced the outline of both areolae, circling her fingertips until the red silk jutted out. Both men nodded

'Yes. That's the sort of thing.'

'Something special, that.'

Shinsawbu turned over, leaning against the pillar and thrusting out her rear. Tightly wreathed in translucent silk, it looked as round and red as an apple. 'What about my behind?' she asked anxiously.

'Now that is just perfect,' said the first carpenter sincerely. 'Just perfect. For a nymph.'

She wriggled it. 'Not too soft?'

He cleared his throat. 'Looks firm to me.'

'Can you tell by looking though?' wondered his companion, a little bolder.

'Well, that is a good point.'

Myrna jumped as a young guard appeared at her shoulder. 'Narathu Min needs to see you,' he said in a low voice.

'Me?'

'Urgently.' He stole a quick glance at the trio on the veranda. 'Regarding ... her requirements for this afternoon.'

Myrna followed his gaze just in time to see a carpenter's hand pass reverently over the proffered cheek. 'My queen?' she whispered. Shinsawbu giggled breathily.

'Come on.' The guard motioned her away. There seemed to be little danger of Shinsawbu noticing and Myrna let herself be led. She felt light-headed, as if what she'd seen could not possibly be real. They didn't go far. Standing just within the shadow of the corridor were Narathu Min and Sao Mor, heads bent together in earnest, whispered discussion. They looked up as she came towards them.

'We're in serious trouble,' said the Captain of the Guard bluntly. His eyes locked on hers. 'All of us. You have to go and fetch Rao Dhammazhedi.'

'What?' That was about the worst thing she could think of to do in the circumstances.

'If they fuck her, he'll go mad,' said Sao Mor quickly. 'He'll kill us, Myrna. All of us. Guards, slaves: everyone.'

'Then stop her!' She looked to the soldier. 'You've got armed men out there. Send them in!'

'Send them – against her? You think she'll let a few guards get in the way of what she's after?'

'You've seen the state she's in. It's her season, Myrna.' Sao Mor's teeth were bared. 'Only the Rao will be able to handle her.'

Myrna had no idea what he meant.

'You've got to get him here before it's too late.'

'He'll kill them,' she said blankly.

'Yes – good gods, yes. It's got to be done now.'

Myrna looked wildly behind her. Across the court-yard, Shinsawbu had her back to the pillar. It looked like both men were leaning in over her, and she was giggling like a girl. 'Why me?' asked Myrna.

Neither man replied to that immediately. She searched their faces, reading the depths of fear there. 'He won't hurt you,' Narathu Min said hoarsely. 'You're her special pet. You'll be able to speak to him.'

She knew from that that it would be far from safe, and that there was every chance that he would hurt her. 'He's in his chambers?' she said bleakly.

The captain nodded. 'It's his meditation time.'

They were begging her help, just as her worshippers had prayed for succour in her temple. But in those days the prayers had never disturbed her equanimity. She'd

147

never before felt their dread so acutely. She nodded. 'All right.'

Leaving Narathu Min on watch, Sao Mor hurried her through the corridors to an area of the palace she'd never entered before. They arrived before a magnificent set of ebony-faced doors inlaid with ivory trees. The two guards stationed outside sprang to attention. 'She brings a message for the Rao from my queen,' Sao Mor said, thrusting her forwards. 'It mustn't be delayed.'

The guards weren't keen to receive such intelligence, but something in Sao Mor's expression must have got through to them and the door was opened just wide enough for Myrna to squeeze through, before being shut again at her back. She stopped there, poised on the balls of her feet, as she took in her surroundings. The rooms of Rao Dhammazhedi were kept dim by drapes hung over the windows. Animal skins were strewn in overlapping heaps over the floor and the furnishings, deadening the sound of her feet and making the air thick with the smells of leather and fur. Sandalwood and spices burned in a brazier nearby. But there was a sourer reek beneath that incense, and as she moved forwards across the soft pile that smell made her throat tighten. It was the smell of old blood, spilt in this place and left to soak into the furs and the floorboards. A gnawed bone turned under her foot. Myrna's spine prickled: it was a long leg-bone and she was unable to tell what animal it might have come from.

It was easy to find Dhammazhedi. She could feel his presence like the heat of an open fire on her skin, and she took the turns through the complex of rooms without error. He was sitting cross-legged in the centre of a large chamber, hands resting on his knees, spine straight and eyes closed, in profile to her. A stray sunbeam lit the thick bicep of his near arm. She hesitated in the doorway.

'My king,' she said softly. Apprehension was making her skin feel hypersensitive to the slightest touch; the brush of silk, the whisper of her own breath. He didn't stir.

She took a moment to study him, feeling the pulse beating hard in her breast and groin. Above the satin waistband of his trousers his heavily muscled arms and chest were naked, his skin golden. Like most of the people of the Twenty Kingdoms he had little body-hair, and there was a sheen to his oiled skin. His pectorals were pronounced. His feet were likewise bare. Each hand loosely grasped a cuff from which curved steel claws protruded. She thought she'd never seen a living man sit so still, so perfectly poised. The curls that rested on the nape of his neck looked like they'd been carved from polished jet. The hairs of his lashes had clustered to points, a jagged black diamond line upon his cheek.

She stepped forwards into the room, feet silent on the carpet of slaughtered gaur buffalo and blue-bull and blackbuck. 'My king,' she repeated; 'your sister needs you.'

He moved without warning, twisting sideways and flinging one arm out in a raking blow. Ferocious amber eyes opened and burned themselves onto Myrna's mind, the teeth below bared in a silent snarl. But he had misjudged; she was slightly out of reach, and the steel claws connected with nothing but empty air. Myrna staggered backwards, pulse crashing. He was on his feet between two of her heartbeats and powering towards her, fist raised anew. She ducked, flinging herself to one side, and the second death-blow missed. He paused long enough to register surprise through his anger, then launched himself at her again.

Fighting Dhammazhedi was the last thing Myrna was prepared for: she knew nothing of fighting. What she did know was the Drought Ceremony dance, performed every year in front of hundreds of her devotees, danced in ritual armour with twin swords in emulation of a battle between the goddess Malia and the demon Sorol Sek fought at the beginning of time. She knew how to feint one way and duck the other, how to slide beneath the natural arc of a blow and roll across the floor and still land on her feet. So she retreated before him, keeping by the utmost effort just beyond the reach of his claws, taking cover behind the heavy furniture where it offered a moment's shelter. Her heart was in her throat and it took all she had to force a few broken words past it, gasping as razored steel carved the air next to her cheek. 'My king! Shinsawbu –'

Steel blades nicked the back of her thigh but the brunt of the blow ploughed into a low table. It cracked beneath the weight and he laughed savagely.

'There are two men ... she can't defend herself!'

With a grunt he scooped up the chest of many drawers that she had ducked behind and threw it sideways against the wall. The cords were standing out in his neck.

'She's lost her mind!' Myrna threw herself backwards, but caught her heel on a thick pelt and tripped to the floor. He stooped over her. 'Her season!' she cried, though she hardly knew what she meant. She scrabbled sideways, tearing handfuls of hair from the furs as she clawed for purchase. Dhammazhedi's fist hit the floor just behind her ear, his blades biting through fur and skin into the boards below, and Myrna's head was wrenched back on her neck. She was pinned by her thick hair beneath his fist.

'Shinsawbu?'

Tears swam in Myrna's eyes from the sudden pain to her scalp. 'Her season,' she repeated as he bent low over her, because it was the only thing that had seemed to get through to him. She could smell the hot cloves of his breath, the masculine scent of his skin. Her heels could find no purchase on the surface beneath her and she couldn't move, could not so much as roll over. 'She needs you.'

Slipping his hand from the steel cuff, he placed it on her throat, cutting off the last possibility of escape. His fingertips seemed to burn her. Even without the weapon he would be perfectly capable of ripping her neck open. She could feel his bulk poised like a rock-face ready to fall.

'Where?' His voice was a growl.

'The courtyard . . .' She didn't know its name.

'Show me.'

With a slight effort he pulled the claws free from the wood, then he grasped her by the hair and lifted her to her feet. He bent to level his face with hers, his lips and teeth almost brushing her skin. 'Run,' he suggested.

She turned and fled. She had no choice. He lengthened his stride, easily keeping pace with her. They came out of the Rao's private chambers and she saw that the guards had gone. For a moment she thought that Sao Mor had abandoned her too, but as she rounded a corner there he was, wringing his hands, and she nearly ran into him.

'My king,' he said, eyes wide. Then his luck gave out: Dhammazhedi, not even slowing, swiped him sideways with the back of his hand, smashing the smaller man into the wall. Myrna stumbled, shocked despite herself. She gaped as the Rao, suddenly thinking better of it, turned back to the steward.

"Where's Anawrahta?' he shouted. 'He was told to attend her!' Anawrahta, Myrna knew, was one of the Rao's cousins.

Sao Mor was struggling to sit up. It was obvious from the angle at which his left arm hung that it was badly broken, but he still managed to bow his head to the boards and gasp, 'I don't know, my king.'

'Find him! Tell him to come now!'

'My king,' said Sao Mor faintly.

Dhammazhedi rounded on Myrna again. 'Hurry!' The chase resumed. They passed not a single guard or servant; the corridors had been miraculously cleared of all human presence. Even when they broke through into the courtyard the only people visible were Shinsawbu and the two artisans. The older one had her pressed up against the wall, her legs around his hips, the red silk sheath pushed right up her thighs. He was thrusting into her with strong, steady strokes. Her head was thrown back to expose her throat and the back of her skull was thumping off the wall rhythmically, but it didn't look as if she felt any pain. Her eyes were half-closed. The other carpenter was at her side, getting a good close-up look, one hand kneading her bare left breast. Shinsawbu had that carpenter's tool tight in her fist, keeping him warm while his companion worked. The head of his prick jutted out from her enfolding fingers and thumb, as dark and engorged and juicy as a plum.

Myrna fell to the floor in an effort to get out of Dhammazhedi's way.

The Rao hit the small group roaring. Both carpenters died within seconds; a mercy in the circumstances that was most certainly not intentional. Hot blood slopped on the boards and one severed head bounced from the veranda and hit the flagstones below with a crack. Shinsawbu screamed with rage and flung herself at her brother, raking at his face and chest, drawing more blood to run out and mix with that already splattered over him. He grabbed at her wrists and they collided, both snarling and snapping. He slammed her against a pillar hard enough to knock any other woman cold; she spat and screamed and cursed him.

'Where's Anawrahta?' he roared. 'He should have been with you!'

'Anawrahta?' With that word she suddenly collapsed forwards against him, panting. 'Oh Dhammaz, please!' she moaned, writhing in his grip. 'Let me go!'

'You shouldn't be out!' he cried: 'Not on your own! I told you!' But his real rage was spent and his grasp though still obdurate was less cruel.

'I need it,' she gasped.

'Shush. Cover yourself up.' Since he had both her arms pinned behind her this was an impossible demand, and he followed it by calling over his shoulder; 'Slave!' Myrna stepped forwards uncertainly. 'Make her decent.'

That was, she thought, just as impossible. The term 'decent' could not be applicable to a blood-flecked Shinsawbu, seemingly drunk and now weeping bitterly. Nevertheless Myrna reached in between them to tug the silk back down over Shinsawbu's hips and pubic delta. She tried to readjust the wrap over her breasts too, but the cloth was in too much disarray and Myrna's hands were shaking. The proximity of the two Tiger Lords, the smell and the horror and the glory of them, was almost beyond endurance.

'Enough,' snapped Dhammazhedi. 'I'm going to take you back to your room,' he told his sister. His voice had dropped to become low and commanding. 'You must calm down.'

'My room?' Shinsawbu's tears stopped as swiftly as

they'd started. When he released her arms in order to pick her up she furled them about his neck.

'Yours,' he said, gently but with emphasis. 'Anawrahta will be here soon.' He scooped her up in both arms and she laid her head upon his shoulder. It was as if she were in a fever of some sort, thought Myrna: as if she were drugged, or acting in a dream.

'Clear the way for us, slave,' he ordered Myrna, indicating the corridor with a jerk of his chin. 'This is a family matter.' She obeyed, running ahead, but it was almost unnecessary. Word had somehow spread and no one was rash enough to linger in Dhammazhedi's path. From side corridors and rooms she heard scurrying feet and closing doors. Only the two guards outside Shinsawbu's room were still in place, the whites of their eyes glinting in the gloom, and she shooed them away as quickly as they could go before opening the doors for the Rao and his burden.

'Attend us,' he ordered. Myrna followed them inside, closing the doors behind her.

Taking his sister through to the sleeping chamber he set her upon the bed, sitting beside her. She clung to his neck. 'My brother ... You always look after me.'

'Get her some wine,' he commanded, but when Myrna fetched a cup from the earthenware cooler Shinsawbu struck it from her hand, sending the liquid across floor and coverlet. Myrna backed off.

'Not thirsty,' said Shinsawbu sullenly as she lay back on the bed, staring up at her brother. Her eyes were huge, her expression smouldering. She tugged at the loose edges of the silk, trying to pull it free, but the wrap was so tangled about her body that the bindings only tightened. She yanked plaintively at the trailing end clutched in her fist, like a trapped kitten.

'He won't be long,' the Rao promised, pulling a fold

up to cover her breasts. He'd never sounded so gentle. Shinsawbu reached out for his hand, which he let her hold.

'I don't want Anawrahta,' she complained.

'You do. He'll give you strong children.'

Her full lips curved teasingly. 'Yours would be stronger.'

Dhammazhedi's shoulders stiffened. 'I'm your brother,' he reminded her. 'Are we animals?'

That made Shinsawbu laugh a deep dirty laugh in her throat. Pulling his hand to her lips she licked blood off it, then sat up and tried to lick his face. He caught her wrists and held her away from him. Then he looked round at Myrna with an expression that was both fury and, she was shocked to realise, naked entreaty.

He hates this, she thought. And he will not forgive me for seeing it.

'Go find Anawrahta!' he rasped.

Myrna backed out, her heart turning over inside her. Outside, the corridors were still deserted, but she headed towards the main palace gates: there were always guards at the main gates. She hadn't miscalculated. Narathu Min was there with his men, and Sao Mor too. The steward was sat upon the steps retching, while a palace physician tried to tend to his arm.

'Where's Anawrahta?' she demanded. The soldiers stared at her. 'The Rao's asking for him!'

'I sent messengers,' replied the captain.

'They won't find him in time,' grunted Sao Mor, head down and shuddering. 'I saw him leave this morning saying he was going to hunt crocodiles up-river.'

'What about the Rao's orders?'

'The Harimau are never very good at following orders. Even from someone like Dhammazhedi.'

So what am I supposed to do? Myrna wanted to ask,

but she didn't speak the words out loud. She looked at the stricken faces of the men and knew they had no more idea than she. They can't help me, she realised. I have to go back.

Every step dragged. Her heart was pounding like a temple drum and making her head swim. They have this effect on me, she told herself: Both of them together, it's too much.

When she re-entered the bedchamber the two Tiger Lords had changed position somewhat. Neither was directly facing the door and they didn't hear her, so locked were they in their mutual torment. Myrna slipped into the shadow by a carved screen. Shinsawbu was kneeling on the bed, facing away from her brother and resting back against him. Her face was a battle-ground of frustration and pleasure. He still had one foot on the floor and was holding her wrists at her sides so that she couldn't turn, but his head was bent over hers so that her short hair brushed his lips.

'Dhammaz,' she moaned, wriggling her behind. The smell of her, of sex and spice and perfume, was potent even where Myrna stood. 'Please,' she begged.

'No,' he growled low in his throat. 'Don't make me hurt you, sister. This is not the way of a great people.'

'But you don't know what it's like! You don't know how I feel. I need it, Dhammaz. I have to have it.'

'You need a proper mate. Not me. Just be patient.'

'Patient? I'll die if you don't touch me! It's agony! I need you, I need your . . .'

'Shush,' he groaned.

'You're so strong. You're so big. You'd fit in me like a hand in a glove, Dhammaz. You'd stretch me wide and fill me up.' Her lips were swollen, her eyes unfocused. She spoke as if her words were sacred liturgy, forming each syllable with reverence. 'I've seen the way you ride your slaves. I need your prick, brother,' she breathed. 'I need your balls, and your hot seed. Don't you need me?'

The silk wrap had all but fallen off and her breasts shimmered as she wriggled, testing his strength. Her nipples stood out like the mahogany studs of a pillar nymph. He ground his teeth and shut his eyes. 'This isn't the way it should be.'

'Am I not beautiful? Don't I excite you?'

'Of course you're beautiful. You're more beautiful than any woman in the world.' The pain in his voice left no doubt as to his sincerity.

'Don't you want me? Don't you want to press me down and mount me and give me everything I crave?'

'There's no man who wouldn't want you,' he whispered, and bit her shoulder. She gasped.

'Oh Dhammaz,' she said in a low voice; 'I'm so wet: feel how wet I am for you, my Rao.' She wriggled against his thighs until she was almost sitting in his lap.

'Shinsawbu. Stop this.' He made no attempt to push her away.

'Are you hard for me? Let me see ... please?' She reached behind her, groping for his crotch. He still had hold of her wrist and should have been able to defend himself, but her fingers crept up the yellow satin trousers and found, under the tightly stretched material, not simply the hard slab of his thigh but the thick cylinder of his erection trapped between cloth and flesh.

'Oh,' she said in a breathless voice, 'it is big.'

'Very,' he admitted.

'And hard.'

'Yes. Hard.'

'And is it hot?'

'Burning.'

'I could quench it.' She twisted her other hand free

from his numb grasp, caught his palm and thrust it between her thighs. 'See?' Then she quivered and whimpered, her eyes flashing as he stroked her.

'Yes.' He pulled his fingers out again, shiny with moisture. 'You are wet. Like you said.'

'Oh ... my beloved.'

'You are ready, aren't you?' He brushed his musk-laden fingers across the line of her lip, letting her smell herself. Then he licked them, one by one, savouring the taste of her sex. It made him growl. She pushed up against him, letting him feel the whole length of her body from arse to neck. He spread his thighs to let her nestle into his crotch.

'This is the way it should be,' she purred, reaching back to touch his face and catch at his hair. 'Can't you feel it in your blood?'

He caught and cupped her uplifted breasts. There were no steel claws on his hands now, just strong fingers to knead her softness. But when he ran his fingertips down her breastbone and belly they left a white line that filled up with little scarlet beads. She groaned and surged against him. 'I feel it,' he replied, his voice thick with desire.

'You are the strength of our people. Fill me.'

'You are my beloved, Shinsawbu.' He bit at her throat and the nape of her neck, his mouth wet, his tongue rasping. 'My queen and my sister.'

She bared her teeth, feral. He put his hand on her neck and pushed her forwards so that he could run his nails down her spine too. She arched her back and opened to him, balanced on her fingertips, cheeks spread wide. He touched her between her legs and she cried out as if he'd burned her. The gap between them gave him space enough to unclasp his belt and open his clothes, releasing the erection pent up so cruelly within.

In the shadows, hidden beneath her skirts, moisture escaped from the full purse of Myrna's sex, down the soft skin of her thigh. That cock of Dhammazedhi's was precisely as promised. He was a big, broad man and his member was perfectly in proportion; thick and dark and curved like a teak beam. Myrna wanted to feel that heavy hotness against her hand. She could imagine the strength in its neck and the way it would kick against her. She wanted to feel the weight of the scrotum that looked bigger than her clenched fist, to find out if it was soft or taut and wrinkled, coarse with hair or smooth. She touched herself through her skirt. Her nipples were aching.

'Sister,' said the Tiger Lord, his voice a rumble, rising behind and above Shinsawbu. His broad hands on her hips made her look small. His phallus, swaying under its own massive weight, thrust forwards blindly to find its target. He nudged into her and she fell forwards onto her elbows. Shinsawbu's eyes were wide, her lips set in an 'o' that echoed the circle of her yoni. She didn't take him easily: he was too thick and she too unused to masculine lovers. He had to feed it into her inch by inch, churning his hips to loosen the clench of her muscles, thrusting up then pulling out. The slickness of her sex lacquered his shaft. He reached forwards to fondle her dangling breasts; his weight at that moment, bearing down through his thick stake, was almost more than she could support. Then he drew upright again and felt round for the front of her pubic mound, stirring her bud. She keened with pleasure and pushed back on him even further, impaling herself.

'Beloved,' he whispered.

They were magnificent, thought Myrna with awe. She had to lean back against the wall to keep her balance, the pulse at her groin thumping against her fingers like the heartbeat of a trapped bird. In their muscular bodies beauty and a terrible strength met as one, lust and power intertwined and fused. It was like witnessing the collision of two towering thunderclouds. Lightning strokes of unbearable arousal crackled between them as he ran his fingers down her back and clawed at her breasts. He bit her shoulders and licked at her spine and raked at her thighs, but despite their mutual fervour he moved slowly, with massive purpose, as if their movements were somehow more than human in significance. It was as if Myrna were watching a god and goddess in divine intercourse, their momentous lovemaking turning the wheel of creation.

Dhammazhedi found his rhythm. Each thrust was aimed with deadly intent. Shinsawbu keened and bared her teeth, her eyes glazing. His hair flapped about his face as he stooped for a moment, and then he straightened, arching his back so that his arse clenched into a hammering fist. His thighs were like slabs of stone, the muscles grinding under the skin. He moved upon her like the ocean battering the shore, like a mountain rising and falling through geological ages. A pulse pounded in Myrna's head; the thunderous dance-beat of the universe. Faster and faster the two Tiger Lords surged together. Shinsawbu met her orgasm pushing and flailing and crying out. He groaned and spasmed, holding himself motionless before collapsing upon her, limbs crashing and sliding, a mountainside plummeting upon the plain. They tumbled into stillness together, intertwined and fused by sweat and sex-juices and blood.

Myrna slid to her knees, her muscles shaking, her joints molten. The hot wetness of her own sex filled her palm. The sandalwood screen made a little scraping noise upon the floorboards as she nudged it with her knee. Above her, Dhammazhedi raised his head from the sheets. His face was flushed and a dark fire burned in those yellow eyes. His gaze fixed upon her. She saw the curl of his lip and gleam of his teeth and she knew her life was balanced on a knife-edge.

'The great lord Anawrahta is out hunting and can't be found, my king.' Her voice shook with desire.

Dhammazhedi pushed himself up from the bed and from his sister's naked body. Myrna saw his cock, still proud, withdrawn from its sheath like a swordblade from a scabbard, flushed dark and gleaming with juices. His scrotum swung heavily beneath him. He said not a word: there was no need to speak to her, because in a moment she was going to be dead. She knew that. He was not going to forgive her for her failure, or for witnessing his.

She was astonished that he should be capable of shame.

Shinsawbu rolled over, reached out a hand and caught at her brother just as he found his feet. 'More,' she said, her voice thick as fur. She raked her fingers through the sweat on his hip and buried them in the dark thatch at his groin. He looked down at her, distracted. She was still intoxicated with that inhuman lust, enslaved to the imperative of her flesh.

Dhammazhedi couldn't help but respond to that. It was etched into the golden metal of his soul as much as it was into hers: an ancient, animal craving. For a moment he hesitated. Then, turning away from a slave-girl who was suddenly no more than an irritant, he sank down upon his sister, belly to belly, his mouth covering and entering hers just as his body did. She writhed beneath him. He growled deep in his chest, a rumble of pleasure and hunger and surrender to an instinct stronger than shame, stronger than wrath, stronger than his own will.

9 Fighting Men

It was late in the afternoon and they were starting to look for a place to camp for the night, when Veraine glanced up and saw a couple standing on the path a little way off, by a shock of bamboo. Their round, nearly identical faces were turned his way. Both were wearing dark clothes, and as he watched they both lifted their arms and made a gesture with crossed hands. Veraine stopped and waved the cart to a halt behind him. 'What does that mean?' he asked sharply.

'What?' asked Rahul from his seat behind the oxen.

He glanced back at his companions and repeated the gesture as best he could. 'They did it.' He jerked his head to indicate the strangers.

Rahul frowned at the road ahead. 'Who?'

'Those two.' Veraine turned back, but they were no longer on the path. The bamboo dipped and shivered in the breeze, sending the shadows dancing. 'They were there, just a moment ago. A man and a woman. They signalled to us.'

'There wasn't anyone there,' said Rahul. 'It's a straight road; you can see a long way.'

'They must have gone off the side then.'

Rahul looked troubled. 'There was no one there,' he said. 'I was looking. There was no one on the road.'

Veraine didn't know how to respond.

'It's a dance gesture.' Teihli was looking as perplexed as her husband, but she repeated the fluid twist of both hands accurately. 'It signifies a threat, or a dangerous character.'

Veraine felt chilly despite the afternoon heat. The two strangers might well have been dressed in indigo-blue. 'A threat?'

'Yes. Are you sure that was it?' She gestured again.

'Maybe I was mistaken.'

'No,' said Rahul. 'You might have seen something.'

'There was no one on the road,' Veraine reminded him.

'But ... perhaps ... it might have been a sign. From someone.'

He didn't like that at all. He'd told neither of them about his hallucinations and the thought that they would take such visions at face-value disturbed him.

Teihli bit her lip. 'Maybe we should –'

'I'm not sure I saw anyone. It was just the shadows moving on the track.'

They both looked at him doubtfully. Those two lived so deeply immersed in their stories, he thought, that they expected miracles and magic in their real lives. 'You said –'

'I was mistaken.' His voice was harsh. 'It was a trick of the light. Forget it.'

'Fine,' said Rahul gently. 'If you wish.' That made him feel worse. He didn't want them watching him with such concern, so he fell back behind the cart as they set off again and walked at the tailgate. He tried again to picture the couple standing on the track. They'd seemed absolutely solid for that short moment that he'd been looking at them. But he knew he couldn't trust his own eyes. Rahul had certainly been right: there was no one there.

Nevertheless, after a few minutes Veraine reached into the back of the cart. He had made a scabbard of split bamboo for his blade and now he took the inno-cent-looking length of wood and wedged it in among the struts of the stage so that it was easily to hand.

Soon after this they turned off the main track and through a field that now carried only a crop of stubble. 'We'll stop at this next village for the night,' Rahul called back. 'We've been here before; they're always pleased to see us.' But his confidence had waned by the time they crossed a streambed over a wooden bridge and drew up in front of the village fence. 'It's very quiet,' he muttered, easing the two oxen to a halt.

'Where is everyone?' asked Teihli. They'd passed no one in the fields. There was a thin haze of smoke over the village as there should be, but no one had come out to challenge them. 'Maybe we should try somewhere further on.'

Veraine had just turned to go round the back of the cart for his weapon when a figure emerged from the village and hailed them. 'Welcome! Welcome!' Even from a distance his saffron scarf marked him out as the village headman. He trotted out to meet them and reached up to clasp Rahul's hand. 'Welcome!' he enthused. 'Come in to the village.'

'We'll pitch our tent here,' Teihli offered.

'No no, you must come inside, all of you. It is not safe for you or the animals outside the fence.' He grimaced. 'There's a leopard in the forest nearby. You're much better inside the village.'

This was unusual but not completely unprecedented. Rahul thanked him. 'Where is everyone?' he asked as they led the oxen through the barrier.

'There's a village meeting. The tax is being collected today, so everyone must attend.'

Veraine wondered why it was the sardar that had come out on his own to greet them.

'Is there a king in Lhanghar City then?' Teihli asked.

Their host shook his head. 'We don't pay to Lhanghar City these days. But there's always a lord wanting his taxes.' They came out into the village square, and there as promised were all the villagers, seated on the caked earth floor. Veraine looked about him. He saw all the usual accoutrements of village life: the shrine to the village goddess set among the hanging roots of a fig tree, the pit-oven, the granary, the neat piles of firewood. But no one jumped up or smiled or called to them, and many didn't even look. They were almost silent, though some were huddled in small groups, muttering. His senses prickled with wariness; he'd never known a village so passive at the arrival of strangers. The storytellers felt it too: Teihli shrank closer to Rahul's side.

There was a knot of people stood on the earthen platform before the headman's big house. Veraine was still trying to work out the pattern to all this when the sardar called to the shadows at his own door, 'The bhopa, as I told you, lord.' Then he bowed low to the floor.

There under the porch sat a man with his knees spread apart and a cup in one hand. He rose from his stool at the headman's salutation and stepped forwards without hurry into the sunlight. It was obvious that he was not one of the villagers: they were all wiry, but he carried a smooth padding of fat over his muscles and his skin gleamed with the shine of one who eats plenty of meat and butter. On his head was a square silk cap with orange and black panels, and round his waist was a sash striped in the same colours.

The moment he saw that Veraine realised that it was a uniform. There were others in the crowd wearing the same caps, some standing and some squatting, but he hadn't recognised the pattern for what it was because he hadn't known what to look for. His muscles tightened. Another glance around the gathering told him that there were at least eight of the men bearing those colours. It wasn't looking good.

The man on the porch spread his arms. 'What luck, for you and for us, sardar.'

The headman pressed his forehead to the bare earth and mumbled, 'Great lord.'

Rahul stepped forwards and made a short, uncertain bow. 'We came in the hope of playing for you tonight,' he said, unable to stop himself glancing at the prostrate headman. 'With your permission.'

The great lord smiled, but didn't answer directly. 'The girl looks pretty enough,' he observed, fixing Teihli with his gaze. 'Come here.'

'What?' said Rahul. 'You're mistaken, sir. This is my wife.'

He was ignored. 'You're used to the company of men, aren't you?'

Teihli drew herself up. 'The gift of the gods is only given after the performance.'

'Afterwards?' He sniggered. 'How could I wait that long?'

'And not at any man's command,' Teihli added with more sharpness.

Veraine was still trying to look around without being obvious about it. A good dozen men in those colours, he concluded, and all armed. Most of them had heavy teak clubs, but their spokesman wore a broad-bladed knife as long as his forearm.

'Ah but, bhopi,' said he, 'we don't work for ordinary men. The Tiger Lords demand their tribute. This village must pay its dues.'

'What has that to do with us?'

The men were closing in slowly on the cart. Veraine turned, very casually, and confirmed that there was one behind him, between him and the tailgate where his weapon was. He turned back and leaned on the cart, affecting a puzzled interest in the conversation. Twelve to one was appalling odds should there be a fight.

'Well, it has to be said the tribute rendered so far has been poor.' The reiver leader indicated the huddle of standing figures on the platform before him. 'Very poor. All skin and bones, most of them, and ugly to boot. Teeth missing. Pock-marked. The Tiger Lords won't be happy. And we can't have that.'

At least there were no bows in evidence, Veraine noted. Bows would have changed the odds from appalling to impossible.

'We're storytellers,' said Rahul, putting his hand on Teihli's shoulder. 'We are under the protection of the gods.'

The reiver boss stepped down from the porch. Everyone shuffled away from him. 'Then tell the gods to take it up with my king.'

Rahul pulled Teihli in so that his arm was around her. He shot Veraine an agonised look, but Veraine shrugged helplessly. There were three reivers within a few paces of him. They were grinning, slouching, and just waiting for the tall man to kick up a fuss. All were armed.

'You mustn't do this,' said Teihli through clenched teeth. 'The gods will punish you.'

'She's quite pretty,' observed the reiver, stopping just in front of her and looking her up and down with disparaging lewdness. 'But mouthy. The boy's nearly as pretty. I'm sure one of the ladies will want him.' He smirked. 'Or one of the lords.' His men sniggered obediently. He put his fists on his hips. 'Come on then, girl, let's get a look at you,' he taunted. 'You've got them out for plenty of men before now.'

'Go screw yourself,' she hissed, eyes flashing.

He reached out and hooked one finger in the front of her blouse. Rahul, goaded beyond endurance, tried to pull his wife away and grab him. It was just what the reiver had been expecting: he punched Rahul straight in the face, over Teihli's shoulder, and the young man crashed to the floor.

Veraine winced heavily. The other reivers laughed, enjoying the humiliation of their victims. A sloppy bunch, he thought.

'Now, as I was saying,' said the reiver boss smugly, yanking Teihli within easy reach. He put both hands to the front of her blouse and tore it open, spilling her big breasts out into public view. 'Nice.'

Everyone looked. It was instinctive. His subordinates gawped and jockeyed for a better view. One even edged past Veraine for a better look.

Stupid, he thought, uncoiling into action. He had his right hand on the man's club in a moment, his fist closing over the slaver's. The man's fingers tightened instinctively beneath his but he was prepared for resistance. His other hand, with the whole force of his shoulder behind it, slammed into the back of the reiver's elbow from behind, snapping the fragile joint like a stick. The heavy club came free and Veraine whirled, turning and lashing out in one motion. The wood was dense and weighted to the far end: it broke open the second reiver's skull like it was a water-pot. That man fell back upon his third comrade and as he staggered Veraine was upon him with the club, smashing his collarbone and forcing him to his knees. Veraine side-stepped his toppling body, jumped for the back of the cart, pulled his blade free and whirled again onto a defensive stance, one weapon in each hand, teeth bared. The steel blade glinted.

It was to his great advantage that the reivers were only half-trained. Their fighting skills, he guessed, had been picked up piecemeal on the streets and they were used to bullying terrified farmers rather than tackling real warriors. Faced with armed resistance some hesitated and some were simply too confused to react. They shouted, hooted, and looked to one another. The bravest one ran in and Veraine stepped to meet him, knocking aside the incoming club with his own and running his blade straight through the man's chest beneath the breastbone. He threw the dying man aside and took the throat of the next with a back-handed sweep of the steel.

The village square erupted as the farmers realised what was happening and floundered to their feet. Most were just trying to get out of the way, but as Veraine ran around the cart to face his next opponent he caught sight of a group of them falling on a reiver from behind. He grinned even as he advanced on a man who tried to turn and run, and cleaved into the back of his neck sending both head and silk cap flying.

The next two reivers had the sense to come at him together and he was forced momentarily on the defensive. He parried up and out with both hands, breaking the force of both blows and throwing the man on the right back on his heels, but a reiver's club scraped up the length of his own and whacked the knuckles of his left hand before flying wide. Numbing pain blazed up his arm and Veraine's club fell to the ground. He jumped in before either opponent had gathered for a second strike and grabbed the man on his left in a hug, wrapping his all-but useless left arm about his neck and smashing his forehead down on the shorter man's face.

The collision of bone with bone made lights flash behind his eyes. The reiver spasmed and they staggered together like drunken kissers before Veraine swung his body round like a shield between him and his right-hand foe. A strike meant for him bounced off the stunned man's spine with a crack and the perpetrator of this assault was still staring when Veraine's blade, coming from below, shore up through the underside of his jaw and out the top of his skull.

Both reivers fell. Veraine chopped down once, hard, into the unwounded one's chest, just to make sure.

'Stop!' howled a voice. 'Stop or I kill her!' Veraine looked up and saw that the reiver boss had Teihli at arm's length and was holding his knife to her. 'You hear me?'

He didn't hesitate: hesitation had been drilled out of him long ago. He charged across the square straight at the slaver, barking a laugh. The reiver-boss did hesitate, just for a moment, with a look of outrage stamped on his face. Then he made the error of drawing back his weapon hand for a good blow at his hostage, and as he did so Rahul rose up behind him and grabbed desperately at his head, dragging him backwards with fingers hooked in his eye-sockets. Teihli tore herself free and fell sideways as the blow, aimed wild and blind, came at her barely missing her head. But Veraine's blade sheared through the reiver's ribs almost to his spine; as he writhed upon the floor Veraine had to put a foot on his chest to yank the weapon free.

Eight down, maybe nine, thought Veraine, spinning on his heel and shaking the hair out of his eyes, ready for the next attack. The square was in uproar, with people everywhere shouting and shrieking. But when he looked for the slavers he saw only fallen men, some lying dead and some wounded, one being battered by a group of peasants, while others crouched with hands over their heads, begging for mercy. He paced a tight circle, adjusting his grip on the slippery shaft of his weapon, fighting to calm his breath. People scattered before him.

It's done, he realised, incredulous. He found himself face to face with the headman, who tripped over his feet and fell backwards trying to retreat. Veraine laughed and turned away, then forced his teeth to unclench, feeling the rictus mask of battle relax only slowly. He drew himself upright, taking deeper breaths. The villagers shrank away from him like dried grass withering before a fire. He tried to lick his lips but his tongue was dry and there was a terrible coppery taste in his mouth. He looked for relief and gratitude in the faces around him but saw only fear. At last he turned back to Teihli. She was standing in Rahul's arms but staring at him, holding her torn blouse closed. There was no smile on her face either. Her expression was one of naked horror.

Reflected in their eyes he saw a monster.

Slowly, Veraine laid his falchion on the ground and then he sank into a squat. The handle of the weapon was as red as the blade. He ran his hand through his hair but when he tried to wipe his face with his forearm he just made matters worse. His left hand felt like it was on fire. The skin was split all across the knuckles and his blood dripped onto the hard earth to make dark puddles.

The headman, on his feet again, passed into his field of view. He watched as the sardar crossed to the fallen reiver lord and knelt. To Veraine's disbelief, the old man was almost weeping as he pawed at the bandit.

'Forgive us, great lord! We didn't mean to do this! We'll take you back to your city, my own wife will tend you, we'll give the gods a bull sacrifice so you will be healed. Three bulls. Only, please have mercy!'

The blood pumping hard and hot through Veraine's veins seemed to turn to bile. He could see that the reiver chief, though still twitching, would be dead within moments but the old man didn't seem to realise that. It was as if he didn't know who'd won, or what that meant. Veraine rose to his feet, strode over and lifted the sardar by the scarf about his throat. The old man squealed with fear.

'What are you doing?' he asked in a terrible voice. 'That man was a slaver. Your people are free now. Why are you asking his forgiveness?' The headman hung in Veraine's grip, his toes barely holding the floor, and gaped. Veraine shook him. 'You're the sardar – isn't it your job to protect your people?'

'They're the Tiger Lords!' he gasped.

'They were only men,' Veraine said and dropped him. 'You,' he spat, 'are not even that.'

There was silence except for the moans of the injured and the wails of a baby. The villagers stared. Even Teihli and Rahul only watched, blank-faced. He retrieved his weapon, shook his head and walked away out of the village, not looking back.

He walked back to the little wooden bridge and then climbed down into the streambed to drink and to rinse his mouth out, grateful for the coolness of the water. The aftermath of the fighting rage was making his arms shake and the muscles of his thighs quiver. The defile fell away rapidly downhill into a steep ravine choked with boulders and trees, and he eyed the shade yearningly before deciding to descend with the stream. He passed under tree-ferns and flowering creepers, stepping from rock to rock until they became too slippery with moss. After that he walked in the streambed on the little pebbles, letting the water surge around his ankles. Eventually he found a pool deep enough to wade into up to his thighs, and he stopped there to wash. He was filthy beyond description and the reflection he saw as he bent was nightmarish.

He didn't remove all his clothes because it wasn't the custom of people in that country to bathe naked, but he pulled off his shirt and sluiced it clean before using it to scrub himself. The touch of the water was sweet and forgiving. He knelt down in the pool to pour water through his hair and down his back, letting the blood and the sweat and the rage loosen and drift away. His forehead felt bruised and tender. He examined his left hand, which was swelling now and hurt too much to clench. He thought it likely that he'd broken at least one of the little bones, but there wasn't much he could do about it other than wrap the whole hand in his wet shirt.

When he'd finished he sat upon a boulder with his face in his good hand, waiting for his skin to dry and his bitterness to evaporate. He had no desire to return to the sunlight and the noise above. When he heard a small noise he looked up sharply, ready to be angry at any intruder.

There was a woman standing among the rocks downstream of him, cloaked in the shadow of the ferns. Veraine's irritation shifted into something else. For the briefest moment he hoped it was Teihli because he was itching for some relief from his tension, but then he realised this was a stranger. She didn't look startled by his presence; she looked as if she meant to be there. But she was naked from the hips up, clad only in a tight skirt of dull and mottled cloth. Her breasts were small and high and dark as if never hidden from the sun, providing a distracting backdrop to an elaborate gold collar that spread below her throat from shoulder to shoulder. She looked at him without a word, then raised one hand and beckoned.

Veraine stood, rather conscious of his wet clothes and wondering who she was. She didn't look like one of the village women, who were inevitably modest in their dress and never wore jewellery so magnificent. He strode towards her slowly across the rocks, but when he'd closed half the distance he halted. Something within him was growing wary of her stillness and strangeness, and the knowledge that he'd left his falchion behind on a rock was preying on his mind for no reason that he could put his finger on. He sized her up. She was just a young woman, unarmed and very slight; she couldn't possibly represent a threat – not in herself. Her skin had a glisten as if freshly oiled. Her hair was so short that on any other woman he'd have thought it ugly, but her bones were so fine and graceful that it seemed to suit her. He looked beyond her, checking for signs of an ambush. 'What?' he said softly. 'What do you want?'

I have something to give you, she said. Her lips hadn't moved: the voice was in his head, sibilant and cool. Veraine felt the water droplets on his spine turn icy. He took a step back as she came towards him, but he couldn't retreat on ground this rough without turning and running, so he had to stand and watch her advance. His heart kicked in his chest. She did not walk across the boulders; she glided, her legs never moving though her hips undulated. Behind her something like a dress-train slipped among the rocks.

'You're not real,' he whispered.

She smiled and clasped her hands at the back of her neck, weaving her torso from side to side as she closed on him, displaying her little breasts to their best effect.

It was almost enough to distract him from that which, below her hips, was so terribly wrong. Almost. He finally realised that what he'd thought of as her skirt was not an item of clothing; from the hips down she was encased in mottled scaly skin, and there was no line of a human leg beneath it – neither legs nor feet. Instead she had the tail of a huge snake, as thick through as her torso and many times her body-length, its coils stirring lazily on the moss. The interlocking pattern on that snakeskin was echoed too in the arrangement of the tight, scalp-hugging knots of her short hair, and a fainter patina on her human skin. He thought he could discern a silvery etching like scales.

He grimaced and repeated louder, 'You're not real, are you?'

Not real? That from a man who doesn't even know what he is?

Her words wiped the smile off his face. 'You're a figment from my mind,' he said grimly. 'The fight, the stress of battle, the heat of my blood ... It's gone and knocked something loose in my head again.' His teeth were gritted. 'You're just a vision.'

Then what do you have to fear?

He couldn't answer that. Her eyes were beautiful; huge black pupils surrounded by golden irises; eyes he felt he might fall into. There was something almost hypnotic about them. But she didn't blink. She hadn't blinked since he'd first seen her. 'What do you want?' he asked harshly. His mouth was dry. He wanted to reach out and grasp her, to prove to his hand that she was real enough to touch, but he dreaded the consequences too much.

I wish to make a bargain with you. I offer... She cocked her head. *Understanding.*

That sounded a little too equivocal. 'Of what?'

Of yourself. Of the past you have lost.

His heart skipped a beat. 'You know?'

The serpent of the mind represents wisdom, and I am nothing but a vision in your mind, am I not? What can I offer on my side but insight?

'In exchange for . . .?'

For a little seed. Seed for my hatchlings. She looked pointedly down at the white cotton of his fouta, still wringing wet; despite the folds of the loose cloth it was translucent where it clung to his thighs and crotch.

He balked. 'Ah.' If not truly erect he was pumped up and distended – partly the result of the fight, partly due to her proximity. Those bits of her that were not serpentine were powerfully attractive. She put her hand on his breastbone and he felt her warmth, like that of an iron blade left in the sun. She reminded him of a knife in many ways; slim and hard and deadly. Now he'd been given the proof of her solidity he'd desired, his skin shivered under her touch. 'You want –?' he whispered. She had no legs, no buttocks; he couldn't even guess where her sexual opening might be located.

She smiled and slid in a circle around him, her hand trailing on his chest. He shuddered but stood still, like a horse too spooked to move, only his head turning. By the time she was behind him her hands were sliding round his waist. He felt the sinews of his legs and buttocks tighten and the skin up his bare back crawl in anticipation. She was looping his feet about with a great coil of her tail.

You fear my poison? She came back round his right shoulder; her palm was splayed across his stomach, pressing upon the hard abdominal muscle, smoothing her way down to the edge of wet cotton that was his only line of defence. She smiled, showing white teeth that seemed quite human, then stretched up to kiss his cheek briefly. *You will take no harm from me.*

He put his hand on her breast – just to be sure. Her skin was neither oily nor cold as he'd feared, but dry and very smooth. She isn't real, he told himself, brushing her hard nipple, but his body believed otherwise and his penis kicked, finding instant comfort in the palm of her hand. There was a taunting glitter in her eyes. Only the twin tips of her pale, forked tongue spoiled the effect as they flickered into view across her lips. It was a narrow tongue no thicker than a finger, and entirely inhuman.

He clenched his teeth. 'No.' A woman could not be a snake; a snake could not be a woman. This was something from a forest legend and he did not have to believe it.

Don't be afraid, she said and slid down before him. She didn't drop to her knees because she had no knees; she simply lowered herself on her huge muscular tail. *I will not bite.* She nipped the skin of his chest between her teeth: *No harder than this.*

The breath caught in his throat. I don't have to accept this, he told himself as she sucked his nipple and teased it to stiffness with that bestial tongue: I can stop her. But his resolve was weakening. When she slipped the knot of his fouta and dropped a fold to uncover his cock he noted that it was already standing, swaying a little. The stream water had done nothing to cool his blood and his flesh looked very dark jutting out against the white cloth.

Oh yes, she said with satisfaction. Her mouth, when it descended, felt like pure liquid pleasure – and with that touch he was lost. No longer capable of resistance, Veraine let his head roll back as the sensation of physical relief washed over his senses. He felt her encompass his cock not just with her lips but also the paired tips of her coiling bifurcated tongue, her grip firm and sure. He surrendered to it completely; unreal or not, it didn't matter in that moment. Above them the stone walls of the ravine seemed to lean in to watch. When he looked down again all he could see was the back of the snake-woman's head rising and sinking as she sucked and licked. As he put his good hand on it and pulled her closer, feeling the hard ridges of her knotted hair beneath his palm, the first memory burst in his skull like a flash of lightning: a glimpse of a sun-drenched courtyard and young men in white tunics involved in some sort of skirmish, armed with dummy wooden swords. He gasped. Then he shut his eyes the better to see, as flash after flash exploded in his skull.

He was riding a horse through grass so long that it brushed his bare shins, straight at a line of foot soldiers with spears. The footfalls of the horse jarred through his spine.

A hard-faced man with long hair drawn back to the crown of his head shouted at him from inches away, spittle flying, and he dared not blink.

He stood on a mosaic map made of semi-precious stones, an Empire beneath his feet.

He was fourteen and was backed into the corner of a room, lashing out wildly with his fists at the boys who crowded in on him, punching and kicking.

He was riding a chariot, and the desert flew beneath his feet.

He was a boy, tied to a fence, and his back was being whipped raw.

He was looking at blood running down the blade of a short-sword towards his hand.

Veraine opened his eyes again, unable to bear the

impact of so many memories. They'd come at him disjointed and without context, as if he were seeing through another man's eyes. Veraine's lips shaped the word Stop, but jolt after jolt of arousal was building to a solid mass at the base of his spine, an imperative pressure that was making him thrust his hips forwards. His hand tightened on the snake-woman's hair. Keeping his eyes open was no defence: other images coruscated through Veraine's mind.

He was holding the reins of a wounded cavalryman, smelling the horse and the leather of the saddle and the metallic tang of blood, almost dazzled by the flash of sunlight on the polished harness-fittings.

He was surrounded by a ring of cadets and was beating the head of a youth a little older than himself against the flagstones of the barracks floor.

He was saluting a man whose face showed him to be in the hearty prime of life, but whose long hair was silver-grey.

She reached up and cupped his scrotum, fingertips plucking at it and teasing the soft skin behind that tight-drawn purse. At the same time she sent one narrow tip of her tongue questing down the narrow mouth of his cock, penetrating him in an entirely new way, overwhelming him with a sensation that he couldn't even have imagined before. He cried out in shock. Hot oil seemed to fill his stones and boil upward. Her coiling tail tightened about his thighs, pushing him up onto the balls of his feet. He groaned aloud and grabbed her head with both hands, the throbbing of his smashed knuckles all one with the pounding in his head and the pulse in his groin as he spilt his semen in scalding waves.

He was standing before ranks of men in white tunics and bronze greaves and helmets, all bearing spears and wicker shields. They raised their weapons towards him as they shouted in perfect unison, like one mighty beast with four thousand heads roaring its approval.

He came back to himself as she pulled off his length, her saliva glistening on the shaft and head of his cock, her lips pursed. The expression in her ophidian eyes was unfathomable. He swayed on his feet, almost staggering as she released him from her coils. Then as she withdrew beyond his reach she did something no human woman could have done; she bent, her spine as fluid as water, and pressed her lips to her own body just where her sex ought to have been rather than flat, burnished scales. For a moment her jaw worked. But even when she straightened again he could see no vaginal opening, just a patch of ruffled scales.

The implications of this strange insemination were far beyond anything Veraine was able to think about. He ran his hand through his wet hair, staring.

The serpent-woman regarded him thoughtfully. *Your mind will not be healed until your heart is made whole too*, she told him as she turned away into the green shadows. She seemed to blend into the dappled light of the ravine with uncanny swiftness. *Your heart is not here.*

Veraine watched the last slim length of her tail vanish among the boulders, then bowed his head, shutting his eyes tight. He remembered the ranks of soldiers, the flash of weapons and the tumult and the excitement and the glory of it all. My heart was not there either, he thought.

A clatter of falling stone behind him yanked him back to the present and he spun, fearing some further nightmare. But it turned out to be Rahul, descending the streambed. 'Did you see it?' Veraine demanded in lieu of a greeting. 'Did you see anything?'

The bhopa shook his head. The blow he'd taken to

the face was coming up as a swelling over one cheek-bone. 'See what?' His gaze dropped to the immodestly loosened folds of Veraine's fouta and his pendent phallus. 'Ah. Regretfully, no. If only I'd got here sooner.'

Veraine's head was spinning. He couldn't speak. He tightened his clothing and turned away to the stream, crouching to splash his face with cool water. Then he sat back upon a stone.

'I came to thank you,' said Rahul after an awkward silence. 'And to tell you we should go. It's not a good idea to stay here.'

With great effort Veraine managed to recall the real world. 'Where's Teihli?'

'She's still in the village.'

'Is she safe?'

'Yes. She's performing a ritual for peace at the shrine. And there's a discussion going on ... They're arguing about what to do with the reivers they've taken captive.'

'They should finish them off,' said Veraine hoarsely, 'and dispose of the bodies.' His mind was in turmoil; fear and confusion and outraged pride were pulling him in every direction at once.

Rahul pulled a face, nodding. 'It's not so easy for us, you know. We're not a violent people.'

Veraine didn't answer that. But I am, he thought. The memory of the fight and its aftermath were still bitter. I'm a violent man of a warlike nation. I can kill without hesitation and in this place that makes me a freak, and a monster fit only for the company of other monsters.

Rahul twisted his hands together. 'What you did ... scared people.'

'I could tell.'

'It was ... amazing.'

He shrugged the words off. 'They were only brigands, not real warriors.'

Rahul looked at his feet and then back up at Veraine again, his face flushed. 'You saved us. Me and Teihli. All of us. Could you teach me to do that – to fight like you?'

Veraine's mouth twisted. 'No. Not even if I wanted to.'

'But I want to be able to protect her –'

'Rahul, you do not want to be like me. And I didn't save Teihli: you did. I was too far off to reach her in time. She'd have died if it had only been me.' He put his head in his hands. He was suddenly exhausted. Tomorrow, he knew, every bit of him would ache.

'We should go find her,' said Rahul, biting his lip. 'She'll be worrying about us. The villagers said you shouldn't have come down here. It's dangerous.'

Veraine blinked. 'This place?'

'They say this stream belongs to a naga.'

'Which is?'

'A water spirit. They look like big snakes.' Rahul glanced around uneasily. 'They guard treasure and sometimes take human life. We don't want to disturb it.'

Veraine drew a deep breath. 'We're fine. It won't hurt us.'

That was clearly not the response Rahul had expected. He turned a frown on the bigger man. 'You saw it?'

Veraine shook his head uncomfortably. 'No. Go back to Teihli. You go on.' Rahul cocked his head questioningly at this and waited until he admitted, 'I think it's time I left you.'

'What, now?'

'It's only a few days early. I have to turn off to Siya Ran Thu anyway.'

Rahul scratched at his chest and turned slowly on his heel as if taking advice from the rocks and ferns. 'No.

We're coming with you.' He looked Veraine in the eye. 'We've decided,' he announced. 'We'll come to Siya Ran Thu.'

'You said it wasn't safe.'

'Safer for you than travelling on your own. Storytellers can go anywhere. What if you don't find her at the slave market? You know, don't you, that if she had red hair and she was pretty enough, she'd almost certainly have been offered at the palace first? To *them*?'

'I can get into a palace.'

'Not as easily as you can with us. Like I said, storytellers can go anywhere.'

'No. Absolutely not.'

'We've already talked it over. And we owe you our lives. We'd be slaves of the Tiger Lords now if it weren't for you.'

'Then we're even. You owe me nothing.'

'You're our friend.'

Veraine shook his head in disgust. 'You don't even know who I am.'

'Balls,' said Rahul briskly. 'We know who you are; we just don't know who you used to be. Anyway, this is what Teihli wants. She worries about you. She likes you.'

Veraine didn't know how to answer that.

Rahul smiled, a little sadly, a little cheekily. 'I like you.'

'I'd noticed,' said Veraine thoughtfully. 'Thank you both,' he added after a moment.

10 **Making His Mark**

Myrna knew he wouldn't forgive, but she had begun to hope that Rao Dhammazhedi had forgotten her. For two days she'd tended the royal lovers in their seclusion as they'd coupled over and over again, barely taking time to sleep. Then life had returned to its normal routine – except that Shinsawbu now lived in her brother's quarters and hung upon his arm when they appeared together in public. She neglected her tiger kittens and had lost all interest in her slaves, who were left to cherish the fragile hours of peace.

On the fifth day, Dhammazhedi sent the palace guard to fetch Myrna.

'I am sorry,' said Narathu Min. He stood flanked by two of his soldiers: it seemed an excessive show of force, she thought, for one unarmed slave-girl.

'Does the Lady Shinsawbu know?' It was her one hope of escape.

He nodded reluctantly. 'I understand so.'

Myrna's mouth was dry. 'What does he plan for me?'

'I don't know. I'm to take you to the Courtyard of the Bougainvillaea.'

It was better than the Arena, she told herself. She wondered whether Veraine would arrive now, in time to save her.

Narathu Min led the way with two guards at Myrna's back to a little courtyard draped with a purple-flowered plant, where Rao Dhammazhedi sat on a carved stool, picking at his teeth with an ivory pin. He looked relaxed and genial – romping with Shinsawbu had been having an effect upon him too – but Myrna didn't take comfort from that. Nor was his mood shared by the three other men kneeling behind him, dressed in workmen's clothes. The soldiers halted and stood braced, eyes fixed on the distance. Myrna was the only one who looked the Rao in the face. He smiled and observed, 'Ah; the Mouse is brought before the cat at last.'

'My king,' she said softly.

'Well, it's time you learned that there are no wild mice in this palace. Even the lizards on the walls live only by my approval, and the crickets here sing my name by night. I think you need a reminder of that, little Mouse.'

She quivered. His gaze slid over her skin like molten gold, burning where it touched.

'Strip her,' he ordered.

The guards pulled off her blouse and skirt, leaving her naked. Myrna caught a glimpse of Narathu Min's expression and thought she recognised reluctance there, but he was no more able to refuse the order than she was. Despite herself she flinched a little as the last garment was thrown aside. She had been naked before men many times and it didn't shame her, but under Dhammazhedi's gaze she had to fight the impulse to cover herself with her hands. Exposed to the air, the tender points of her breasts tightened up. The Rao flicked his toothpick away, got to his feet and paced around her, nodding his satisfaction. His amber eyes seemed to strip her even further.

'Will she suit you?' he called. The three kneeling men looked up, their faces betraying their fear. The eldest nodded vigorously. Three boxes lay on the floor next to them. 'Not too dark?'

They shook their heads.

Dhammazhedi put one fingertip on the nape of Myrna's neck and drew it slowly down her spine. She nearly screamed. It stopped just above the crease at the top of her buttocks and she felt the touch, gentle as it was, boring like an awl into her pelvis, all the way to her yoni. Her backside clenched and her thighs jumped. Her nipples hardened so much that they hurt. She could feel the warmth of his breath on her neck.

This is what the deer feels just before the tiger bites, she thought.

His breath was hot on her ear as he stooped. 'I am going to mark you,' he said in a voice so deep that it made her bones vibrate. 'I'm going to mark you as Harimau property, permanently.'

She shuddered and he laughed.

'Put her on the bench,' he commanded, and suddenly she was bereft of his torturing touch upon her skin and the guards were leading her towards a leather-topped bench much like the one she was shaved upon every day. 'Face down, and tie her.'

The men were efficient rather than rough, but they didn't give her time to catch her breath or her bearings before they pushed her belly-down onto the leather. Her legs hung off one end of the bench but they drew them up against the wood so that her arse was thrust out, and lashed her in place with tethers tight around her knees. Then they slipped leather cuffs about her wrists and tightened them, trapping her hands down at floor level. There was neither comfort nor dignity in the pose: her breasts were squashed beneath her, the blood was running to her head, and her naked sex was spread wide and inviting for anybody walking past to see. She could feel the chill on the moist places of her body. She clenched and squirmed, but it was useless. Her hands strained against the cuffs.

'You'll be glad of the restraints soon enough,' remarked Dhammazhedi, strolling around to admire the view. He laid his fingertips upon the small of her back and she froze.

Was this how it was going to happen? she asked herself, aghast.

'Shinsawbu chose the design, by the way; I thought you'd like to know.'

Myrna didn't understand what he meant, even when one of the workmen flipped open his box to reveal a small wooden mallet, an array of coloured ink-blocks and a stone to grind them upon. There was a small container made from a section of bamboo too, which let out a sharp reek of brandy when he unstoppered it: with unsteady fingers he drew out a clutch of bronze needles from the liquor. One of the needles he fixed in the slot at the end of a flat piece of wood.

'Oh,' she breathed, eyes wide.

Dhammazhedi grunted his amusement. 'I'm sure you'll love it.' He stretched and yawned, then turned to the craftsmen. 'Don't worry, I won't stay to watch you work. I'd hate for nerves to make your hands unsteady – the final result must be perfect.' The threat in his words was barely veiled.

Myrna closed her eyes and pressed her face to the leather, trying to regain her composure. She didn't succeed. Dimly she heard people moving around and then men talking in low voices and, fainter, the scrape of ink-blocks being pushed back and forth on stone and the glug of water. Then came footsteps close by her head and she lifted her neck up to an uncomfortable angle to see Narathu Min kneeling down before her.

'One of my men will be here, always,' he said in a low voice.

She had nothing to say. From the corner of her eye

she could see the pallet of colours being prepared: soot-black, lapis lazuli blue, crimson, yellow and malachite-green.

The tattoo artists started high up on her back, marking and pricking and blotting. Each time the mallet struck the back of the wooden slat the needle bit into her skin. It hurt, but not unbearably so – at least not at first, though it was worse where the bone was tight up under the skin, around the edges of her shoulder-blades and the nubs of her vertebrae. The prick of the needle was not so bad as, say, the sting of a bee. Myrna remembered the bees' nests on a west-facing wall in Mulhanabin: knobbly little hillocks of spittle-bound mud plastered to the sandstone. The dark brown bees lived solitary lives and each defended her own nest fiercely. When she was very young the priests had made Myrna trap a bee beneath her palm and hold it until it stung her. Then they had made her do it again, and again. It had been an early lesson in pain – one of many lessons. She had become intimate with pain, as was only right for the earthly incarnation of the Goddess Malia. She had been taught its strength, and its fragility. She had been taught to use it to purify the mind. She had been taught that it is a hollow crust full of anger and fear, and that once the anger and fear are drained then pain becomes nothing more than a shell that can be set aside. And here in the Courtyard of Bougainvillaea this was not, by any standards, a truly great pain.

But it went on. She couldn't tell what design was being worked on her skin, only that it was broad across her shoulders and then narrowed to descend her spine. It was intricate, involving many interlocked lines. The artists worked in turns, the first setting an outline, the other two infilling detail. Whenever a section was completed they would wipe her skin with crushed fern, which stung. They worked so close to the pattern that she could feel their breath on her skin, and they didn't stop, for hour after hour. As each grew tired he would step aside, rubbing his wrist and flexing his cramped fingers, wiping the sweat from his face; he might sit down for a while and eat from the trays of food provided. One of his companions would step into his place and begin anew, dabbing and piercing and wiping.

The artists didn't look at her while they rested, as if they saw her only as a blank canvas.

Myrna received no such respite. A slave sometimes brought her a cup of watered wine, but she was never permitted to sit up and rest. Her cramped limbs grew numb. The red mist of blood in her head thickened and throbbed. Her lips cracked. She eventually cut herself off from the world around her, hanging in a twilight trance. She was only dimly aware of the change of the light as the day wore on, or of one of the lesser Harimau lords speaking over her head, and the guard at the time warning delicately, 'She's slave to the Lady Shinsawbu, great lord,' and of the Harimau passing hurriedly on from the courtyard.

The work progressed from the top of her spine to its base and paused just at the top of the cleft of her buttocks. Then it moved between her thighs, stuttering pinpricks jabbing into the soft folds of her outer labia. It hurt less here than over the bone but somehow seemed more irrevocable too: some simple yet precious beauty was being taken from her. Fear and sorrow rose up in her and tears prickled under her eyelids for a while. She mastered that too, unravelling the knot of her loss and casting it out upon the void.

Later, they turned her onto her newly tattooed back and worked upon her shaven mound, without consideration for her discomfort.

Then, long after she had given up hope of it ever ending, she felt hands upon her wrists pulling her upright. Opening her eyes she saw that the courtyard was roofed over by the night sky and lit by flambeaux. It must be very late, she thought: the palace lay in silence. She blinked at the man holding her arm, recognising the captain. Behind him stood one of his men. There was no one else in sight.

'Have they finished?' she mumbled. Her mouth was arid and her back felt as though it had been sanded down like a piece of new parchment. It burned as with the touch of the sun.

'It's all done,' he said gruffly.

She looked down at her mons with dread. It was covered with a dark diamond in which she could make out no detail, and looked unpleasantly swollen. Her sex-lips were puffed up and throbbing. She shuddered. Her body was sticky with half-dried sweat and her limbs were shaking. All she could think of was water. 'I'm thirsty.'

Narathu Min gestured and the soldier hurried to fetch a cup of buffalo milk. Myrna gulped it down, wishing there was a barrel of it, wishing there was a bathful so that she might slide into the cool liquid and soothe her burning skin. She felt filthy; all the more so because she knew there was no way to wash this stain from her.

'Let's get these off,' the captain said, kneeling. Somewhere during her ordeal, presumably when they had turned her over, the restraints had been moved from her legs to her ankles, though she had no memory of that change. Judging by the ache in her limbs and the abrasions, though, she'd been straining against the ropes. She looked down at him as he slipped the loops free.

'How touching,' said a voice, and there suddenly was Dhammazhedi striding through the torchlight. Narathu Min lurched back, but it was too late to conceal his actions. 'You seem to have a soft spot for her, Captain. How very sweet.'

'My king,' he said stiffly.

Dhammazhedi reached out, snagged Myrna by her hair and tipped her forwards off the bench so that he could get a good look at her back. She bit back a gasp as her knees hit the stone. He pushed her head down hard.

'Hm,' he grunted. 'Not bad. It'll look better when the redness goes down, no doubt. What do you think, Captain?'

'My king?'

'Do you think it's attractive?' He smirked. 'Do you think she's beautiful?'

The captain's frozen stare didn't shift. 'My king, all your slaves are beautiful.'

The Rao draped his arm around the other man's shoulders and grinned. 'Well, I think you should fuck her,' he confided. 'Go on; give her one.' He glanced round at the younger soldier, who was trying to fade into the background. 'In fact, I think both of you should fuck her. That would be fun, wouldn't it?'

Myrna's heart crashed into her stomach. From down on her knees she could see the fat bulge at his crotch and knew that he was finding this entertaining in more than one way. Narathu Min had gone pale, but didn't respond. Clenched in the Rao's embrace, he didn't dare move. The young guard, less wise, stammered, 'But the Lady Shinsawbu . . .'

For a moment wrath flashed in Dhammazhedi's eyes before it turned to cruel amusement. 'Well, you'll just have to hope she's in a forgiving mood,' he said cheerfully.

'My king?'

'Go on: get on with it!'

Myrna clenched her fists to stop them shaking.

The young man put down his halberd and fumbled at the bindings of his trousers for a moment before his movements, slow to start with, ceased altogether and he froze, looking stunned.

'My king,' said Narathu Min in a small voice, 'there are some things a man simply cannot do, in – in your mighty presence.'

Dhammazhedi considered this, pursing his lips, then laughed derisively. 'Fair point.' He released the captain from his brotherly embrace. 'I'm going for a drink. If you've not both managed it by the time I get back then, well, you won't have to worry about Shinsawbu, either of you. Does that sound reasonable?'

'My king,' the captain rasped. As soon as Dhammazhedi had gone he turned away, swore under his breath, then turned back to Myrna. 'I'm sorry.' His eyes burned. The other soldier started praying through gritted teeth.

'Why do you let them do this?' she asked. 'There are so few of them, and so many of you. Why don't you rise up against them?'

He shook his head. 'You don't understand. It's impossible to fight them.'

'They're flesh and blood, aren't they?'

'Are they?' His jaw was clenched. 'Rao Dhammazhedi was on the throne when I was born; did you know that? They don't grow old. They don't die, or at any rate –' He broke off, chewed his lip and then continued: 'The only time we've ever seen one of them killed was when one of the lesser Harimau challenged Dhammazhedi. They took it to the Arena and the Rao tore his heart out. But that's one demon killing another.' He shook his head as if to clear it. 'Even if you can kill them, how many men do you think he'd be able to take down on his own before we made even a scratch? Ten? Twenty? A hundred? Who's going to volunteer to do it?'

She stared at him.

'Oh gods,' the young soldier said, knuckling his forehead. 'If we don't do it, he kills us. If we do, she will.'

'Be quiet, Shwe,' his captain said.

'What do we do?' Shwe groaned.

'Soldier!' Narathu Min snapped: 'Shut up! This slave shows more courage than you do – though by the tiger's balls, girl, I don't know where you get it from.'

She smiled a tiny, sad smile.

'Ah gods. You're going to need it.' He grimaced. 'I'm sorry.'

She spoke softly: 'It's all right.' She pulled herself back up onto the bench. If she sat with just her cheeks on the edge, it was not too uncomfortable.

'You shame us.' His face was burning.

'I don't mean to.'

'We're dead meat,' Shwe whimpered.

He was very young, she thought, and very scared, and simply less able to hide his fear than his captain. She shivered. Their fear and outrage and helplessness were the same as hers; the only difference was that she was able to master her feelings. She was stronger than them. 'No,' she said. 'It's all right. Do as the Rao told you.'

'She'll know!'

'No she won't. I'll make sure of that. Trust me.' She held out her hand to Shwe, who stared at her blankly. 'Come here,' she told him: 'Come on.'

He came to her warily like a feral puppy approaching food held out by a stranger. She reached to his clothes and pulled open the last of the knots with numb, rather clumsy fingers, and eased his member out. It was flaccid and as soft and warm as a fledgling in her hand. She took it gently in her mouth, nursing upon it. He tasted a little sour. She put her hands on his thighs to steady herself and drew his length down her throat, holding him in her warm inner clasp, caressing him with her tongue. She felt him respond with a sudden thickening surge, and then he caught her head and pulled her against him, pressing her nose into his glossy pubic thatch as if he were trying to lose himself in her embrace. He didn't even thrust; he just clung to her.

A cock, she thought, easing him from the deep places of her throat as he hardened and laving him with her tongue, has no idea of past or future; it knows only the present. She felt him heave and tense, and she delighted in his lustiness, and in her power to evoke it. The taste of him, the strength and the solidity of him, the way he shuddered under her hands and jerked under her tongue – all these were a simple pleasure. She missed Veraine's cock so much. It was so good to feel a man in her mouth again.

She heard the captain's long intake of breath and she withdrew from Shwe far enough so that she could look up at him. The glazed knob of Shwe's prick rested against her lips as she turned her eyes questioningly upon his officer. Narathu Min stood with his arms folded tight across his chest, transfixed. 'Don't stop,' the captain said hoarsely.

'No, don't,' echoed Shwe, trying to feed his length back into her mouth. She held him back and used her tongue to trace the contours of his glans. Then she reached into his uniform and cupped his balls in her palm, teasing the soft skin with her nails, rolling the ripe plums in their scrotal sac. Shwe had responded to her touch with the blind urgency of youth and he came now with shocking swiftness, spilling copiously. She caught the first gouts of semen in her mouth, then pulled away and lifted her chin so that succeeding jets flicked his pearly ejaculate on her throat and breasts. She was astonished by the quantity. The droplets clung to her, momentarily solid but quickly melting from the heat of her skin and dribbling down her soft curves. One strand hung from her nipple like a bead of milk. She swallowed the salty burden in her mouth, savouring it. Shwe let out a long breath and pressed the swollen head of his prick back to her lips. She kissed the last drops from him, her tongue delicately probing the tiny slit offered up to her, and he groaned in appreciation. When he finally drew away she became aware of her own wetness: it must be a side-effect of the burning in her tattooed labia, she thought.

When she looked up, her eyes met those of Narathu Min. His expression was too complex for her to read, but the warmth of it was unmistakable. He knelt and touched her feet in the sign of respect. 'Which way is least uncomfortable for you?'

She wanted to kiss him for that. 'From behind,' she whispered. The silver of his hair reminded her far too much of Veraine.

He nodded, unwound the sash from about his waist and, folding it, laid it on the stones by the end of the bench. 'Kneel on that,' he suggested, and took her by the hand to help her into position. She braced her forearms on the padded leather, trying to prepare herself for the ordeal to come. Her sex felt so raw and swollen that she didn't even want to imagine what it looked like, but she knew that nothing remained veiled. She could feel the night air on her moist tissues, and she spread her thighs wider to welcome its touch. She heard Narathu Min working at his belt and clothes, then felt him kneel down behind her. One hand clasped her upthrust cheek, while the other guided the head of his phallus to her yoni. There was no question about him being hard enough. Her abused flesh stung at his blunt probing.

'You're beautiful,' he said softly.

'You should do it quickly,' she replied, 'before the Rao returns.'

He was not quick; he was too old for that lightning discharge. What he was, and it brought hot tears brimming to Myrna's eyes, was as considerate as he could be in the circumstances. He entered her smoothly and took her with short, careful strokes. His hands gripped and squeezed at her buttocks and hips, but he took care never to touch her sore back and he didn't slam into her – and she found that though her labia itched and burned, it was not with real pain. The firm pressure of his penis was first comforting, then comfortable, then pleasurable. Her body welcomed him, and a flush grew in her cheeks as she realised this. She leaned into him, opening herself up, meshing with his rhythm until his strokes grew staccato and his hands on her waist became heavy as stone. She clenched her inner muscles, squeezing him, and was rewarded by feeling his crisis take him in a grip even fiercer than her own clasp. He spent with a groan, lurching forwards and leaning hard into her, but even then not touching her painted back.

It took him a long time to get his breath back, and during that time he remained deep inside her, almost motionless. She could feel his balls brushing her fat lips and she longed to reach back and touch them.

'Oh nicely done, Captain. I knew you wouldn't disappoint me.'

Myrna's eyes snapped open and there was Rao Dhammazhedi, arms folded, looking at them with satisfaction.

She wondered how on earth a man that big could move so silently.

Narathu Min withdrew, to stand and tuck himself away with cold military professionalism, but Myrna couldn't help the escape of a tiny moan of loss. The burning in her flesh was becoming a wet boiling and the emptiness inside her was almost unbearable. Dhammazhedi straddled the bench and sat down right in front of her face, his crotch framed by his splayed thighs.

'Satisfied?' he asked her conversationally.

'No. Not yet,' she whispered, because she'd never been any good at lying.

He raised an eyebrow. 'Gods, woman, you're an insatiable slut.' He twisted his hand in her hair and pulled her towards him. 'How many men is it going to take?'

She didn't answer. He was wearing loose trousers this night and she could see the cloth lifting over the tumescent length beneath. He liked her like this, she knew: tear-stained, exhausted, shaken and in pain.

He stooped to sniff at her throat, pulling her head to a near-impossible angle. His tongue rasped across her skin, right over the jugular. It felt incredibly rough, like wet sand: she was sure that a few more strokes would start her bleeding, and she knew he could feel the pulse rocketing beneath his lips. 'I know what you really need,' he whispered, and the bass rumble of his voice made her spine turn to water. She sobbed out loud. He slackened his grip enough to allow her head to fall back to a natural angle, as he leaned back and delved in his own clothing. And there it was; that monstrous phallus, drooling and bobbing, its engorged plum-dark glans pushing out from the foreskin. 'You need a bit of this, don't you?' He had her head in one fist and his member in the other: he forced them together, rubbing his prick over her face, stabbing at her eyes, bludgeoning her lips until she yielded to him and he entered – far too briefly – the sanctum of her mouth and pillaged it. He pulled it out again before she could suck it properly and wiped her own spittle on her cheeks. 'You want a really big one, don't you?' he mused. 'You want something big enough to fill your greedy, desperate snatch and treat it the way a whore's should be treated.'

She whimpered with frustration, unable to contain the pathetic noises.

'Tell me you love my cock,' he demanded.

'I love it,' she moaned, trying to catch it with her lips.

He laughed and slapped her with his prick, first one side of her face then the other, before pushing her away. She collapsed to the floor, gasping. 'You dirty little cunt,' he sneered, hefting his balls and caressing the proud shaft. 'You're ready to melt, aren't you?' Then to her utter bewilderment, he put it all away and, smirking, made to leave.

Myrna's head was spinning with shock. For a moment she could only think of the terrible demand in her own flesh, and could not begin to understand what he was doing. It was clear that he found her arousing – the physical proof of that, hard as teak and hot as blood, had been stuffed in her helpless mouth and left her bruised inside and out. What she could not understand was why he didn't consummate that itch. She was not his natural preference, she knew that: Dhammazhedi preferred his slaves virginal, terrified and, finally, broken. But he had been – he still was – hard for her.

She was just enough of a novelty to pique his interest, she realised. But there was something about her that repelled him: her desire.

She couldn't hide the fact that she burned at his

touch, his glance, his presence. And he didn't like that. He wanted her to fear him. The fact that she had the temerity to feel lust in his presence, not terror, actually offended him.

Myrna tried to swallow. He was standing up and walking way, leaving her awash in sex-juices and reeking of the palace guard, to crawl before Shinsawbu and take her punishment. Her heart felt like it would crack her breastbone. She couldn't pretend to fear him; it was far too late for that. She couldn't make him believe that she recoiled from him, which was the one way to make him take brutal advantage.

But, she thought, she could make him angry. And for Dhammazhedi wrath and lust must be nearly indistinguishable. 'You're worried you might not impress?' she rasped.

He stopped dead in his tracks. 'What?' he hissed, swinging to face her.

She tried to get to her feet, but her legs were still shaking and she staggered like a drunk, clutching at the bench for support. 'Well, your bed-slaves are mostly so young, my king, that they'd find anything bigger than a finger a shock.'

His eyes widened and his lips peeled back.

Myrna took a deep breath. 'And as for the great Lady Shinsawbu, she's not what I'd call choosy –'

She got no further because he reached her in three strides and slammed her down upon the bench, his whole weight on top of her. The breath went out of Myrna with a cry and her back seemed to explode with shock, but that was as nothing to the horror of having him bent over her, his hand hard on her breastbone, his face inches from hers. His eyes caught the flicking light of the flambeaux and shone like moons. 'Bad move,' he hissed. For a few pounding heartbeats he studied her face, then his free hand found her thighs and forced them open. There was a moment's fumbling and then his cock was out in his hand, and then it was forcing the gate of her vulva, and then it was boring into her and his weight was on her pelvis and her shoulders. Myrna couldn't stifle her cry. A distant part of her mind was saying it was good that Narathu Min had already opened her up and greased her with his cream, because Dhammazhedi was much bigger, bigger than anything she'd ever had to bear, and he took her absolutely without mercy.

He did it without emotion too, his face set like stone, his thrusts savage but measured. For Myrna it was like being ground under a millstone, and every pore of her body screamed its protest. Her back was on fire, her thighs felt as if they were torn from their joints, she could hardly breathe for the pressure on her ribcage, and her sex – her sex felt as if it were being struck over and over by lightning. For hours her body had been starved, cramped and abused, glutted with discomfort, kept upon a sweating, shivering plateau of sensory stimulation. Her vulva was swollen and itching, its heat communicated directly to her clitoris. Then she'd been sexually aroused but not satisfied, her mouth filled with the taste of semen, her throat stretched by an eager prick, her yoni thoroughly opened and primed and pumped full of spunk. Now her every fibre was congested and yearning: her body was desperate not for rest but for some sort of release, a final cleansing immolation, the more brutal and overbearing the better.

The Tiger Lord gave her that. At the best of times she was wet for him, her thighs slippery with shameless need. Now she swallowed the terrible battering of his cock like a fire swallows oil; it set her ablaze. She writhed beneath him, tearing at his flanks with her nails, opening to his every punishing thrust. He thought he was hurting her and he loved it, redoubling his efforts. She cried out and he assumed it was with agony. She bucked and twisted and he imagined she was trying to escape. The knowledge of his own glory brought him to orgasm and he was so wrapped up in the fire of his own triumph that he didn't recognise her transfiguration, mistaking ecstasy for torment even as he spasmed and filled her to overflowing with his hot essence.

Myrna was smashed beneath her climax like a swimmer beneath a breaking wave, and when she emerged she could hardly breathe or see. She felt Dhammazhedi cover her breasts with his big hands, his nails biting her flesh, but the roar of the waters in her ears and the salt in her eyes left her too stunned to react. Then he detached himself and she felt the bite of the air upon her abraded flesh. She felt like she'd been tumbled among rocks by a terrible ocean surge.

He straddled her head. 'Satisfied now?' he asked, his voice reeking of self-congratulation. She couldn't reply because her breath was catching in her throat, but she whimpered in affirmation, bringing a broader smile to his lips. He lowered himself so that he could wipe his cock on her face again, pushing its glistening, turgid length into her unresisting mouth. She could barely lick at it. When he withdrew she could taste the faint tang of her own blood and she winced. He laughed, well pleased with himself, and then stepped away, preening his cock and balls. 'Got more than you bargained for?'

She moaned.

Grinning, he took his cock in his right palm, set his legs and began to piss on her. The hot jet struck her throat and she jumped in shock. He played it up on her face and she choked and spasmed. 'Drink it up, Mouse.'

She opened her mouth to the acrid liquid splashing on her swollen lips and tongue.

'Good girl.' He filled her then kept pissing; on her eyes and forehead, back down across her lips to her breasts, all the way down to her navel. The last fall of the dying stream was reserved for her battered pudenda. He had marked his territory in the most basic and animalistic manner, and at the same time displayed his utter contempt. He had also, she knew as she swallowed the golden fluid, swamped the scent of the other men in his own pungent odour, far more effectively than anything else she could have engineered. She smiled.

'You love this,' he said idly, 'the humiliation.'

She looked up at him, completely quiescent except for her heaving breasts, her pupils vast. It hadn't occurred to her that she should be humiliated by any of this.

'You love being my slave.' He touched her between the legs, casually, and she quivered with shock. 'You love it when I hurt you, and when I use you and violate you. You love to crawl for me. You love to be my whore. You just can't stop being wet for me.'

She could not have denied that last even if she had been able to speak.

'I'm the only thing in the world that can fill that hungry cunt of yours.' He stooped lower so his lips hovered over hers. 'You love me because I'm your master, and you need to be mastered. You need it. You need to be on your hands and knees with your mouth worshipping my almighty prick.'

Myrna gritted her teeth, because it was the only way she could get her mouth under enough control to speak. 'You're like a god,' she slurred. 'Just a bit.' It wasn't meant as a compliment; like all gods, he made a piss-poor excuse for a man. But that was what she responded to: the monolithic ego, the unfairness, the detachment from lesser mortals, the inexorable execution of power. 'You're like ...' she managed to whisper, but broke off.

He was amused. Inevitably, he'd taken her words as well-deserved flattery. 'Like what?'

Like family, she'd meant to say. But the likeness was a little closer than that. She responded to him, she realised, because he was a mirror in which she could see the goddess Malia. *You're like me*, she thought. Wide-eyed, she shook her head.

He cocked an eyebrow, snorted and laughed. The glow of orgasm had blunted his temper; he found the mad little Mouse peculiar but no longer irksome. 'I'll have to buy Shinsawbu a present now,' he said, more to himself than her, and ran a finger down the length of her torso. 'And you, my luscious little whore, should wear a permanent reminder of tonight.'

He spun on his heel, shouting for the guards to find the tattooists. 'Do they think they've finished for the night?' The sound of running feet echoed from the courtyard walls. The night seemed to spin in circles round Myrna and she closed her eyes. When she opened them Dhammazhedi was tugging at his ear. 'Here,' he said, slapping his hand down on her stomach and addressing someone out of her field of view; 'there's more work for your needles. My toy must carry my marks.'

Myrna tilted her head up to look down her body and nearly drowned in a wave of dizziness. There on the damp plain of her belly, colder than her skin but glinting warmly in the torchlight, lay three gold rings taken from Dhammazhedi's ear.

11 **Bring Him Back to Me**

Sitting in the great kitchen courtyard, Veraine tried to look as if he was busy with the bowl of noodles he'd been presented with. In fact food was the last thing on his mind.

Their visit to the slave market of Siya Ran Thu hadn't gone well. Not only had no one recalled any red-haired Yamani woman being offered there, but Veraine had nearly had a fight with a merchant and his bodyguards. He'd struggled to keep his temper since he set foot inside the market, reacting with a deep visceral revulsion to the whole place, and he'd very nearly been goaded into starting a brawl. Teihli and Rahul had drawn him away just in time. The intensity of his distress had taken him completely by surprise. It wasn't based on compassion either; his pity for the slaves – stolid labourers or scared children or grieving young women – was a distant, abstract thing.

This is about me, he'd admitted to himself. I'm angry for my own sake. I've been in this position myself: I was a slave, and I hate these people for it. The conclusion had left his mouth dry.

It had been, in the end, surprisingly easy to gain access to the Palace of the Harimau. Their greatest obstacle was the surprise evoked by their offer to perform an entertainment there: such volunteers were clearly not common. They'd applied at the servants' entrance and a succession of officials were sent for, each better-dressed than the last, who each in turn listened to the offer, looked astonished and doubting, then vanished to seek the advice of someone further up the palace hierarchy. Eventually they had performed a truncated version of *Two Brothers* before a thin man with weary eyes and one arm bound up in a sling. He'd been pleased enough to offer them a show that night in the gardens, and to give them a purse of coins with another promised should the performance prove popular with his masters.

Veraine hadn't been impressed by the excessive generosity of their hosts, any more than by the opulence of those parts of the palace they'd glimpsed. Its beauty meant little to him. He'd been busy studying the faces of the slaves they passed, the layout of the corridors, the access afforded to the upper storeys and, surreptitiously, the guards in their lacquered armour. There was, he thought, something subtly wrong about the guards. He kept his eyes open for the famed Tiger Lords too, but saw no demons.

They'd been taken to the kitchen courtyard and fed while they waited for nightfall. The place was filled with people, some of them involved in food preparation but most of them passing through, catching a bite to eat or a moment to sit, gossiping or dozing. Teihli and Rahul's ability to join in any community came to the fore here, and soon they were circulating among the palace staff, laughing and conversing. Veraine could only watch in admiration and stay put, sitting with his back to a pillar where he could watch the main doors. He didn't altogether avoid attention because even clean-shaven he couldn't pass for a local man, and more than a few people came over to ask where he was from and chuckle at his accent. Several of the women seemed quite taken by him and brought him different drinks and dishes to try. He thanked them politely but refused anything that smelled of alcohol, which made them laugh.

Eventually Teihli, in one of her passes across the floor, dropped down beside him and passed over half a flatbread stuffed with almonds and fruit. 'There is a red-haired woman among the slaves,' she said, keeping her voice low. 'They don't know if she's Yamani, but she is a foreigner.'

His stomach tightened. 'What's her name?'

'Mouse.'

He shook his head: it didn't sound familiar. 'Is she likely to pass through here?'

'No. She's a personal slave to one of the Tiger Lords; they don't hang around in the kitchen. Maybe you'll get to see her tonight.'

'Maybe.' He chewed his lip. 'How on earth did you find all that out?'

Teihli grinned and wiggled the indigo-blue tuft at the end of her braid at him. 'I just got into a conversation about hair-dying.' Veraine had to resist the impulse to lean over and kiss her hard on the lips: it wouldn't have gone down well in public.

Eventually Teihli and Rahul sat and started on a serious discussion of what elements to include in their performance that night. Veraine, half-listening, happened to glance up and his gaze was caught by another's. It was one of the serving-women. She'd brought him food before and been flirtatious then, but now, across a table laden with chopped vegetables, she was definitely giving him the eye. Veraine raised a questioning brow. She turned away, but glanced back to make sure he was watching. It wasn't easy to make out much of her figure under the heavy wraparound skirt and blouse she wore, but there was no mistaking the graceful, exaggerated play of her hips as she headed out of the courtyard.

Veraine excused himself quietly and followed. She led him down a short corridor and then disappeared into a side room. He glanced round once to make sure there was no one watching and then slipped in behind her. The chamber beyond was a small storeroom, with shelves up the walls and sacks and barrels piled all over the floor. The woman was waiting for him, one hand on her hip. 'Why did you follow me?' she demanded.

Veraine shut the door and leaned on it, smiling. Light in this room came only from windows high up under the eaves and the air was dim and dusty. 'I thought you might need some help.'

'Doing what?' Under her pout was a sly smile trying not to betray its presence.

'Well,' he said, looking around the room. 'Getting something down off a high shelf, perhaps?'

She bit her lip, eyes glinting. Her hair was tied up in a bright scarf, but black wisps had escaped around her temples. 'I do need one of the big platters,' she said, and turned her back on him to point high up the wall. 'One of those.'

He came up close behind her, unhurried. 'The wooden ones?' He was so close he was brushing against her clothes. Her headscarf held the scent of toasted spices.

'The one with the carved vine-leaves.'

He reached up past her and it was a stretch even for him, so that he had to lean forwards into her, his chest against her shoulders, his thighs bumping her rump. She didn't flinch. He put his hand lightly on her hip to steady himself, taking his time, his cock essaying a thickening surge. Her stance was firm, and he found he could press against her and make quite sure of the roundness of the buttocks beneath the fabric. She sighed pleasantly. The platter was heavy; he passed it down with both hands, his arms encircling her.

'It must be useful to be so tall,' she admitted, taking the plate and resting the weight against her hip. The motion swung her slightly side-on to him. She smiled up from under her long lashes.

'Hm. It allows me to reach all sorts of places most men can't,' he murmured, putting one hand around her waist and stroking the other up her bare arm to the sensitive skin of her inner elbow.

She sighed again, her lips parting breathily. 'Naughty.'

He stooped to nuzzle the skin of her cheek and throat and the nape of her neck. There was a braided leather slave-collar around her throat and beneath it she tasted of spices and sesame oil from the kitchen, but he didn't mind; his cock stirred impatiently, butting up against her. He tightened his grip, pulling her in.

'Don't,' she said weakly, and he stopped kissing her to take a better look, though he didn't loosen his grip. She was nestled, hip and one cheek, snugly up against his groin, her eyes and her lips both half-open, sleepy and unresisting. He touched her mouth softly with his finger, tracing a circle in unspoken token of what he would like to be doing to her other more secret lips, and she flicked out the point of her tongue to moisten his fingertip. He pushed into her mouth, feeling the ridge of her teeth and the hot soft wetness beyond.

'Don't?' he asked softly, withdrawing from her mouth and tracing a gentle, inexorable line over her chin and down to the well of her throat. Her heart was thumping hard.

'We musn't.' She lifted her chin, exposing her throat

further. He ran all five fingers down the sensitive skin, but the coarse cotton of her blouse stopped him exploring further towards her breasts from that direction. Instead he took the platter from her hands and laid it aside, and then approached from below, sliding his hands up from her waist, under the cloth. Her skin was a little damp and she shivered under his touch.

'Why not?' Her breasts were small but that didn't make them any the less sensitive. He circled her nipples, teasing them.

'It's not safe.' Her eyelids fluttered and she wriggled against him deliciously.

'Hm?'

'It's the Tiger Lords.' She grimaced and captured one roving hand, pinning it against her breast. She meant to thwart his caresses, but she couldn't prevent him squeezing her as if testing her downy fruit for ripeness. 'Oh gods, how can I think straight when you're doing that?' she complained. 'They can smell it when you've had sex. It makes them hot, and when they're horny they get mean. It's not safe.'

This sounded like rank superstition to Veraine. 'They really do turn into tigers?' he wondered, pressing his other hand down the gentle swell of her belly and sliding a couple of fingers under the waist of her skirt. He could just feel the topmost tufts of her pubic fleece.

'Of course.'

'You've seen them do it, then?'

'Well, not me. I only work in the kitchens.'

'And you can't ever have sex?' he said, trying not to laugh. He bit her earlobe very gently.

'No, of course not. Just not if you're likely to go near them. I'm safe enough here.' She was melting against him. 'But you aren't. You'll be seeing them tonight.' She whimpered. 'Listen, you should be grateful; I'm trying to protect you.' She made a token effort to extract herself from his embrace.

Several objections to this statement occurred to him but he voiced none of them. He didn't let her go either. 'What about later?' he whispered: 'After the show?'

'Yes.' Her nipples were as hard as dried peas. 'Come back here afterwards.'

'It could be late. I don't know how long it might take.'

'I'll wait.'

He teased her erect nipple between his fingers, not giving her space to catch her breath. 'Is it safe to walk around the palace at night, if I was to try to find you?'

'Yes,' she moaned. 'No. The Lords like to be awake at night; they like the moonlight. But they sleep late in the morning. We'll have time then.'

'That's good; we'll need it. But I don't even know where I'm spending the night. They might throw us out after the show. Could I get back in? Are there guards on every gate?'

'Oh ... the guards!' She writhed in delightful frustration. 'They are nothing to worry about. They don't patrol between dawn and noon because Dhammazhedi doesn't like being disturbed. There's no guard on the kitchen door anyway.'

'Really?'

'Just old Yashwant the porter. Tell him you're coming to see me, Zjar. He won't mind. I'll tell him to let you in.'

He grinned, breathing hot against her ear. 'Won't he be jealous, Zjar ... thinking of me coming down all hard on your body?' She giggled. 'I want you right now, you know,' he said, as if there could be any doubt about that.

'I know. Oh gods, I want it too. But we can't.' She bit

at his lips and he kissed her warmly, invading her mouth. She yielded without a struggle.

She was weakening: Veraine sensed the danger. In another minute she'd cease objecting and then ... and then if there was any truth at all about she'd said of the Tiger Lords, it would be too late for him. And if he tupped her properly now and gave her blood a chance to cool, she might think more carefully about exactly what she'd just told him. 'But we can do this,' he whispered. He strummed his fingers across the covered mount of Zjar's sex, like a man striking music from a stringed instrument. She moaned and tried to wrap an arm round his neck, leaning hard into him as he scratched his nails across the coarse weave of the cloth and she danced under his touch. He stirred her whole soft mons against the bone and she pressed into his palm, gasping. The cloth was thick: he had to work without fine detail or lubrication, but Zjar was highly aroused and he made up for lack of intimate contact with unrelenting teasing that eventually became a torture of frustration, as bad for him as for her, as she ground her backside into his thigh and crotch. His other hand never let up on her so-sensitive breasts, and he took his time until she finally juddered and whimpered and collapsed heavily against him, her skin damp and dewy. He chuckled and cupped the mound of her sex in his hand, feeling her heat through the cloth. Knowing just how plump and soft and creamy she would be right now, should he care to lift that skirt, was both tormenting and deeply satisfying.

'You do know how to scratch an itch,' she sighed.

'Ah. But itches don't go away that easily, do they? Not after one little scratch.'

Zjar wriggled on his fingers. 'What do you recommend?'

'Heavy, prolonged pressure,' he said, nibbling her earlobe. 'Don't you think?'

She whimpered. 'Promise you'll come back tonight?'

'If I can. Wait for me.' He released her, not without regret, and brushed his lips over hers one last time in token of his promise. She looked a little disappointed at his self-control and cast longing looks at the tumescent bulge of his groin, but she seemed to accept the postponement of their consummation. Straightening her clothes and retrieving the platter, she left the room, whispering, 'Don't forget!' from the doorway.

When she'd gone Veraine's smile faded quickly. He sat down on a sack of rice and waited for his erection to die. If Zjar had chanced to come back into the storeroom, she would have been shocked by the grimness of his expression.

They set up the stage in the gardens after dark, before a red-lacquered pavilion. The gardens were lush and overgrown, like a miniature forested landscape, and made dreamlike by the light of paper lanterns and the fragrant clouds that rolled out from braziers where gums and the dried leaves of herbs were tended upon burning sandalwood. Veraine found that too long in that smoke made his head spin. They were not the only people providing entertainment that night; in different niches about the garden dancers and fire-eaters and musicians made ready. Veraine picked a place in the shadow of a tree, where he could see without drawing too much attention to himself. Before they began he warned his companions: 'Whatever happens, whether we see her or not, you must get out of here tonight and get as far away as you can. Don't wait for me.'

Teihli kissed him on the cheek.

'And,' he'd added, 'you must not offer them the gift of the gods after the performance.'

'Don't worry about that,' she said. 'I'm not bringing down a blessing upon this house.'

The performance went well, at first. Perhaps because they were a novelty, several Tiger Lords drifted in and took their leisure in the pavilion, lounging upon couches of carved rosewood while they chatted and kept a casual eye upon the show. Others came and went, pacing the garden with stately grace. There was no mistaking the rulers of Siya Ran Thu, not once he'd seen one. They were all fine, big-boned people, gloriously dressed, with handsome faces and curious amber eyes, but under flickering torchlight it was the way that they moved that really marked them out; with a muscular grace like the roll of a deep river over boulders. At one point there were three of the Harimau women in their audience as well as a youth and a younger child. The youth had a mongoose on a noose, which he swung and jerked about his feet. The half-strangled animal didn't look like it would survive long. One of the women held a tiny tiger kitten in the crook of her arm and was nursing it at her swollen breast. The cub purred in contentment and kneaded at her golden flesh with white paws, and the sight made Veraine's mouth go dry.

That was the first real tiger Veraine saw that night. It was not to be the last. He was drumming along with a battle-scene when a fully-grown beast paced into the lamplight from a darkened path: as big as a pony but low-slung, its heavy pelt hanging like cloth-of gold barred with shadows over a muscular frame, its face a mask of black and white and red-gold that framed eyes like burning gemstones. Veraine faltered involuntarily although the puppeteers carried on, unable to see what had happened. The animal swung its massive head in their direction for a moment, and Veraine felt its gaze lance through him, burning a hole in his soul. He went rigid. It was not precisely fear that surged through him at that moment – the burning gaze cauterised mere fear: it was the instinctive conviction that this was the predator of which he and every human in the garden was the rightful prey. He was dimly aware that his hands lay still and numb on the drum-skin.

Then the tiger looked away, bored, and it felt like an iron hand which had seized his heart had loosed its grip again. He watched it move off, muscles rippling. The beast was flanked, he finally noticed, by two slave-girls in green and saffron silks, who walked at its side with eyes lowered, as if nothing could be more fitting than to give such an animal human homage. And as the slave-girl in green passed before a flambeau, her long hair caught the gold light and blazed out, crimson as rubies. Veraine caught his breath like he'd been kicked in the guts.

The woman turned her head. She didn't break her stride, but for one moment her expression went from studious submission to shock and then, for a fraction of that moment, to horror. Then it snapped back, absolutely blank again as if she'd donned a mask. She turned away and kept walking, keeping pace with the tiger until they all vanished into the garden shadows.

Veraine forced himself to look at the drum. His hands brushed the skin, following the rhythms of the puppet-drama by instinct but without force, a stuttering excuse for a drumbeat. That was her! he thought. It must be! He hadn't recognised her, she didn't look remotely familiar to him, but there was no question but that she'd recognised him. It didn't escape him that she'd looked far from pleased, and for the first time it occurred to him that maybe she didn't hope to see him again, that perhaps he was no friend – that he'd done something to her in his previous life that made him a source of dread. I am capable of it, he thought, his mind racing: more than capable. Bile rose in his throat.

He could hardly bear to sit there pretending to play, and was thankful when that piece finished and Teihli came forward to sing. Veraine stumbled into the darkness behind the stage, dropped the drum and rubbed his hands over his face, trying to force some sort of coherence back into his thoughts. He had to find her. He had to speak to her. He couldn't think of anything else. Even the threat of the tiger chaperone hardly mattered. He gathered up a bundle of props from the discard pile and shoved his sword among them. Teihli and Rahul didn't need him for the performance, not really. The possibility that he was walking out on them for good didn't make him hesitate.

He passed several guards and had his excuse half-formed, something about taking props back to the cart, but no one challenged him. He'd already worked what was wrong with the palace guard. Give a man a weapon – any man, any weapon – and he will naturally respond with a swagger, a surge in confidence and pride, however misplaced. But not these men. They were well-trained enough, but somehow they'd had all the confidence kicked out of them. It was, Veraine assumed, something to do with their overlords, but what mattered was that it gave him an edge. As he walked, and as the shock to his gut faded, his own resolve hardened.

Even the sight of more tigers didn't shake him. He gave a wide berth to a grassy clearing in which five naked people, two women and three men, were engaged in deliberate and unrestrained sexual play, coupling with extravagant athleticism. All the participants were tightly blindfolded, which lent their touch more purpose and sensuality, but what they didn't see was that beyond their little circle of warm torchlight two adult tigers lay close by, watching intently, mighty jaws resting on their forepaws, shoulders hunched with tension. Dry-mouthed, Veraine lingered only long enough to be sure that the slave-girl Mouse was not among them, before slipping away into the night.

I must find her, he told himself as caged birds cried from the darkness like ghosts. Green skirt, green bodice, gold necklace, that pointed little chin; she should be easy to spot. I will find her.

And he did.

The shock of seeing Veraine was so fierce that Myrna could hardly breathe. She had to clamp her lips shut in order to hold back a cry, and she had to bottle up the pressure of her shock with every ounce of her will, because the one coherent thought in her head was that Shinsawbu must not know, must not hear and must not smell it on her. So she emptied her mind and forced her limbs to submit to her, and she didn't allow any thought of him to intrude as she walked away. Only when the Tiger Lady bade Harzu and her to wait under the orchard trees, while she dallied with Dhammazhedi in a limestone grotto, did she at last allow the confused voices and images in her mind's eye a free rein.

What was he doing here? What was he planning? This was not how she'd pictured their reunion. She'd dreamed that she would wake to find him lifting her in his arms, carrying her out to a boat waiting upon the river. Or imagined him striding into the throne room to confront Rao Dhammazhedi, in all the finery of his battle-armour, his hand heavy and threatening upon the hilt of his sword – not glimpsed drumming for itinerant entertainers. 'Fool,' she said to herself, clench-ing her fists as she paced beneath the mango trees.

'What's wrong?' Harzu asked, looking up anxiously.

'Nothing.' Fool, she repeated, silently this time, but no less bitterly. You spin illusions to trap yourself, as if there weren't enough snares here. He's here, that's all, and you must be ready. But she wasn't ready. She had no idea what the gods expected of her now, and her own mind was in a whirl. He was in terrible danger here, and panic was threatening to blind her.

He must not fall into their hands! she cried silently. *Protect him!* she demanded of the silent, watchful gods. Then she turned on her heel and opened her eyes and there he was, standing under a swaying paper lantern, looking at her. The blood roared in her ears. She took one step towards him but her legs faltered.

Veraine was not as she remembered him. She'd always seen him as a big man, well-muscled – but after Dhammazhedi he looked slight. And there was more grey in his hair than she remembered. He stood on that orchard path dressed in simple workman's clothes, bare-foot, a bundle of sticks and cloth under one arm. His head was tilted back at a proud angle, but there was such a look of pain, almost of despair, in his eyes that she quailed. The cords of his neck stood out in tension. It was the look he might have worn just before con-demning her to death.

'Do you know me?' he asked. His voice was hoarse.

'Veraine,' she whispered, taking another step. His eyes widened. 'Veraine.'

He looked as if she'd slapped him. She could see the muscles of his jaw working. 'You do!' he said, baring his teeth. Then he came suddenly forwards, reaching out his free hand to grasp her.

'Don't touch me!' she gasped, flinching away. It was

ingrained training; and she realised as she said it that he didn't understand and that he wasn't going to obey. His hand closed on her upper arm with a grip like iron.

'I have to talk to you –'

'Let her go!' It was Harzu, fluttering among the trees in her yellow silk. 'Don't touch her!'

'Shit,' said Veraine softly to himself.

'Oh dear gods,' Myrna groaned. 'Let me go.'

He looked from woman to woman in dismay. 'I'm not going to hurt you,' he insisted.

'Guards!' screamed Harzu. 'Stop him!'

At that moment, if she could have struck Harzu dead Myrna would have. 'You have to run,' she told Veraine. 'Now.'

'Touching my cousin's property?' said a new voice. 'You really don't know the rules, do you?' It was Lord Anawrahta, strolling towards them across the grass. He was neither so important nor so muscular as the Rao Dhammazhedi, but at the sight of him Myrna's heart dropped and Harzu abruptly stopped screaming. The Harimau's reputation was far uglier than his sculpted face. Dressed in pale green satin, the young Tiger Lord wore a sneer of anticipation. Veraine turned to meet him, shoving Myrna behind him. 'Here,' said Anawrahta, 'let me show you,' and he drew back one arm lazily as he closed to striking distance.

To Myrna it looked like Veraine pulled out a stick as he dropped his bundle, but it was a stick that glinted in the dim lamplight, and when it met Anawrahta's arm it sheared straight through flesh and bone. The upper arm continued its trajectory but the lower part of the limb, its fingers still locked in a fist, flew wide into the grass. Anawrahta, carried by his own momentum, stumbled to a half-crouch as Veraine stepped smoothly aside. For a moment there was complete silence, then Anawrahta opened his mouth in a roar of outrage and pain. Veraine, backing off, turned to Myrna and she saw that his expression had set in hard lines, all doubt and confusion wiped away.

'You have to come with me. I won't hurt you,' he repeated, though she had no idea why he should say that. He caught her wrist and they began to run, across lawns and through stands of shrubs. They dashed over an ornamental bridge and ducked to run beneath low branches. Myrna felt his hand tight around hers and despite everything her heart sang in time with her pulse. But all around them guards were on the move and shouts of alarm were going up. They could run but they could not avoid being spotted. A knot of guards appeared in front of them as they rounded a boulder and they turned aside across an open moss lawn towards the nearest building. They were nearly at the gate to the servants' corridor when more guards came out of that. Veraine came to a sudden halt and Myrna piled up against him.

'The Arena gate!' she cried, tugging at his arm. If they could get into the Arena there was a wooden gate leading out onto the hillside which was used for the disposal of bodies; it was the only route she could think of in the circumstances. Veraine came with her, but they were beginning to slow. In another few moments a line of guards swung across to intercept them. They halted, breathing hard, turning in every direction. There were guards all around, advancing with halberds lowered. There was no way past. The first soldiers got within striking distance but when Veraine lunged hard at them with his sword they backed off nervously. Veraine circled like a leopard in a cage, eyes blazing, the blood on his blade black in the torchlight. She kept close to him, and he tried his best to interpose himself between her and the nearest of the soldiers. The cordon tightened. Myrna searched the faces of the men, looking for Narathu Min. It seemed unfair, she thought crazily: not one of the soldiers was willing to run in and risk his life in close combat; too wary of the armed stranger. Yet there were so many of them that it was impossible for him to fight his way out.

She saw the face she was looking for. 'Captain!' she called: 'Let us pass!' Just for a moment hesitation showed in Narathu Min's eyes. Perhaps he might have negotiated, but at that moment Anawrahta staggered in. He was clutching his stump to his chest and his shirt was shiny with gore. He was swaying on his feet, yet he'd caught up with them.

'He hurt me!' the Tiger Lord yowled. 'Take him!' The guards wavered, aghast at the sight of a Tiger Lord injured. 'Take him!' Anawrahta shrieked again, then: 'Keep him pinned down so I can do it myself!'

The guards gave every appearance of preferring this option. The cordon became a palisade, the halberds pointed inward to prevent escape. Veraine and Myrna were back-to-back. 'Captain,' she mouthed, holding Narathu Min's eyes, letting him see the pleading in hers.

Then some of the guards peeled back to allow Anawrahta access, and the Tiger Lord stepped into the gap. His face was pallid. Veraine lifted his blade and pointed it mockingly. 'You want this, kitty-cat?' he spat.

Anawrahta slipped to one knee, the snarl on his lips sliding away to be replaced by a look of confusion. It seemed for a moment that Veraine had cast some kind of magic upon him. The guards stared. Everyone was waiting for one of the men to strike; everyone except Narathu Min. As all eyes were locked on the Tiger Lord, he stepped in, reversed his halberd and swung the haft. It struck Veraine on the side of the head and he went down like a slaughtered ox, measuring his length on the earth.

For a moment Myrna froze. A scream only she could hear began to ricochet around inside her skull, faster and faster. There was no blood spilling from Veraine's head, but he lay perfectly still. *This is not what you promised me!* she cried to the Sun God, but he was miles away beneath the benighted earth and didn't hear her. Myrna did the only thing she could think of then: she dropped to her knees, clasping Veraine with her hands. She looked the Tiger Lord in the face and warned, 'Not unless you crave the wrath of Lady Shinsawbu.'

Anawrahta blinked several times and frowned. He seemed to be having difficulty working out what was going on. 'Kill him,' he slurred at last. 'Kill them both.'

None of the guards moved. They feared Shinsawbu more than they did him; Myrna was Veraine's shield. She cradled his head and shoulders, feeling the weight and the solidity of his unconscious form and tasting the familiar scent of his skin. Her wrist circled his throat and she could feel his pulse. She wanted to moan for longing and weep for despair. She bowed low over him, her hair sweeping the ground. 'I knew you'd come for me,' she whispered. 'I won't leave you.'

She heard footfalls and then Narathu Min squatted down in front of her. 'Myrna,' he said; 'you have to let go.'

She lifted her head. 'Kill him and kill me,' she said, her voice like the grave. 'One blow will do for the two of us.'

'I can't do that.'

'You won't separate us.' She was putting him in an impossible position, and she knew it, but she no longer cared. He could not so much as touch her.

'What,' said Shinsawbu's voice, cold and angry, 'are

you doing with my slave?' The captain snapped back to his feet, and Myrna felt her heart contract. When she raised her head she saw that the circle of guards had peeled back and was standing to attention, and that Dhammazhedi was looking down on them all with his sister draped upon his arm. The Rao looked faintly amused; his lady did not.

'He hurt me,' Anawrahta complained. He'd sat down and was trying to staunch his stump.

'He did?' Dhammazhedi raised an eyebrow and stepped forwards for a closer look. 'How?'

'Took me by surprise.'

'Haven't you finished him off yet?' He looked disgusted. 'What are you waiting for?' Anawrahta tried to climb to his feet but his legs gave out beneath him. Shinsawbu sniggered. Dhammazhedi's eyes narrowed and he turned back to the guards. 'Kill him.'

The soldiers wavered. Even in the face of the Rao's direct order, every eye went to Shinsawbu. She licked her lips, irritated. 'What do you think you're doing, Mouse? Get out of the way.'

Myrna shut her eyes. 'He's more than a match for any Tiger Lord.'

'What?'

A susurrus of dismay swept around the circle. She spoke clearly, making sure everyone could hear. 'This man is a battle-hero of the Irolian Empire.'

Frowning, Shinsawbu stooped for a closer look and realisation lit up her face. 'Good gods; this is him, isn't it?' She laughed, incredulous. 'This old man! It is – this is the one you've been waiting for!' She hooked one foot under Veraine's unconscious body and flipped him over with little effort. He sprawled limply, his throat bared to the night. Myrna kept hold, one hand cradling his neck and jaw, his stubble rough on her palm. 'Not all that old then,' Shinsawbu admitted, reappraising. 'And not so bad-looking.'

Dhammazhedi growled. 'I don't care what he is: he's dead meat. It only pains me Anawrahta hasn't done it himself.'

'He'd be a match for you,' said Myrna loudly; 'man to man.'

The night seemed to grow very silent. It was Shinsawbu who broke the hush, by sniggering. 'Oh Dhammaz, you're being mean. The poor girl's waited months for her hero to come and rescue her, and now she's going to be so disappointed. You can't have him butchered by a servant!'

'I can't?'

'It's not very romantic. At least do her the favour of seeing him killed properly in the Arena.'

'I feel you indulge your slaves too much, sister.'

'I'll do it,' slurred Anawrahta. Two of his slaves had hurried in and were attempting to bind his stump.

Shinsawbu cast him a glance of pure contempt. 'You couldn't kill anything bigger than a frog.'

'Meet him in the Arena,' said Myrna, looking the Rao in the face, 'and he will win. I give you fair warning.'

His yellow eyes were like chips of the moon. 'One day you will cease to amuse, little Mouse,' said he.

'Oh come on,' Shinsawbu said, running her hand down his arm. 'Don't you think she's sweet? Think how funny her expression will be when she sees her beloved disembowelled on the Arena sands.'

Dhammazhedi, smiling, lifted her hand and kissed it. 'If it will give you pleasure, my queen, I'll do it for you.'

Letting go of Veraine was the hardest thing the Harimau had ever made Myrna do. Every fibre of her flesh wanted to hold on to him; her hands clung on even

223

when she told herself she must withdraw. Watching the guards drag him off to the cells, his head hanging on his breast, it felt like her insides had been ripped out and vinegar poured into the raw wound. But she'd achieved as much as she could for the moment. The Tiger Lords had lost interest for the time being and gone about their own business. She forced down the seething acid of her emotions, collected her thoughts and then asked Narathu Min for a word aside.

'Don't blame my men,' he said. 'They had no choice.' She looked at him speechlessly, gathering herself for the leap she was about to make, and the captain squirmed under her gaze and eventually grunted, 'I'm sorry for your grief.'

'May we talk in private?'

He was surprised. 'Alone?'

She took the leap. 'You, me, and Sao Mor.'

12 **The Arena**

When Veraine woke he was lying face down with his hands manacled together behind his back. It took some time before he was capable of thinking much further than that and the fact that his head ached. There was a strong smell of leather from the padding on the broad bench-top. No sound but his own breathing reached his ears.

I must have a skull like a cracked egg by now, he said to himself.

He rolled cautiously onto his side and then sat up. A chain clinked. The small, rock-cut chamber came into focus; there was a wooden door in the plastered wall opposite him. The only light came from a barred window high up which revealed no view but a few tufts of grass. Veraine flexed his shoulders and tried vainly to separate his arms, and then attempted to stand – only to find that his wrists were chained to a ring in the wall behind him, and that there wasn't enough slack to allow him to do more than lie down on his bench or sit on the edge. He could just about stand with his heels and calves braced against the bench and his shoulders pulled back, but he had no balance in that position. He licked his rough lips.

Very neat, he thought. My first memory is waking up parched with my head half staved-in, and now weeks later I'm back to the same position. Everything before, and likely after, is darkness. A short, short life.

The difference was that this time he remembered

how he'd got into this position, but the memory was bitter rather than comforting. The woman – Malia: he'd found her only to lose her. He'd acted without caution and squandered his chance. The memory of her piquant face and the pain he'd seen there made his heart clench. So close, he thought. And now he was a prisoner.

Squinting over his shoulder revealed a barrel-lock keeping the manacles in place. If he could get hold of a nail or something, he thought, there was chance he might be able to work it into the lock mechanism.

He was bent over, trying to identify some way to get a purchase on one of the pins holding the leather to the bench, when a noise from the door caught his attention and he sat up fast. His pulse hammered in his ears like someone drumming on his skull, and as the door opened the room swam about him. Beyond the door was darkness and beyond that, a hundred miles away, light: framed against the darkness and the light was a woman wreathed in flame. The air shook around her, warped by heat and the howls of despairing souls. Drums roared at her every step. She was a hundred foot tall, and in her eight hands were blades, and her feet were painted with blood. A garland of severed arms encircled her famine-shrunken waist, blackened skulls made a necklace for her breasts, and from her staring eyes flame and blood poured out like tears upon a face mummified to a rictus-grin. The stink of burned bones rolled into the room before her. Veraine shrank back with a groan of horror.

Then she stepped into the tiny room, and she was no colossus, no hag; just a young woman, dark and slight, carrying a brass tray in her hands. The perfume she brought with her was the smell of jasmine, and though the hair falling about her shoulders was red as venous blood it was not aflame. She closed the door behind her. He sat paralysed.

'Veraine,' she said, folding to one knee before him, her face tilted up, her eyes brown and clear and framed by dense black lashes and heavy kohl. Her face was still; only those eyes betrayed her emotion. She laid the tray upon the end of the bench and he vaguely noted that there was food upon it. His pulse was rocketing.

'Malia,' he said hoarsely, when he was able to ungum his throat.

There was the slightest hesitation. 'It's been a long time since you called me that.'

He searched her face, trying to outstare that terrible visionary moment. It had been so brief, yet the visceral shock of it had left him trembling. Why should he have seen her like that, so terrible and so ugly, when this woman was neither? She was as pretty as any slave-girl might be expected to be, and he guessed she was some years younger than him. It was the first time he'd had a chance to take a proper look at her – in the garden he had been too hurried – and he drank in those arresting eyes and that generous mouth. Her hair was drawn up to a gold filigree net interlaced with tiny white flowers of jasmine, from which it tumbled in thick, loose curls. There were malachite beads on her leather collar and on her clothes too; a full skirt from which her smooth thigh emerged in a dark sweep, bare almost to the crotch, and a blouse so brief that it only just covered her breasts and was closed by a single lace. There was a narrow golden chain about her waist. Framed by that blouse, the cleft of her breastbone was threaded with gold and emeralds. Clothing like that was as provocative as nakedness, he thought.

He'd hoped with all his heart that when he met her,

he would know her. But he didn't. Only his flesh responded to her, with a deep ache that billowed up through the pain and the thirst and the fear. His mouth was as dry as ashes. He met her eyes again.

'Veraine,' she whispered, raising her hand as if to touch his face but faltering, leaving it suspended in the air. Henna lines traced foliage patterns upon her palm. 'Oh, my love . . .' And with those words he heard all her pain and her need, and it was like a window opening onto a place so intimate that he had to look away for a moment as the breath clotted in his chest.

We were lovers, he thought, and now he really was trembling. 'How long?' he asked hoarsely. 'Tell me. How long have we known each other?'

It was a brutal question to throw in her face. Her hand fell away. 'A year, maybe,' she said at last. 'I'm not sure. The seasons are different here. Veraine?'

'But you know me well.' He didn't mean to hurt her, but there wasn't any gentler way to do this and he had to know. He had to know. He would have liked to have taken her in his arms and held her tight until everything was revealed; that would have made it easier. When she nodded, he took a breath and spoke, his words broken and staggering under the weight of that imperative. 'I don't. I woke up. I woke up in the forest. I was on my own. I'd taken a blow to my head and I'd lost everything. Everything, do you see? The words, the names . . . I remember nothing.' He gritted his teeth. 'I don't remember how I got there. I don't remember you.'

She stared.

'It took so long. I recall bits and pieces, like broken pottery, but I can't put it together to make its true shape. I've no past. Nothing before the forest. And I don't know where I'm going. The only time I know what I should be doing is when there's a sword in my hand. Do you understand that? I know nothing. I came to find you. I needed you to tell me who I am.' He grimaced. 'It's too late now, isn't it? Too late to do any good.'

He waited for her to show surprise, horror, derision – to blame him or to weep for him, to reject him or shower him with questions or break down. Her face remained smooth, like a rock polished by the wind: watching.

His mouth tasted of wood-ash. He struggled on. 'Ah … I remember soldiers in white uniforms; I was among them. I remember your name, but not your face, just the red hair. And there are things I see in dreams,' he confessed uncomfortably; 'I don't know if they're memories or not. A pool of water, burning with flames. A cliff so high that you can hardly believe it, and I'm stood looking down terrified that I'll fall. A face, but it's blue. It doesn't make sense.'

'Yes, it does.' Her lips shaped the words gently. 'It was a mask. The blue face, I mean. One of my ritual masks from the temple.'

He exhaled. A priestess? he wondered. 'Who am I?' he whispered. The bare cell seemed to close in around them, cupping the fragile moment. 'Tell me – who am I?'

She tilted her head a little, measuring her words. 'You're General Veraine, commander of the Eighth Host of the Irolian Empire. When the Horse-eaters marched upon the Empire, you came to defend the Yamani holy city of Mulhanabin, at the edge of the desert. You held the city through siege and plague, and then led your men against the enemy host even though they far outnumbered you. Then the earthquake came and struck at the Horse-eaters, and you achieved victory where none could be sought, destroying them utterly.

You're a hero of your people. And in the moment of your triumph you left them, and you stole me from the temple, and we fled westward across the desert.' She paused, giving her words a moment to sink in. His face had gone stiff with shock. 'You're a legend,' she concluded.

He was speechless. He blinked, and he searched for a response, and then when he found none he shook his head and answered the preposterous news the only way possible; by laughing. His throat was sore, and his chuckles came out ragged and hoarse.

'Why's it funny?' she asked, not rebuking him as he thought for a moment, but with simple, almost childlike curiosity.

'A legend?' He raised his eyebrow to indicate the room, the predicament, his own helplessness, unable to keep the smirk off his face. 'A hero? Right.' The smirk became anguished. 'Right.'

She watched him as his smile died. For a while there was silence.

'Why?' he asked at last. 'Why did we leave them? Why come west?'

'You had a choice. You couldn't keep me and stay where you were.'

And it seems I chose you, he thought. Looking into those eyes he believed her, not because she was straining to convey the weight of conviction, but because she didn't. She spoke as if it were simple fact. He'd chosen her over acclaim and glory and his own homeland. He didn't understand it, but he believed. It frightened him a little. I must have wanted her very much, he thought. 'I loved you, then.'

'As the rain loves the earth.'

And he believed that too. Even now, across the space that separated them, her flesh pulled upon his. She drew him like the earth pulls at the falling rain. 'And what happened then?'

'We came through the Twenty Kingdoms, looking for a place to live. We were ambushed one night in the forest. Slavers. You were just starting a fire, blowing on the tinder, and – oh – we didn't hear them coming until too late.' For the first time she looked really agitated. 'They knocked you out and left you for dead. They brought me here. But I knew you'd find me. I knew you'd come.'

He grimaced. Her faith in him was tormenting, and his emotions were at war within him. This information was what he'd been waiting for, working for, all these weeks – but now he had no idea what to do with the knowledge. Did it make any real difference to hear his existence confirmed by another? Relief and guilt and frustration curdled together in his chest. Every muscle ached. His head ached. He was so close to her that he could smell the lemon-grass on her breath and feel her warmth. His cock, curbed like a champing horse, ached. We were lovers, he thought, and it was like a fist grinding in his guts. She knew every little thing about him; his habits, his peculiarities, his flaws. And he knew nothing at all about her. The lack made him squirm. He had no memory of the taste of those lips, the shape of her under his hands, the little noises she might make as her body yielded to his. He needed to know. Why, he wondered, had he loved her so much?

'I thought my heart had been torn apart,' she whispered.

'Come here,' he murmured. He could lean forwards, but the chain stopped him reaching her. 'Kiss me.'

She pulled back. 'I can't.'

'I want to remember your kiss.' His voice was husky. 'They would know.'

He clenched his jaw. He was very close to begging. 'Does it matter? Would it be much worse?'

'Much.' She turned aside and took a wooden fork from the tray. 'I'm not supposed to be here. Someone else was supposed to bring you food.' She was trembling. Piercing a sliver of mango, she kissed it, then held it to Veraine's lips. He took the sweet, moist flesh with his tongue and swallowed. The juice glistened on her full lips, warming him as the cool fruit could not. But it was unnerving to be so much at her mercy.

'Good?'

He nodded, tonguing a second piece. 'I'm very thirsty.'

She took up a wooden bowl then and, kissing the rim, offered it to him. His lips caressed the smooth wood where hers had rested. The liquid within was water sweetened with honey, and after a few sips he gulped greedily, draining it to the dregs as she held it up for him. A little water spilled down his chin, so needful was he, but she couldn't wipe his face.

'Malia,' he whispered, his eyes burning. 'Let me see you.' Her unattainable lips, softly parted in question, were a torment to him. She brushed her fingertips across the tie of her blouse, uncertainly. 'Please,' he groaned.

Without a word she stood. She moved gracefully, but her fingers as she tugged upon the knot of her blouse were gauche, almost clumsy. The top, which had been stretched tight across her breasts, swung open enough to allow a glimpse of silk-smooth curves and glimmering gold beneath, making the pulse leap in Veraine's veins. Stepping away, she turned her back so that he was transfixed by the jut of her buttocks, from which a curtain of green silk hung to her ankles. For a moment she paused. She slipped off the tiny blouse and let it fall, then pulled her hair forwards over her shoulder leaving her back, narrow and lithe with muscle, naked though far from unadorned.

Veraine took a deep breath. Printed across the width of her shoulder-blades was a fan of feathers; a peacock's tail inked in shimmering colours on her cinnamon skin, blue and green and purple and gold. It narrowed at its base to form a tail, but not the tail of a bird. Instead a snake's, feather-scaled in peacock-blue, wound in sinuous curves down her spine. As his eyes followed that path she released the tie of her skirt and let that slowly fall too, to pool around her feet. He saw that the snake's body disappeared into the cleft between cheeks as round and sweet as peaches. She was stunning. From behind, perhaps in contrast to her pert rear, her waist looked even narrower, the golden chain sitting snug just over her hips. Her skin was from top to toe as smooth as polished wood. Spiralling curlicues of painted henna clasped her heels and ankles and trickled up her calves like wisps of smoke.

She waited, wordless, for his verdict.

She was, Veraine thought, absolutely flawless. His erection surged and ramped like a war-stallion at the sound of the signal-trumpet. The breath died in his throat and his muscles knotted up unconsciously in response to his desire to put his hands on that slender waist and those smooth hips, to kiss and bite each staring eye of the feather bouquet and trace with his tongue the long path of the snake all the way to its lair. He wanted to feel that behind pressed into his groin. He wanted to send his own serpent delving into that secret cleft where the first had gone. He made an inarticulate noise in his throat and she looked over her shoulder at him. And now he saw trepidation in her eyes, as if she were awaiting judgement.

'Turn around,' he whispered.

Slowly, very slowly, she turned. He saw first where the serpent re-emerged: its jewelled head, the scales delicately detailed, lay over her shorn pubic mound – with the vertical slit of her sex forming its mouth. It would have been a very cruel joke, he thought, if it hadn't been so beautiful.

The second thing he saw was her jewellery. He had assumed she wore a necklace of gold strung with emeralds. It was a little more complex than that, and when his eyes had worked out what they were seeing it took his breath away. From her slave-collar hung a short chain to a sun-disc that rested flat upon her breastbone. From that two loose curves of chain led away across the sweep of her exquisite breasts to where her dark, erect nipples were pierced by gold rings. Another length of chain described a parabola below, from nipple to nipple. Three chains, enclosing a curved triangle. Her breath was coming hard as she stood beneath his scrutiny, and the little emeralds shook and quivered.

'Ah,' said Veraine involuntarily. The blood was charging to his groin and he was fully erect now, hard as rock, his warhorse armoured and frantic for the fray. He felt light-headed with the desire to take those chains in his mouth, to feel the hard links upon his tongue and lips as he gently pulled them. She would feel every individual link as they slid over his teeth.

The chain around her waist was no mere belt, either. Its circuit of her hips met at a link just beneath her navel, and from there descended to another ring pierced through her flesh. The tattooed serpent was hooked upon the gold ring that peeped from its mouth. Every time she took a step, he realised, the chain must tug softly upon her clitoris. The intention must be to keep her in a permanent state of arousal – or of frustration.

He had to look away in the end. He couldn't touch her, though she stood less than a stride from him, and it was unbearable. He couldn't even lift a hand in her direction, or to touch himself. 'I had no idea that you'd be so beautiful,' he whispered.

'They made me beautiful.'

He bit the inside of his cheek. 'Have they hurt you?'

'Many times.'

His chest tightened. He braced his wrists against the manacles until the metal bit into his skin. 'Forgive me,' he said, in a voice so hoarse it didn't sound like his own.

'What for?'

'For not protecting you.' His mouth was pulled into a tight line. 'For taking so long to find you. When I met you in the garden, I should have got you out of the palace. I should have taken you away. There were ways out.' He shook his head. 'This is all of my making. I've failed you.'

'Not yet, you haven't.'

He looked at the floor. I cannot bear this, he thought. His cracked soul was breaking up into fragments; even as he reeled under the burden of his culpability another part of him was avid with lust: he longed to feel those soft breasts beneath his lips, the firm buds of her nipples and the tiny gold links webbed between them, cool where they hung in midair and warm where they lay upon her skin. He wanted to kneel before her and press his face to the satin of her flat belly, and tongue that taut vertical chain until she cried and quivered from the insupportable sensitivity of her captive flesh. He yearned to taste the salt on her breastbone after their rutting. He wanted to kiss the serpent's mouth, and feel it open to him.

'Our options are limited from here on, I think,' he said, shaping his mouth carefully around the bitter syllables. Lust and guilt and fury churned below, and across the pitching surface rode his rational mind like a tiny boat in a heavy sea. 'Have you any idea what they plan to do with me?'

'Veraine . . .' She knelt back down before him, but she was naked now – and if he'd thought her desirable before, by this time she was like a flame burning in his head; an open furnace, too hot to look at directly. His spine was locked tight, his balls were so turgid with his cream that they must have been blue, and his cock was seeping. 'They are going to put you in the Arena; tomorrow or in a few days.'

'The Arena?' He had to ignore it. He had to concentrate on the practical. His body was insistent that if he could just hold her, if he could get his hands on her arse and get her thighs wrapped round his and his prick planted deep in the rich hot darkness between them, that if he could only take her to the floor and cover her, then everything would be all right, that nothing else would matter again.

'You're to face Dhammazhedi in combat.'

He tried to focus on her words and not to listen to his prick. 'And he is?'

'Their Rao: the king of the Tiger Lords. He kills people in the Arena for the sport of it. He's the strongest of them all, and you'll have to defeat him.'

'I see.'

'You don't see, yet. There are so few of the Tiger Lords, Veraine, in the midst of so many others. Only a score of them altogether, even including the small children, and they're hated in the city and the palace and all across the Twenty Kingdoms. They favour no one, not even their own guards. If we all rose up against them they wouldn't be strong enough to hold onto power – but no one will rise. The people don't know what it is not to fear, and not to obey. They don't even believe it is possible to slay one of the Harimau. They need hope. They need proof that it can be done.'

'Any man can die in battle.' Half his mind was on the way those chains quivered as her breasts rose and fell, the tiny emeralds shivering. 'No one's invulnerable.'

'Dhammazhedi is ruthless, and he holds his place as leader of the Tiger Lords by right of combat. He's bigger, stronger and faster than any normal man. If you kill him, in public, then you'll tear out the strength of the Harimau.'

Veraine was perplexed. 'You don't make it sound like I can.'

'I know you can. It's why you're here.'

He couldn't help wondering if the tattooed snake continued right down between her buttocks. 'I came to find you,' he reminded her, aching to mingle his tongue with hers and taste her breath as she yielded to orgasm.

'You were brought here by the gods to destroy the Harimau.'

He shook his head, and for a moment irritation overrode his lascivious imaginings. 'Oh no. Not the gods; don't you start that. The gods have nothing to do with this.'

She blinked. 'You haven't changed, then.'

'Why's that?'

'You always refused to acknowledge them.'

That he found perversely comforting. He snorted.

'I made a bargain on your behalf, Veraine.'

If there were gods, he thought, then they had shaped her lips expressly for the purpose of being pursed about a cock. And those eyes with those long lashes, downcast in concentration upon that task; could he picture anything more lovely? He cleared his throat. 'Wasn't that a little foolish?'

'You can do it, I promise. I know you. Do you trust me?'

He took a deep breath. 'I have no idea,' he confessed.

Ruefully she acknowledged this. 'I promise you; kill Dhammazhedi and there are many among the palace servants and the guards that will rise up and turn against the Harimau. It's been prepared. They're waiting. All you have to do is prove that it is possible, and they'll kill all the others.'

Her expectations seemed out of all proportion to his situation. He started to laugh. 'Even including the small children, I suppose?'

'All of them.'

He stopped laughing. He looked into her face and for the first time realised that behind that sweet desirability and that unearthly calm there was something altogether more disquieting. And finally he asked the question he should have voiced long before: 'Who are you?'

'I am the Malia Shai,' she answered.

Malia. Exactly what sort of temple had he stolen her away from?

Before he could say anything else she cocked her head. 'Someone's coming.' She jumped to her feet, snatching up her clothes. He didn't want her to go and the chain rattled as he tried reflexively to grab her. He had a thousand more questions and above all he needed to ask what had happened to Teihli and Rahul, but she laid her finger across her lips as she fled into the corner behind the door. The sound of armoured footfalls clashed in the corridor. Then the door was flung open and two guards walked in, taking up their stations at either side. Between them emerged a man so big that he had to duck his head to make it through the doorway.

Veraine gaped. He didn't have to fake it; this was the

biggest man he'd seen, considerably taller and broader-shouldered than he was himself, and not a fistful of that mass was superfluous fat. He didn't try to contain his surprise, and perhaps that helped to keep the Tiger Lord from noticing Malia slip from the corner behind his back and hurry away down the corridor, still naked and clutching her clothes. The eyes of the two guards flitted to her, but they didn't stir.

The Tiger Lord cocked one eyebrow, sneered, then sniffed the air. 'Have you had a woman in here?'

Veraine could smell the lingering perfume of jasmine too, but it was common practice for women to wear the fresh flowers in their hair. He looked deliberately at the tray of food and waited for the other to realise what a stupid question that was. His pulse was coming so hard he could feel it thudding in his skull.

'Ah.' The big man snapped his fingers. 'Shut the door,' he said and the guards retreated from the room, leaving him alone with his prisoner. 'Do I need to introduce myself?'

Veraine shook his head once. 'Rao Dhammazhedi.' If this wasn't the Tiger Lords' king, if there was someone bigger and meaner-looking than this man, then he truly didn't want to know.

'Well, given the circumstances we'll dispense with the formalities.' He folded his arms. 'I won't insist you get down on the floor.'

This one's a real bastard, thought Veraine. In other circumstances he might have wanted to stand up and meet this man on his feet but the chain made that all but impossible and in order not to still be looking up at him he'd have to be standing on the damn bench. Besides, if he straightened now it would be only too obvious that he had an erection that was far from appropriate in the altered circumstances.

'I thought I might call in before our terminal meeting. I like to see those I'm to be matched against, and let them see me.'

The Rao's canine teeth were quite pronounced, Veraine noted, light-headed. How the hell was he expected to fight this man? What was Malia thinking of?

'They tell me you can fight. It'll certainly make a change to find someone in the Arena who can. What's your weapon of choice?'

'A crossbow and a bloody tall tree,' he answered through gritted teeth.

Dhammazhedi laughed. He paced to the slit window and squinted out. 'You injured Anawrahta fairly badly – I'm still not sure how.' He clicked his tongue. 'But I find it quite irritating.' When he glanced back his eyes had trapped the sunlight and now glinted yellow. 'Do you have any idea how long it takes to build up a decent fighting force of my people? We breed slowly and mature slowly, and you've just crippled one of my best hopes for the next generation. I'm going to have to make a thorough example of you.'

Veraine held his tongue. He could tell a short fuse when he saw one. This man felt deeply dangerous – having to sit meekly in his presence with his hands tied outraged his every instinct.

The Rao circled the cell, dragging his fingers across the walls. His nails scored tracks in the plaster. Back in front of Veraine, he stopped to glower down. 'It's not going to be that much of a show though, is it? Me against a sorry-looking old man like you. Shall I give you some sort of weapon advantage? Or shall we just go at it tooth and nail? Which would you prefer, Mouse's Man?'

He met the Tiger Lord's eyes in silence, refusing to quail. It took all his self-control not to recoil when the

Rao dropped to a squat just where Malia had knelt so recently, grinning at him face-to-face.

'You look like you've seen better days, frankly,' Dhammazhedi purred. 'But hell, it's no wonder you've gone grey, old man. The girl's insatiable.'

Veraine's skin crawled.

'I've never met anyone who needed cock so much,' mused Dhammazhedi. 'She's wet for it all the time, wide open like a split melon. Begs for it. Moans for it. I have to keep slapping her off me.'

The taunting was stupidly crude, thought Veraine, and the Rao was mistaken to assume that he could be jealous of a woman when he didn't even remember her – but that didn't mean it didn't work. His fists clenched behind his back.

'She likes it best from behind; have you noticed? Like a bitch on heat. Head on the floor and arse in the air, cheeks spread wide. Hey, it works for me. You can get in good and tight that way, can't you, right to the root ... Really feel your rocks banging.' He savoured the words, then winked conspiratorially. 'And you get a choice of targets, of course. Her cunt's incredible, isn't it? Don't you miss it? So hot and juicy-wet ... It's like boiling honey; sweet and dark and so fucking good you can't get enough of it.' Dhammazhedi lips curled. 'And you've got to give it to her hard: that's the way she wants it. Slamming in all the way, like you're trying to beat her brains out.'

Veraine's expression was like stone, but his whole body seethed.

Dhammazhedi grinned ruefully. 'It's not so tight though, these days, as it was before I started on her. She got a bit ... stretched, you know. I've probably ruined her for other men.' His eyes twinkled. 'You want tight, you have to go for her other hole. She likes it that way too – and gods, the grip on her! You can hardly believe it, can you? She gets a hold and she just wrings the spunk out of you. That sweet little round arse could drink a gallon of hot jism.' He paused, running his tongue across his lips, his eyes upon Veraine's flushed face. 'You know, just thinking about it is giving me the bone.' He ran his hand up the inside of his thigh, patting what was clearly a tumescent ridge beneath the cloth. 'What about you?' he whispered playfully.

Veraine, his muscles rigid with tension, was starting to shake. Despite the coolness of the cell sweat was standing out on his temples.

Dhammazhedi reached up and grabbed his prisoner by the hair, yanking him to the full extent of the chain. His other hand went straight for Veraine's crotch. 'Thought so,' he laughed, squeezing cock and balls savagely. 'You like the idea of me on your woman, don't you? Did you think I couldn't tell?'

'Wrong.' Veraine's lips pulled back into a snarl. 'I'm thinking of the moment when I'm going to cut your throat.'

For a moment Dhammazhedi didn't seem to react. Then he bunched his fist and drove it into Veraine's groin, almost casually, once and then a second time. 'I wouldn't count on that,' he grunted. Veraine convulsed, defenceless and unable to escape; the pain was blinding. Dhammazhedi punched him again, in the guts this time. 'Remember this, Mouse's Man,' the Rao said as he stood and prepared to leave the room. 'You think about it as they put you into the Arena.'

Veraine lay silent, his whole body clenched with pain. He was fighting an overwhelming urge to vomit. Let the bastard think he's broken me, he said to himself, his face pressed to the bench and spittle running through his bared teeth to make a wet patch on the leather. It will give me that much more pleasure when I kill him.

The terrace above the Arena was filled for the day of Veraine's death. Displays of Dhammazhedi's prowess were always a source of fascination for family members. Rugs and cushions in a rainbow of colours were spread upon the stone tiers, and lounging on them were many of the Harimau; Myrna counted six of the women, each with her own entourage of slaves and officials. Rather fewer of the male Harimau were in attendance, though there was as usual a little cluster discussing the Rao's form that day and the perennial question of when, if ever, his dominance would start to slip.

Myrna knelt at Shinsawbu's hip as she reclined upon her cushions. As the Rao's favourite sister, her mistress had the choicest position on the terrace and their view of the rock-cut Arena was unrivalled. They could see every part of the enclosure except for that directly before them, where the overhanging wall dropped to the sandy floor. The terrain within was almost natural, with tumbled boulders and sparse shrubs providing some cover. In places the bare soil was darkened by the stains of prior combats. There were only three ways into the Arena: the gate in the palisade on the far side; a flight of steps leading down from the terrace; and – unseen beneath them – a tunnel through the rock by which human prey were introduced from the cell-block.

As she watched, guards brought out two prisoners and chained them to a dead tree in the centre. Myrna's heart jumped painfully, but neither was Veraine. There were guards stationed at intervals all along the lip of the terrace, theoretically there to prevent anything climbing out of the Arena. Narathu Min had picked his men carefully that day.

This is it, thought Myrna. Today everything changes, one way or another.

Shinsawbu ran her hand idly up Myrna's bare back, tracing the line of the serpent to its feathered tail. In other circumstances the touch might have been pleasurable. She shivered.

'Excited, Mouse?'

'I'm sure you can tell, my queen.' Myrna didn't try to hide her anxiety. She'd been able to think of little else but this hour. He would be fighting for his life and every fibre in her body was stretched like a wire. That was, of course, what Shinsawbu would expect, and Myrna hoped that it would help distract her from the tension exuded by others. Sao Mor stood behind his Lady, gazing into the Arena and fanning himself, his expression locked shut and unreadable.

Shinsawbu chuckled and reached up to pluck the jewellery at Myrna's breasts, tugging the chains until fire ran across her skin and tears jumped to her eyes. 'Thinking of him?' she purred.

'Yes, my queen.'

'It shows. Maybe I should have them gilded, they stand so proud.' The Tiger Lady chuckled and relaxed back on her side. 'Make the most of it. He'll not last long.'

Myrna looked down from under her lashes at the jut of Shinsawbu's hip and the sweep of her bare thigh. So far she showed no physical sign of pregnancy, but she spoke often of how she would bear Dhammaz's children this year – twins, naturally. I will never have to see that, Myrna thought. After today, she will not touch me again. One way or another.

Seeing Veraine had thrown her emotions and her body into turmoil; Shinsawbu was right about that. And she couldn't stop thinking of him. Of how he'd looked chained in the cell, haggard and grim like a caged hawk, his shoulders pulled back, the breadth and the strain of his chest emphasised by the pinning of his arms behind him. The scent of his skin, so familiar to her, had instantly evoked the warmth between her thighs. She'd been desperate to touch him, to clasp his face and kiss his lips and bite the lobes of his ears, to smooth back his tangled hair from his temples and bury her face in his neck, to feel his stubble rasping against her cheek. It had been an almost insupportable temptation.

Remembering it, she ached for him, softening like warm wax.

Chained, he couldn't touch her. His strength was constrained by his bonds. Yet even that had tempted her: standing over him, feeling the heat of his gaze upon her naked flesh, she had imagined herself pushing him back and baring his crotch and taking her pleasure with mouth or with yoni upon it, taking full advantage of his lack of control. He wouldn't have been able to stop her. He would have submitted to her, helpless and ecstatic.

The realisation that his vulnerability aroused her had shaken her to the core.

And his eyes ... they had shaken her too. Hot with desire and then aching with torment; eyes that both burned and bled. And then so cold, so filled with distrust. When she'd first entered the cell, she'd thought for a moment that he looked at her with horror. It was a long time since she'd seen him look at her with that expression. It had happened before. She had hoped it would never happen again.

He had forgotten her. He did not love her.

As if from a great distance she saw Dhammazhedi emerge onto the terrace and salute his admiring family. Everyone applauded. His feet were bare and he wore no armour, only shirt and trousers. Steel waghnakh glinted on his hands. He came down the tiers until he was standing within arm's reach, then he stooped to kiss Shinsawbu. 'You are lovely, my queen.'

As he turned away, he spared Myrna a glance. He smiled. No words, just a knowing, wicked smile that promised her a world of grief.

'This is what you've waited for,' murmured Shinsawbu, watching him descend the stairs. 'I hope you appreciate it.'

Myrna swallowed. She couldn't imagine living without Veraine's love. Not now. If that had been possible she would have stayed in the desert. There was nothing else that mattered to her in this incarnation. She would not live without him – one way or another.

They gave him some time to prepare for the fight, unshackling him the night before so that he might stretch his muscles and sleep more comfortably. Then in the morning guards brought him, to his surprise, new clothes and armour: a linen tunic, hob-nailed sandals which wrapped right around the ankles, greaves for his shins and vambraces for his forearms, a kilt of stiffened leather strips and a breastplate. A design of stars was embossed on the bronze. He wasn't going to complain at the unexpected generosity. The armour was unfamiliar to him but his hands knew exactly what to do, pulling and buckling on the pieces in the right order, adjusting each so it gripped snugly and didn't rub. He would have appreciated a helmet of some kind too, but that wasn't on offer.

He waited for hours until they finally marched him to a holding room cut from unfaced stone. The guards were uncommunicative; they seemed on edge. Veraine looked for Malia but there were no women in sight. He wondered if her planning for the rebellion was going well, but then dismissed the thought. It hardly mattered to him. Whether he lived or died was down to how well he could fight Dhammazhedi. The guards lined up to block the passageway behind him, while ahead was a wooden door with light leaking through the jamb. His stomach churned with pre-battle nerves and he longed for a drink. His bladder complained even though he'd already emptied it. His arm muscles twitched, desperate for action. Give me a weapon, he urged silently.

An officer, an older man with a close-cropped beard who looked faintly familiar, came and stood toe to toe with him. 'Give your eyes time to adjust to the light,' he said in a low voice. 'He's already in the Arena, waiting for you, but he won't make his move straight away. He wants to make a show of it. That's why he's not likely to pin you against the wall either.'

Veraine drew a deep breath, his eyes locked on the other man's.

'There are two shields hanging out there,' the officer continued. 'Don't go for the bronze one: it's fixed in place. Don't try for any of the exits; they're barred.'

Veraine nodded slightly.

'The Rao fights with his guard wide open and always leads with the right hand. Don't underestimate him – but if you're any good, chances are he'll be underestimating you.'

'Right.'

'Good luck.' Then he handed over a short-sword with a bronze blade. It was designed for stabbing rather than slashing, and hardly the best weapon to take up against a man with as much reach as Dhammazhedi. Nevertheless he felt such a sensation of relief that he could have laughed out loud.

The only time I know what I should be doing is when

247

I've got a sword in my hand, he'd told Malia. Battle, once joined, left no room for doubt, for thought, not even for fear.

'You're used to one like that?' the officer asked.

'Oh yes.'

The other man stepped aside and signalled. The door was pulled open and light – the kind of harsh sunlight that Veraine hadn't been exposed to in days – roared in to the dim room. He blinked hard, remembering the advice he'd been given, and stepped out only once he had some idea of what it was he was facing; a landscape of sand and rocks and curved perimeter walls. There were three dead trees at equal spacing from his doorway. Well above his head the rock-face belled out into an overhang: there was no escape that way. To his right stone stairs hugged the wall. He stepped from the narrow strip of shade, feeling the sun warm on his shoulders, moving in a half-crouch, ready to leap aside. His eyes searched the Arena, distrusting every shadow and bush and boulder.

The tree to his left had a metallic shield lodged in a low branch. The one on the right held a grey shield. And chained to the base of the third were Teihli and Rahul, staring at him.

'You piece of shit,' he whispered.

He moved cautiously out into the open. Above his head came a swell of sound, the belling of an audience; but he spared them no more than a moment's glance, long enough to take in the sentries posted round the top of the wall. Then a flicker of movement to his left caught his attention and he whipped round. It wasn't Dhammazhedi. Lying on top of a boulder, its paws crossed in front of it, was a full-grown tiger.

Veraine felt sick. He'd not anticipated having to fight more than one foe, and he rated his chances against an animal of that size as very slight indeed. The tiger yawned, displaying teeth like yellow knives, and the crowd above howled in approval. It sat up, its barred pelt rippling. Veraine fell back in a defensive crouch, the short-sword held at guard position before him even though he suspected it was going to do him no good at all. If a thing that size jumped him there was no way he could keep his feet. He had to get a shield.

The tiger slipped down from its rock, muscles flowing like molten gold. The crowd howled encouragement. It stalked Veraine as he retreated, its head low and shoulders hunched. Its muzzle wrinkled in a derisive snarl and thin strings of drool slid out. Its pupils were narrowed to slits.

Don't turn your back, he told himself, feeling for each step. He didn't dare take his eyes from the animal: their mutually locked gaze seemed to be the only force holding them apart. Step by shuffling step he retreated towards the tree with the grey shield.

The tiger paused. Then it turned aside, twitching its tail, and walked away. Veraine gained a few hasty yards of ground, breaking into a shuffling sideways trot before he realised what had distracted the beast: it was heading for Rahul and Teihli. The dry lining of his mouth grew sour. The choice was stark: his friends or a shield. He could almost think that the tiger was doing it from deliberate malice. Teihli began to scream, throwing herself back and forth in her bonds and shrieking as if by sheer volume she could scare the predator off. Rahul didn't scream until the tiger reached up to hook a paw in his shoulder. It moved lazily, with casual brutality, letting its weight tear those claws through the skin. Veraine stooped and grabbed a stone. He threw it with all his might and it struck the tiger behind the ear just as it closed in to gnaw. Golden dust flew from its fur and it turned, spitting and shaking its head, forgetting Rahul as it launched itself towards the stone-thrower.

Veraine ran. He leapt as he reached the bare tree and his fingers made contact with the shield, knocking it loose, but it caught against a branch and didn't fall into his grasp, flying wide instead. He had no time to try and retrieve it: he threw himself round the trunk of the tree just as the tiger closed in and its first blow raked down the barkless wood, leaving parallel furrows. Veraine kept the trunk between him and it as it struck twice more, and on the third blow its claws bit too deep and momentarily caught there. He took the chance, darting out on that side and stabbing as he ran past its shoulder. It whirled, spitting. He felt the point of his sword hit bone, jarring his wrist, and then he stooped to seize the shield handle and threw himself across the sand in a rolling dive. He came up on his feet scored all up one side with gravel and had just enough time to register that the shield was made of thick curved plates of rhinoceros hide and get it up between him and the tiger, before the beast hit him, staggering him backwards. But it hadn't thrown its whole weight into the attack; it was batting at him with its front paws, crouched on its hind legs. He turned the first blow aside and, as the second scraped off his breastplate, thrust up at its throat. The blade bit deep.

Not deep enough, though. For a moment he hoped he'd got up through its jaw and into its skull, but the tiger lurched backwards, spitting and shaking its head in confusion. Blood gleamed on the white fur of its throat and more ran from its mouth as that opened in a squall of fury, but the animal didn't fall. Veraine caught sight of the crumpled tip of his sword and realised that the soft bronze had folded over when it had hit solid bone.

He didn't waste time cursing. He had a moment of respite now while the tiger gathered its wits and he used it to find firm footing and brace himself. The tiger roared. The sound seemed to punch into Veraine's breastbone and stop his heart; he barely reacted in time as it came forwards, slashing at him low this time. If it hadn't been for the greaves he would have had the legs taken out from beneath him. It was all but impossible to strike back during the following flurry: the animal came in hard and fast with blow after blow that slammed his shield arm back against his body and kept him on the retreat. If he'd had more leisure to think about it he might have puzzled at its style; it hit much harder and higher up on his shield side, barely swinging with its left paw, and making no attempt to bite. But he didn't have time to mull this over; only to react with a warrior's instinct, finally seizing the split-second chance to parry the tiger's offhand blow with the sword-edge. He felt the blade bite.

Yowling, it threw itself upon him with its entire weight. There was no way he could stand up under that assault: before he knew it he was on his back in the dirt with the shield mashed into his jaw and his sword-arm pinned under the furry bulk. He felt something in his left wrist snap. The hot coppery stink of the tiger's breath nearly choked him as he struggled, and its teeth filled his vision, and because he couldn't get his sword free he simply resorted to letting it go and punching the animal in the head with his fist, aiming for the eyes. The weight pinning him slackened momentarily. He struggled free, rolling over in the dirt. For a moment just being able to breathe clean air was enough, then he blinked the grit from his eyes and forced himself up onto his knees, his lungs heaving. There was a hot sensation down the outside of his right leg that he knew without even having to look was his blood running free. He spat some more into the dust. Somehow he still had the shield but he wasn't holding it right; his hand wasn't working properly and though he couldn't feel any actual pain his whole shield-arm was ablaze with a white inner light that he knew well enough would be pain very soon.

He didn't have the sword at all. It lay in the sand, out of his reach, the bronze blade gleaming like gold in the sunlight. Over it the tiger crouched with tail lashing and lips drawn back in a snarl, gathered to spring.

Myrna saw Veraine go down and nearly cried out: when he got to his knees again it felt like her heart was restarting. Even from where she sat high up among the spectators the injuries of both antagonists were quite clear, and great dark runnels were staining the dust they were both plastered in. The audience seethed.

Sao Mor's casual suggestion to his mistress, that the Irolian might look best dressed for the part, had paid off. From somewhere they'd found him armour – nothing like so fancy as his General's equipage, but authentic enough – and though what really mattered was that it gave Veraine an advantage in the battle, to Myrna it brought back all the wonder and the strangeness of him. Her heart had been in her mouth. He was beautiful, she thought: the white tunic glowing against his skin, the muscles of his long bare legs, the proud and watchful tilt of his head.

And he'd drawn first blood. She'd never seen that done to Dhammazhedi. Nobody had ever seen a genuine fight between the Rao and a prisoner go on so long or so viciously before. Both men were now battered and bloody, and Dhammazhedi was clearly furious. It was written on his face and proclaimed in his savage, unconsidered attacks; it was painted in gore down his throat and chest. This was not what he'd been expecting. His arrogance in entering the fray against an armoured opponent had been richly punished.

But now he had the edge. Veraine faced him swordless, and with his shield-arm hunched awkwardly. It was going to be over in seconds. Myrna was on her feet as soon as she saw the sword fall. Hesitation was impossible; she dared not let Shinsawbu catch an inkling of her plan. Even as she sprang down the steps, skirts flying, she expected the slice of nails in the skin of her back.

'Mouse!' The Tiger Lady's voice, some way behind her, sounded exasperated.

The guards were, like everyone else, intently watching the combat below. They'd all been briefed by their captain, but Myrna ran for Shwe, the young man who already owed her his life. She slammed into his arm and seized his halberd; he released it instantly and suddenly she was only a pace from the lip of the wall. She launched the weapon almost without breaking stride, hurling it as far as she could towards the centre of the Arena. Then she jumped out into space after it, falling in a whirl of green silk. For a moment she hung above the golden oval of the sand, bathed in light, the air cupping her like the hands of a lover. Then the earth rose to meet her, hard.

The halberd came from nowhere, striking the oblique surface of a boulder and skittering across the ground. As far as Veraine was concerned it might have fallen from the hands of the gods. Just for a moment the tiger glanced to Veraine's side. He stooped and swept up a handful of sand and tiny stones, flinging it into the animal's eyes, and then he sprinted for the new weapon. The shield, so precious a moment before, fell from his slack grasp. The tiger, spitting in fury, seemed only a hair's breadth behind him as his fingers closed round the halberd's wooden shaft. Then he turned, dragging the broad spearhead of the weapon up. Nothing had ever seemed to move so slowly. He didn't have time to brace it or himself before his enemy was on top of him, just to get it pointed in roughly the right direction before the impact staggered him backwards. His feet slid from under him and he half-fell; only the fact that he was clinging to the wooden shaft kept him from going over completely. The butt of the spear wedged up hard against a rock. The other end drove up into Dhammazhedi's chest.

Veraine very nearly let go then. He blinked the stinging sweat from his eyes, not understanding what it was that he was looking at. It was no tiger impaled on the end of the weapon; it was Rao Dhammazhedi. The shaft had entered his body just under the right collar-bone and the tip of the blade was jutting out behind his shoulder. The man's jaw was set and his teeth bared in a rictus grin of pain.

Not for one moment had Veraine given credence to the stories of tiger-demons who shifted shape between man and beast. Not for a moment. The shock nearly paralysed him. He didn't react as the Rao placed one hand on the shaft – it was the left hand and the thumb and first finger had been shorn off – nor when he raised the other. He wore steel tiger-claws, Veraine noticed dumbly.

Dhammazhedi struck the spear-shaft with the heel of his hand. The wood snapped between his hands and he roared in pain. Veraine, still clutching the butt-end, fell back and rolled away, his body taking over where his mind seemed unable to get a purchase. He found his feet and shifted his grip on the wood. Dhammazhedi swayed.

You should be dead, Veraine thought: You've got a spear through you. Lie down. Lie down, monster.

For a moment Dhammazhedi touched the slippery stub of the halberd as if contemplating whether he could pull it out of his body. His hair hung down around his face in wet ringlets. Then he grunted and grinned at Veraine, his teeth red from gum to gum. Blood was still welling out from the puncture wound on the underside of his jaw, and had painted him crimson to the waistband of his trousers. The speed and the whirlwind fury of the tiger had gone out of him and he was unsteady on his feet, but he was still armed and very much a threat. His eyes were as yellow and bitter as poison. It wasn't over yet.

The two men began to circle, facing each other across the trampled, clotted sand. Veraine could feel the sweat running down his spine. The piece of wood he'd been left holding was about the length of his arm and he spun his wrist, getting used to the relatively slight weight. Peripherally he was aware that the spectators above were on their feet, screaming at the two of them. Then he became aware of the figure of Malia, crouched on the Arena sand near the shadow of the wall. She was gasping for breath. His heart flipped over.

As if sensing Veraine's weakness, Dhammazhedi glanced her way. 'She's come to die with you?' he asked softly. 'How sweet.'

Veraine forced himself to smile. He'd heard the tightness in the Rao's voice and the bubbling note in his throat: the bigger man was bleeding into his lungs. Given enough time, he'd go down for lack of breath. The trouble was that Veraine didn't have time: he was tiring badly.

'I think I'll screw her across your corpse,' said the Rao, and without warning lunged across the space between them. It was lucky for Veraine that the spear through his shoulder was weakening his right arm; Veraine managed to catch the blow on his vambrace and throw it off, all but a few scratches. Then he struck back, smashing the Rao on the side of the face with the wooden shaft, putting everything he had into that blow: by rights it should have felled the other man. Dhammazhedi just staggered. 'Not good enough,' he snarled.

Veraine's muscles felt like they were filled with lead. He hit him again, but not on the head – this time he struck the broken shaft protruding from his chest.

That hurt. Dhammazhedi arched his back, his mouth opening in a silent scream. Veraine reversed the piece of wood in his hand and drove the splintered end up beneath the other man's diaphragm, deep into his chest. Dhammazhedi folded to his knees. Veraine, weaponless, kicked him in the guts as hard as he could, staggered back a few steps while he got his breath again, then kicked him in the head.

The crowd went suddenly silent.

I need to sit down, Veraine thought, but rage kept him going. He walked away, looking for the abandoned short-sword. Every step he took on the coarse ground sounded loud in his ears.

When he turned back, Dhammazhedi had still not fallen. The Rao was kneeling, one hand on the ground, one pressed to his torso. Right in front of him stood the slave-girl he called Mouse, her gaze locked on his. For a moment Veraine feared that he was still capable of slashing her with those steel claws, but no one moved. The slender woman, bare-breasted and beautiful, stood motionless, only the green silks of her skirt stirring. Her face was expressionless, like polished stone.

She has desert eyes, Veraine thought: bare earth, hiding nothing and offering nothing.

Dhammazhedi's mouth was slackly open, his face grey.

He sees *her*, realised Veraine. He sees death.

Then he stepped in with the blade and opened the Tiger Lord's throat.

It's done, thought Myrna. He did it. She turned and looked up at the audience. Everyone was on their feet now, from Tiger Lords to slaves. They stood staring. Not a whisper broke the silence.

'He did it,' she said. Her voice was hoarse. Some of the guards were stealing their first glances at one another, but they were the only ones moving. Come on, she urged, clenching her fists. She was shaking.

Shinsawbu took three paces towards the lip of the terrace. In her ashen face was the first presentiment of what she must be feeling as she looked down on the corpse of her beloved brother and lover and king. Then Sao Mor stepped up behind her, drawing from the sling on his arm a narrow steel blade which he drove up with all his might between his Lady's shoulders.

Myrna shut her eyes. The silence exploded into tumult.

'It was a tiger,' Veraine's voice said harshly, and when she turned he was glaring at her. Under the crust of sand and the glaze of sweat his muscles stood proud from the fighting. But he didn't look triumphant. His mouth was twisted and there was a warning glitter in his black eyes. 'A tiger!' he repeated, closing on her.

'Yes,' she said. 'Dhammazhedi.'

'No – not Dhammazhedi.' His eyes were locked on hers; he didn't even seem to notice the strife that had erupted on the terraces. 'Not a Tiger Lord,' he said vehemently; 'not a man at all. A tiger. A hulking great cat. Is that what you saw me kill?'

'I saw Dhammazhedi.' Her belly was molten but she didn't dare reach out for him. The world seemed to shrink to a tiny bubble containing only her and this raging man. She scrabbled for some sort of understanding. 'He looked like a man to me, just as ever.'

'Not to me.'

'You saw his spirit, maybe.'

Veraine stopped in his tracks. The whites of his eyes flashed. If it had been any other man she would have thought from his expression he was about to strike her. His breath hissed out from between clenched teeth. 'No spirit. That was no spirit. It had stripes and teeth and a tail. I smelt its stinking breath. I felt its fur and the weight and the heat of it. It was real.' He grimaced violently, baring his teeth. 'There's something wrong with me!' he groaned, and Myrna suddenly saw the terror that underlay his fury. 'I see things that aren't there. I can't tell the difference between vision and reality. I don't know what's real and what's illusion.' For a moment his eyes pleaded with her.

She had only the comfort of her temple upbringing to offer. 'All the material world is illusion,' she said softly. 'There is nothing real but the Divine, dancing in the void.' But she saw the anger and contempt snap back into his gaze like she'd slapped him.

'This isn't real, then?' He wiped his palm across a cut on his forehead and brandished the blood at her. Then he caught her by the throat, his fingers in the angle of her jaw, and he wasn't gentle. 'What about this?' he snarled into her face.

Her whole body cried out for his touch, wrenching her breath away.

'Is this real?' he cried.

Myrna caught his face in both hands and pulled him down to her. 'This is,' she whispered, her lips meeting his.

The melting warmth of her mouth; the softness of her lips on his rough, torn, dry ones – he felt it burst in his head like the opening of a flower. The world spun, and for a moment he could barely respond. He felt her pulse racing beneath his hand and felt the trembling strain in her body. The honeyed tip of her tongue melded with his. With searching kisses, her mouth sweet and supplicant, she peeled back layer after encrusted layer of his distrust and wrath and hurt until she uncovered the clean, hot desire that lay beneath. Then she ignited it.

His whole body, every fibre of it, caught fire. The sword dropped from his hand. Scooping her up he backed her against the wall, into the embrace of its shadow, pinning her slender frame between him and the rock. She wrapped her legs round his hips and her arms about his shoulders and bit his lower lip passionately. He turned on her with devouring kisses, stealing her breath with his own as if he would eat her soul. Frantic messages of pain signalled all over his body from nicks and strains and sundered flesh, but he ignored them and pressed his aching hand upon her breast where it so needed to be, and the pain drowned beneath the rising tide of his lust. He felt the hard jewellery under his palm but the only jewel that really mattered was her nipple, jutting from the warm wave-swell of her breast. She cried his name. He wanted to rip off his armour and press his skin against hers, to feel those breasts soft against his bare chest, but there was no time for such niceties: his need was too urgent.

This was going to be quick, he realised. In another situation he might have felt embarrassed. This was going to be swift, unsophisticated, and to the point.

She was slight, her weight negligible, and he held her easily against the rock face. She wore no chain about her middle this time; her waist was smooth to the touch. Her skirts offered no obstacle to his hand, no more than his own tunic and kilt. Under the tumble of fabric she was smoother than silk, and every inch was warmer and tighter and more irresistible than the last until he found that narrow cleft, slippery and yielding, which was the goal of his desire, of his hope, perhaps of every step he had taken since waking in the forest. She was like butter melting on his hand and the smell of her sex was spicy-hot and utterly intoxicating. A tiny noise, almost a whimper, escaped her at his touch. He brushed against the ring in the serpent's mouth as he guided his cock into her, and the gold was just as warm as her flesh and as slick with her juices but far harder, drawing a line of heightened sensation down his length as he entered. She twisted her hips, opening herself to him, a fluttering gasp escaping from her throat.

Just for a moment after penetration, secure in his possession at last, Veraine paused. Malia's face was turned up towards his, her mouth a little open and her lips swollen with desire. Under her thick lashes her pupils were dilated with a fearful joy. He brushed his lips slowly against hers, soundless, even his breath held. The time for words was over; only his cock could speak for him now. It was thick with unexpressed desire, turgid with the burden of the secrets it longed to spill.

Malia clenched around him. His cock surged of its own accord, and then there was no holding back any longer. He pressed into her, the muscles of his arse knotted like fists, with quick trembling strokes. Her bare heels drummed the back of his legs. With his good hand he gripped the firm flesh of the back of her thigh. Soft moans fluttered in her throat. Light flashed behind Veraine's eyes and he closed them, sinking swiftly into the river of sensation. The waters were dark and deep and swift, sweeping him towards the white spume of the rapids and the final dizzying fall. Every thrust pushed him further on towards that drop. Every thrust nailed him to her. Every thrust was a blow upon a door whose lintel was bleeding light.

'Oh!' she gasped. There was little room in her lungs for breath.

With every blow the door buckled, letting the light in. There were things behind the door he recognised. 'It's . . .' he groaned, but never finished. 'Oh gods.'

Malia licked his throat, her tongue rasping on the stubble beneath his jaw. 'Veraine –' She licked him again, in a long shivering stroke. He hadn't been wrong about the swiftness of his approaching crisis. The door crashed back on its hinges. He came with his eyes wide open, hardly seeing the rough rock wall or the curve of her cheek. And in the whirlpool midst of his ecstasy all the doors in his head flew open, one after another, and the light fell upon him in hammer blows, blinding white.

He remembered everything.

Piece after piece of his past slid into place, and he saw himself as if for the first time: Bastard-born son of a noble of the Eternal Empire and one of his many concubines. Raised as a slave on his father's estate. Adopted on a narcissistic whim at fourteen, and thence thrown into the savage world of the Imperial Army's officer cadets. An outsider in a barracks where every other boy was a firstborn son of pure blood. Always an outsider, all his life. He'd had to earn the respect of his military superiors and fight for every ounce of it from his peers. He'd been a good soldier, a talented officer, and finally a rising star of a general. His men had trusted, even liked him. Then he'd betrayed them all.

They had been right, the ones who'd said a slave-born man would never be truly loyal to the Empire.

He remembered the city in the desert. He remembered the great temple of Malia, goddess of the killing earth, of famine and drought and plague. He remembered battling the Horse-eaters. He remembered everything he'd done; things to be proud of and things of which he was bitterly ashamed.

He remembered her, the Malia Shai. The fey, half-crazed girl, worshipped as the living incarnation of a goddess by her people, who had driven him halfway to madness himself with desire and carnal frustration. How he'd in turn been filled with pity, infuriated and then repelled by her, how she had made him challenge everything he thought he knew about himself, how no attitude of his had been sufficient until he'd surrendered to his obsession and his need and he'd held her beneath him and heard her gasp, 'I want you.'

And he knew at last why it was so important that he reclaim his past. Not because it told him who he was – he knew who he was, and if he'd had the sense to listen to Rahul then he'd have recognised that long ago – but because it showed him what he was not. Not a ruthless overlord like his father, cold-hearted enough to watch his own children kill one another. Not a slave like his mother, broken and embittered by fate. Not a brutal spoke in the Empire's iron-shod wheel of conquest and control. Not an ambitious young commander. Not even a loyal servant of a power and a dynasty far greater than himself. He might have been any of those things but he had renounced them all, for good or ill, when he had chosen her; the Malia Shai.

He was hers, just as she was his.

He had remade himself for her. Nothing else, he thought, would have been adequate for the extraordinary woman who had surrendered herself, heart and flesh, to him, but whose soul was no man's – was hardly of this world at all. She was as innocent as Mehetchi, as terrible as the Rani Mirabai, as passionate and loving as Teihli. For a vertiginous moment Veraine wondered if any of those women had been real, or if they were not just fragments of his dream of her. Then he laughed at himself, still dizzy with wonder. He saw every woman in her. Wasn't that the way with goddesses?

Veraine blinked his eyes back into focus at last. He was still under the Arena wall, still holding her. Her body was moulded to his. Damp tendrils of hair clung to her temples. 'Myrna,' he whispered.

She smiled tremulously, and he saw the tears that had been brimming in her eyes spill softly down her cheeks. He kissed them away. She touched his face with her fingertips and they kissed again tenderly. Then he set her down, slipping from her and encircling her waist with his arm, offering her support as her legs threatened to give way beneath her. He had besmirched her coppery skin with the grime of his own, he noticed, and was unable to resist brushing his fingers across the soft mound of her sex one more time. She shuddered and flushed, suddenly heavy in his arm as the aftershocks of pleasure shook her. He laughed, moved by delight and wonder.

For a time they held each other. Veraine was still trying to get to grips with the vistas of memory laid open in his mind, and revelling in the newly discovered familiarity of her scent, her form, her touch. He thought he might hold her forever. But slowly the sounds of the world above, the shouts and screams and grasps of conflict, filtered back into their charmed circle. What had seemed to him to have changed the whole world had taken only a few moments.

Myrna spoke first. 'They need you. You should go and help them.'

'I'm not leaving you again.'

She traced the broken outline of his lips with her fingers. Her eyes were huge and serious. 'You won't be. Go on – give them a leader.'

She was right of course. He couldn't hide under the overhang of the wall until it was all over, merely hoping that the battle had swung their way. Regretfully he released her and went to retrieve the sword for a second time. A glance towards the centre of the Arena showed him that Teihli was kneeling over Rahul, staunching his wounded shoulder with her shawl. He seemed to be conscious and talking to her. That would have to be dealt with later: for the moment it was good enough.

Veraine flexed his shoulders, girding himself for another effort. He was tired, but the real pain hadn't kicked in yet; his blood was singing in his veins. With one last glance at Myrna, a glance that held an aching unspoken promise, he hurried for the stairs.

Myrna leaned back against the wall, glad for the moment of its solidity. She ran her fingers down her breastbone and belly, feeling the fire of orgasm still fizzing beneath her skin. Then she stepped out from the shade and raised her face to the sun, welcoming its fierce caress upon her closed lids and her bare breasts. The slippery chrism of Veraine's anointing seeped from her and ran down the inside of her thighs. 'Thank you,' she whispered, ecstatic. 'You brought him back to me. Thank you.'

Then she turned to the stairs too, not moving swiftly as Veraine had, but with a measured, deliberate pace. The fire under her skin didn't die; it drew heat from the sunlight and danced up her spine and along her bones. It blazed in her belly like a second sun. She could not hide in the relative safety of the Arena any more than Veraine could. Her place was in the midst of the destruction that she had wrought.

Wreathed in flame, the goddess Malia trod the battlefield.

13 **A New Song**

Myrna opened the birdcage door and pinned it up with a sliver of bamboo. Inside, the bulbul hopped from perch to perch nervously. Myrna didn't attempt to reach for it, but she left the cage open when she walked away. She'd opened all the birdcages in the garden, one by one. There were no prisoners in the palace now.

Customs many decades old were being overthrown throughout Siya Ran Thu.

As she walked back through the flowering shrubs, the silk orhni that was her only garment greener than the most verdant leaves, she heard music among the trees a little way off: a single line of song, repeated several times with slight hesitancy. It was, she realised, Veraine's friends the storytellers, already composing a new song about the overthrow of the Harimau. The man, Rahul, was only a day out of bed, but was managing with his shoulder bound up tightly. He was lucky.

Myrna's bare feet knew the way back to Shinsawbu's chambers. They knew every one of the flagstones on the path. The sun warmed her skin through the loose silk drape, smoothing away her shiver of sadness. Others hadn't been so lucky as Rahul. In the chaotic struggles that had taken place through the corridors many people had paid dearly for freedom, with blood and with their lives. Sao Mor lived, but would never see the changes he'd wrought; even while dying with his blade through her heart Shinsawbu had managed to turn and rake at his face. The steward had lost both eyes.

Myrna mounted the steps to Tiger Lady's bedchamber. They'd taken that one for their own. No one had laid claim to Dhammazhedi's, or to anything in it: that whole suite had been torn down timber by timber and burned.

Narathu Min had been wounded worse than his co-conspirator, though considering that he'd been at the forefront of the skirmishes it was no surprise. Myrna intended to visit him again later in the day. The physicians were keeping him in an opium stupor while they waited to see if his body could heal itself. If he lived, he would not walk again without the aid of a crutch: he'd been torn open from hip to calf all down his left leg.

The garden doors stood wide. Myrna trod softly across the polished floorboards, unwinding the orhni as she went and letting it fall from her naked body. She glanced down once at herself and realised that it was for reassurance, which both amused and saddened her a little. She'd removed the Rao's rings, and although she suspected that Veraine rather regretted their disappearance he'd said not a word about it. She'd thrown the rings onto Dhammazhedi's funeral pyre: let anyone who wanted the gold go raking about among the ashes in the Arena for them.

She'd not yet decided whether she would let her pubic fluff grow back to conceal the serpent's head. There was nothing she could do about its feathered tail. She wore her hair in a loose braid this day, and it rested between her shoulder-blades like a reminder of the beast tattooed down her spine.

She stepped into the shadow of the room.

Veraine slept flat on his back in the middle of the bed. It was still a shock to see him in that place and she hesitated mid-stride, collecting her feelings. The raw silk of the sheets made a pale nimbus about his dark figure.

His left hand, bandaged from fingers to forearm, was cradled against his ribs while the other lay palm-up upon the coverlet, fingers gently curled. His legs were spread a little. His eyelids were still bruise-purple with exhaustion under the black arches of his brows; it would be a while yet before he was fully recovered from his exertions and they'd had little sleep, even in the time they'd had to themselves. It was as if he'd been trying to make up for every night they'd spent apart, all at once.

Myrna closed upon the bed, moving silently on her bare feet. Her heart was pounding hard in her breast. Just the sight of him lying so still woke in her a desire that was close to terror. There was such trustfulness implicit in his supine posture, and even tired and battered he was beautiful. His muscles stretched beneath his skin like the rocks that define the contours of the land. His penis lay quiescent like a sleeping animal in its nest, flushed and full and dark with bruises. The narrow line of hair that marched from his groin to his navel was a path for her finger to trace . . . or her tongue.

She smiled inwardly. She would have to get used to masculine body-hair again; on his belly and his long legs and his hard forearms, and scattered across the upper reaches of his chest like a shadow. It made a change from the flawless smoothness of the Tiger Lords. Nobody could have described Veraine's body as flawless.

She counted his scars; the ancient silvery ones and the dark contusions, some still scabbed with dried blood, from the Arena. Two lines of silk stitches ran up his thigh now. There were bruises everywhere. If it hadn't been for the armour Dhammazhedi would certainly have killed him, and that knowledge now made her dizzy. He was so terribly vulnerable; never more than the thickness of his own skin from death. She wanted to kiss the satiny softness of his throat, and his flat belly, and just inside his hips, and where the pouch of his scrotum met the root of his phallus – as if she could offer them some sort of divine protection.

She knew she couldn't. He would always be vulnerable. It was enough to rend her heart. She'd once thought him strong enough to endure anything, to master any challenge of fate, but that wasn't what she'd seen in the garden or the Arena, and it wasn't what she saw when she looked at him now. And she knew that it was not he who had changed: it was her.

Myrna had grown up in a temple where the gods, with their rampant personalities and excessive moods, had seemed more real to her than any living thing. Her inner spiritual life had been so vivid that everything else had faded to dust tones, and she'd been more familiar with the person of the Sun Lord than that of her High Priest. Then Veraine had found her, and he was the one living man that could overwhelm her senses and her emotions just as the gods did. When they'd fled, whatever lands they crossed and however many people they'd met, he'd still been the only thing that seemed truly forceful and bright and alive. In her inner eye the world was still the colour of dust. It was as if they were the only two real people in her universe, and all others were puppets painted onto flat strips of rawhide, just like the shadow puppets she'd seen at play in the garden.

Then he'd been taken away. And without his protection she'd been forced to recognise that both she and he had more in common with the mass of humanity than she'd ever realised. She'd learned that she shared her fears and her hopes and her comforts with others, and that she needed them. That Veraine was human too. That she must learn to be human, however poor she was at it, however lacking in practice.

Because the alternative to being human was to be Dhammazhedi.

She now knew Veraine's vulnerability, and she loved him the more for it.

Myrna knelt up very carefully on the bed and walked forwards on her knees, straddling his right leg. He woke as she brushed against him and opened his eyes slowly. He smiled, and she wondered what it was about his smile that was still so devastating.

'I had the strangest dream,' he said softly: 'Someone went and made me king.'

'It wasn't a dream,' she said, then realised too late he was teasing her: she'd never been able to get her head round the habit. 'Ah.'

He studied her and his eyes grew more serious after a moment. 'We don't have to stay,' he said. 'We can move on if you like.'

Myrna understood: he was offering to steal her away again to a new life, one without the memories embedded in this place. She considered for a long moment. But she knew she couldn't learn to be human in isolation. 'No,' she said. 'We ... I ... think we need to stop running. Besides, you'll make a good king.'

'I'm glad you think so.' The pucker of his brows betrayed a certain trepidation. Then the glint came back to his eyes. 'What about you? You used to be a goddess; isn't queen a bit of a come-down?'

For answer she bent low and laid a kiss in the centre of his chest. She planted her kisses like tiny footprints down his breastbone and his abdomen and he stretched beneath her as if to prolong the distance and the sensation. The heat of his body was like a blush on her face and her plait slipped forwards over her shoulder and slithered onto his stomach. She found her way to his navel and circled it, exploring with her tongue. He squirmed. Then she pressed onwards down the path defined by the narrow line of hair to his groin, where his thick locks smelled of her sex from their last coupling. He parted his thighs slightly at the brush of her hand.

'Ah,' he said plaintively.

His penis stirred at the first touch of her lips. She planted teasing kisses all the way to its tip. It was heavy with sleep and glutted with pleasure but it somehow responded again and Veraine's breath caught at the back of his throat as his member grew harder, flesh incarnating out of nothingness and bone out of flesh, the primordial miracle re-enacted once more. She drew him out until he was stiff and then released him so she could sit up and straddle his hips.

His eyes were wide open now, and there was no trace of a smile in his expression; rather an agonised awe.

'I am still a goddess,' she reminded him.

He put his good arm about her and pulled her down onto him. He was very strong. 'Oh, yes,' he admitted: 'You are.'

Visit the Black Lace website at
www.blacklace-books.co.uk

FIND OUT THE LATEST INFORMATION AND TAKE
ADVANTAGE OF OUR FANTASTIC FREE BOOK OFFER!
ALSO VISIT THE SITE FOR . . .

- All Black Lace titles currently available
  and how to order online
- Great new offers
- Writers' guidelines
- Author interviews
- An erotica newsletter
- Features
- Cool links

BLACK LACE – THE LEADING IMPRINT
OF WOMEN'S SEXY FICTION

TAKING YOUR EROTIC READING
PLEASURE TO NEW HORIZONS

LOOK OUT FOR THE ALL-NEW BLACK LACE BOOKS – AVAILABLE NOW!

All books priced £7.99 in the UK. Please note publication dates apply to the UK only. For other territories, please contact your retailer.

STELLA DOES HOLLYWOOD
Stella Black
ISBN 978 0 352 33588 3

Stella Black has a 1969 Pontiac Firebird, a leopard-skin bra and a lot of attitude. Partying her way around Hollywood, she is discovered by Leon Lubrisky, the billionaire mogul of Pleasure Dome Inc. He persuades her to work for him and she soon becomes one of the most famous adult stars in America. Invited on chat shows, dating pop stars and hanging out with the Beverly Hills A-list. But dark forces are gathering and a political party is outraged and determined to destroy Stella any which way they can. Soon she finds herself in dangerous – and highly sexually charged – situations, where no one can rescue her.

Coming in February 2007

THE BOSS
Monica Belle
ISBN 978 0 352 34088 7

Felicity is a girl with two different sides to her character, each leading
two very separate lives. There's Fizz – wild child, drummer in a retro punk
band and car thief. And then there's Felicity – a quiet, polite, and ultra-
efficient office worker. But, as her attractive, controlling boss takes an
interest in her, she finds it hard to keep the two parts of her life
separate.

Will being with Stephen mean choosing between personae and
sacrificing so much of her life? But then, it also appears that Stephen has
some very peculiar and addictive ideas about sex.

GOTHIC BLUE
Portia Da Costa
ISBN 978 0 352 33075 8

At an archduke's reception, a handsome young nobleman falls under the
spell of a malevolent but irresistible sorceress. Two hundred years later,
Belinda Seward also falls prey to sensual forces she can neither
understand nor control. Stranded by a thunderstorm at a remote Gothic
priory, Belinda and her boyfriend are drawn into an enclosed world of
luxurious decadence and sexual alchemy. Their host is the courteous but
melancholic André von Kastel; a beautiful aristocrat who mourns his lost
love. He has plans for Belinda – plans that will take her into the realms of
obsessive love and the erotic paranormal.

Coming in March 2007

FLOOD
Anna Clare
ISBN 978 0 352 34094 8

London, 1877. Phoebe Flood, a watch mender's daughter from Blackfriars, is hired as lady's maid to the glamorous Louisa LeClerk, a high class tart with connections to the underworld of gentlemen pornographers. Fascinated by her new mistress and troubled by strange dreams, Phoebe receives an extraordinary education in all matters sensual. And her destiny and secret self gradually reveals itself when she meets Garou, a freak show attraction, The Boy Who Was Raised by Wolves.

LEARNING TO LOVE IT
Alison Tyler
ISBN 978 0 352 33535 7

Art historian Lissa and doctor Colin meet at the Frankfurt Book Fair, where they are both promoting their latest books. At the fair, and then through Europe, the two lovers embark on an exploration of their sexual fantasies, playing intense games of bondage, spanking and dressing up. Lissa loves humiliation, and Colin is just the man to provide her with the pleasure she craves. Unbeknown to Lissa, their meeting was not accidental, but planned ahead by a mysterious patron of the erotic arts.

Black Lace Booklist

Information is correct at time of printing. To avoid disappointment, check availability before ordering. Go to www.blacklace-books.co.uk. All books are priced £7.99 unless another price is given.

BLACK LACE BOOKS WITH A CONTEMPORARY SETTING

☐ ALWAYS THE BRIDEGROOM Tesni Morgan   ISBN 978 0 352 33855 6   £6.99
☐ THE ANGELS' SHARE Maya Hess   ISBN 978 0 352 34043 6
☐ ARIA APPASSIONATA Julie Hastings   ISBN 978 0 352 33056 7   £6.99
☐ ASKING FOR TROUBLE Kristina Lloyd   ISBN 978 0 352 33362 9
☐ BLACK LIPSTICK KISSES Monica Belle   ISBN 978 0 352 33885 3   £6.99
☐ BONDED Fleur Reynolds   ISBN 978 0 352 33192 2   £6.99
☐ BOUND IN BLUE Monica Belle   ISBN 978 0 352 34012 2
☐ CAMPAIGN HEAT Gabrielle Marcola   ISBN 978 0 352 33941 6
☐ CAT SCRATCH FEVER Sophie Mouette   ISBN 978 0 352 34021 4
☐ CIRCUS EXCITE Nikki Magennis   ISBN 978 0 352 34033 7
☐ CLUB CRÉME Primula Bond   ISBN 978 0 352 33907 2   £6.99
☐ COMING ROUND THE MOUNTAIN   ISBN 978 0 352 33873 0   £6.99
     Tabitha Flyte
☐ CONFESSIONAL Judith Roycroft   ISBN 978 0 352 33421 3
☐ CONTINUUM Portia Da Costa   ISBN 978 0 352 33120 5
☐ DANGEROUS CONSEQUENCES   ISBN 978 0 352 33185 4
     Pamela Rochford
☐ DARK DESIGNS Madelynne Ellis   ISBN 978 0 352 34075 7
☐ THE DEVIL INSIDE Portia Da Costa   ISBN 978 0 352 32993 6
☐ EDEN'S FLESH Robyn Russell   ISBN 978 0 352 33923 2   £6.99
☐ ENTERTAINING MR STONE Portia Da Costa   ISBN 978 0 352 34029 0
☐ EQUAL OPPORTUNITIES Mathilde Madden   ISBN 978 0 352 34070 2
☐ FEMININE WILES Karina Moore   ISBN 978 0 352 33874 7   £6.99
☐ FIRE AND ICE Laura Hamilton   ISBN 978 0 352 33486 2
☐ GOING DEEP Kimberly Dean   ISBN 978 0 352 33876 1   £6.99
☐ GOING TOO FAR Laura Hamilton   ISBN 978 0 352 33657 6   £6.99
☐ GONE WILD Maria Eppie   ISBN 978 0 352 33670 5
☐ IN PURSUIT OF ANNA Natasha Rostova   ISBN 978 0 352 34060 3

❏ MAD ABOUT THE BOY Mathilde Madden   ISBN 978 0 352 34001 6

❏ MAKE YOU A MAN Anna Clare   ISBN 978 0 352 34006 1

❏ MAN HUNT Cathleen Ross   ISBN 978 0 352 33583 8

❏ MIXED DOUBLES Zoe le Verdier   ISBN 978 0 352 33312 4   £6.99

❏ MIXED SIGNALS Anna Clare   ISBN 978 0 352 33889 1   £6.99

❏ MS BEHAVIOUR Mini Lee   ISBN 978 0 352 33962 1

❏ A MULTITUDE OF SINS Kit Mason   ISBN 978 0 352 33737 5   £6.99

❏ PACKING HEAT Karina Moore   ISBN 978 0 352 33356 8   £6.99

❏ PAGAN HEAT Monica Belle   ISBN 978 0 352 33974 4

❏ PASSION OF ISIS Madelynne Ellis   ISBN 978 0 352 33993 5

❏ PEEP SHOW Mathilde Madden   ISBN 978 0 352 33924 9

❏ THE POWER GAME Carrera Devonshire   ISBN 978 0 352 33990 4

❏ THE PRIVATE UNDOING OF A PUBLIC SERVANT   ISBN 978 0 352 34066 5
     Leonie Martel

❏ RELEASE ME Suki Cunningham   ISBN 978 0 352 33671 2   £6.99

❏ RUDE AWAKENING Pamela Kyle   ISBN 978 0 352 33036 9

❏ SAUCE FOR THE GOOSE Mary Rose Maxwell   ISBN 978 0 352 33492 3

❏ SIN.NET Helena Ravenscroft   ISBN 978 0 352 33598 2   £6.99

❏ SLAVE TO SUCCESS Kimberley Raines   ISBN 978 0 352 33687 3   £6.99

❏ SLEAZY RIDER Karen S. Smith   ISBN 978 0 352 33964 5

❏ STELLA DOES HOLLYWOOD Stella Black   ISBN 978 0 352 33588 3

❏ THE STRANGER Portia Da Costa   ISBN 978 0 352 33211 0

❏ SUMMER FEVER Anna Ricci   ISBN 978 0 352 33625 5   £6.99

❏ SWITCHING HANDS Alaine Hood   ISBN 978 0 352 33896 9   £6.99

❏ SYMPHONY X Jasmine Stone   ISBN 978 0 352 33629 3   £6.99

❏ TONGUE IN CHEEK Tabitha Flyte   ISBN 978 0 352 33484 8

❏ TWO WEEKS IN TANGIER Annabel Lee   ISBN 978 0 352 33599 9   £6.99

❏ UNNATURAL SELECTION Alaine Hood   ISBN 978 0 352 33963 8

❏ UP TO NO GOOD Karen S. Smith   ISBN 978 0 352 33589 0   £6.99

❏ VILLAGE OF SCRETS Mercedes Kelly   ISBN 978 0 352 33344 5

❏ WILD BY NATURE Monica Belle   ISBN 978 0 352 33915 7   £6.99

❏ WILD CARD Madeline Moore   ISBN 978 0 352 34038 2

BLACK LACE BOOKS WITH AN HISTORICAL SETTING

❏ THE AMULET Lisette Allen   ISBN 978 0 352 33019 2   £6.99

❏ THE BARBARIAN GEISHA Charlotte Royal   ISBN 978 0 352 33267 7

☐ BARBARIAN PRIZE Deanna Ashford ISBN 978 0 352 34017 7

☐ DANCE OF OBSESSION Olivia Christie ISBN 978 0 352 33101 4

☐ DARKER THAN LOVE Kristina Lloyd ISBN 978 0 352 33279 0

☐ ELENA'S DESTINY Lisette Allen ISBN 978 0 352 33218 9

☐ FRENCH MANNERS Olivia Christie ISBN 978 0 352 33214 1

☐ THE HAND OF AMUN Juliet Hastings ISBN 978 0 352 33144 1 £6.99

☐ LORD WRAXALL'S FANCY Anna Lieff Saxby ISBN 978 0 352 33080 2

☐ THE MASTER OF SHILDEN Lucinda Carrington ISBN 978 0 352 33140 3

☐ NICOLE'S REVENGE Lisette Allen ISBN 978 0 352 32984 4

☐ THE SENSES BEJEWELLED Cleo Cordell ISBN 978 0 352 32904 2 £6.99

☐ THE SOCIETY OF SIN Sian Lacey Taylder ISBN 978 0 352 34080 1

☐ UNDRESSING THE DEVIL Angel Strand ISBN 978 0 352 33938 6

☐ WHITE ROSE ENSNARED Juliet Hastings ISBN 978 0 352 33052 9 £6.99

BLACK LACE BOOKS WITH A PARANORMAL THEME

☐ BURNING BRIGHT Janine Ashbless ISBN 978 0 352 34085 6

☐ CRUEL ENCHANTMENT Janine Ashbless ISBN 978 0 352 33483 1

☐ THE PRIDE Edie Bingham ISBN 978 0 352 33997 3

BLACK LACE ANTHOLOGIES

☐ MORE WICKED WORDS Various ISBN 978 0 352 33487 9 £6.99

☐ WICKED WORDS 3 Various ISBN 978 0 352 33522 7 £6.99

☐ WICKED WORDS 4 Various ISBN 978 0 352 33603 3 £6.99

☐ WICKED WORDS 5 Various ISBN 978 0 352 33642 2 £6.99

☐ WICKED WORDS 6 Various ISBN 978 0 352 33690 3 £6.99

☐ WICKED WORDS 7 Various ISBN 978 0 352 33743 6 £6.99

☐ WICKED WORDS 8 Various ISBN 978 0 352 33787 0 £6.99

☐ WICKED WORDS 9 Various ISBN 978 0 352 33860 0

☐ WICKED WORDS 10 Various ISBN 978 0 352 33893 8

☐ THE BEST OF BLACK LACE 2 Various ISBN 978 0 352 33718 4

☐ WICKED WORDS: SEX IN THE OFFICE Various ISBN 978 0 352 33944 7

☐ WICKED WORDS: SEX AT THE SPORTS CLUB ISBN 978 0 352 33991 1
    Various

☐ WICKED WORDS: SEX ON HOLIDAY Various ISBN 978 0 352 33961 4

☐ WICKED WORDS: SEX IN UNIFORM Various ISBN 978 0 352 34002 3

☐ WICKED WORDS: SEX IN THE KITCHEN Various ISBN 978 0 352 34018 4

❏ WICKED WORDS: SEX ON THE MOVE Various   ISBN 978 0 352 34034 4
❏ WICKED WORDS: SEX AND MUSIC Various   ISBN 978 0 352 34061 0
❏ WICKED WORDS: SEX AND SHOPPING Various   ISBN 978 0 352 34076 4

BLACK LACE NON-FICTION
❏ THE BLACK LACE BOOK OF WOMEN'S SEXUAL   ISBN 978 0 352 33793 1   £6.99
      FANTASIES Edited by Kerri Sharp

To find out the latest information about Black Lace titles, check out the
website: www.blacklace-books.co.uk or send for a booklist with
complete synopses by writing to:

> Black Lace Booklist, Virgin Books Ltd
> Thames Wharf Studios
> Rainville Road
> London W6 9HA

Please include an SAE of decent size. Please note only British stamps
are valid.

Our privacy policy
We will not disclose information you supply us to any other parties.
We will not disclose any information which identifies you personally to
any person without your express consent.

From time to time we may send out information about Black Lace
books and special offers. Please tick here if you do <u>not</u> wish to
receive Black Lace information.   ❏

Please send me the books I have ticked above.

Name ....

Address ....

....

....

....

Post Code ....

Send to: Virgin Books Cash Sales, Thames Wharf Studios, Rainville Road, London W6 9HA.

US customers: for prices and details of how to order books for delivery by mail, call 888-330-8477.

Please enclose a cheque or postal order, made payable to Virgin Books Ltd, to the value of the books you have ordered plus postage and packing costs as follows:

UK and BFPO – £1.00 for the first book, 50p for each subsequent book.

Overseas (including Republic of Ireland) – £2.00 for the first book, £1.00 for each subsequent book.

If you would prefer to pay by VISA, ACCESS/MASTERCARD, DINERS CLUB, AMEX or SWITCH, please write your card number and expiry date here:

....

Signature ....

Please allow up to 28 days for delivery.